Underground

Underground

Revolution

František Kotleta

TABLE OF CONTENTS

From the sewers…

I tapped the mask and turned on the night vision device.

Splash!

"Maybe you'd…"

Looking at Belch, standing waist-deep in a liquid formed by sewage, mazout, dirt, dead rats, people and who knows what else flowed from the world above, immediately my anger that he had given this surprising and most importantly, loud sound passed.

I carefully explored the area between us, looking for a solid foothold. We were moving on some old pipes with an uncertain bottom under them. The Pole was slowly falling down, like DEZATEG's shares after its owners had mysteriously left this world.

"Maybe you should help me," he growled.

"Maybe I should let you die for what you add to the hunter's stew." I smiled, though he couldn't see it through the protective mask.

"By the sacred bones of Lech Kaczyński, Czechs, you sōm blank ciule!" a man from Katowice swore in Silesian and Czech.

Due to the fact that during the second war for Cieszyn Silesia, I learned some Polish and Silesian - languages still used on the border, I guessed that we were to become something like a gang of dicks, but I gave him my hand. Even if he pissed on my head, I would still help him. I don't have many friends left in this fucking city.

I shook his hand and pulled him out of that slime muck. Dark, slimy slurry ran slowly over him. Luckily we were wearing smart waterproof pants and jackets and old but damn reliable military nano leather boots.

"You know it smells like your Varsovian mushroom sauce?"

"You know you lost the war, pepik?" He replied.

But at that moment, another splash sounded nearby.

We shut up right away. Belch cleaned the mask. We were in what used to be part of the sewage system and collectors, and it must have been over a hundred years since the last conservator had come here. Since then, shit has just been dripping from bursting pipes and sewers. But there were also people living here. Prague - strongly separated from the rest of the world by autonomous combat drones, bunkers and wire entanglements - could not grow wide, so the rich moved up and the poor down. Always been like that. Life in the castle towers was different from life in the slums outside the castle, even under regimes that darkened to introduce equality. After all, there were always new bigwigs, and with them, people were pushed to the margins. And a lot of blood and pain.

"Hold it," Belch snapped me out of my futile philosophizing.

He unzipped his plastic backpack and handed me the gun. There was a five-pointed star on it.

"What is this?"

"Makarov. Soviet classic," he said.

"Soviet? You mean that Soviet Union that disappeared before my great-grandfather had his first erection?" I made sure and checked the gun. It had a magazine for eight rounds, caliber nine.

"I doubt anyone in your family will ever get an erection, but yes, it's from the Soviet Union. Stalin was scratching his balls with it, while Beria sucked his dick," he replied and took out the second antique. I knew it from childhood-read black and white comic books printed on a hundred times recycled paper - the Thompson submachine gun, a favorite weapon of the American mafia from ancient times. Hot dogs, burgers and Al Capone are my old love.

"You robbed the museum?" I asked, still checking Makarov's gun. It looked functional.

"Something like that. One collector replaced it with me for hunter's stew."

Needless to say, a good hunter's stew made of real meat and cabbage was more valuable than an outdated gun, and now the latter is needed. What do we need hunter's stew in the sewers.

* * *

I struggled cautiously through the standing liquid. We were silent as we walked a good three hundred meters. We heard dripping water and distant scratching sounds that gradually increased.

I paused, waiting for Belch to reach me. He was no longer the youngest. During the Polish-Czech war, which ended in what could be called a Polish victory - when the Czech Republic fell apart and lost interest in fighting its northern neighbors - he served in special units. Their specialty was to obtain provisions for fighting units. Then Belch founded a Polish restaurant in Prague to somehow use the experience gained during the war in acquiring exclusive food products, such as: meat, eggs and cabbage. When I mentioned my work today, he persuaded me to take him with me. He was panting loudly now, audible even through the mask filter.

"Do you still want to: 'Experience a little bit of this excitement like in the good old days?'," I recited his words from memory.

"Fuck your old woman. Better focus on what's in front," he whispered, checking the condom on the thompson's barrel.

Such measures were once implemented by US troops in Vietnam to protect their weapons and ammunition from moisture. So the smell of the Vietnamese Civil War was a mixture of napalm and burnt rubber. As a result, syphilis has spread in the US military due to the lack of condoms, but this is the price to pay when a person is betting on survival, here and now, even if it would cripple a person's future.

We walked another two hundred meters. The scratching grew louder and a new muffled sound was heard at the same time. I sped up.

* * *

Out there, the world could be cruel and uncivilized, plunged into ruin and corruption, and Prague may be the pinnacle of modern European civilization, but what was hiding in the guts of this city would not even survive in the wild. But somehow it was vegetating here, hidden from daylight in what might once have been a warehouse or an electrical switchboard.

Meanwhile, someone had broken through the tunnels that could be used to get outside otherwise than through the slurry in which we were now waist-deep. In the dark, thanks to the infrared camera in my mask, I saw the outline of a tall, hunched figure.

"Sewer man," Belch concluded.

They were labeled differently, but the word "sewer man" probably best reflected their essence. People who lived outside the system usually stayed at U-metro stations, the lowest of the three routes. Contrary to the overground S line and the luxury N line, which connects the new center of Prague with the elegant suburbs via a magnetic expressway, admission to the U metro area was free. Only ordinary people traveled to work on this line. So, when someone had gotten too much of a wreck, even for a U-level, a few of the beefy types - what they couldn't do better than working twelve hours in a fake meat factory and beating drooling human wrecks - sent them still deeper. And so, they became sewer men. Some have lived below the surface for several generations. There were strange creatures among them. Few could afford real food, such as meat or (God forbid) vegetables, while everyone ate what was produced in DEZATEG or ARKAS laboratories - but the sewer men could not buy or dig out even that from the garbage can.

From this there were ordinary homeless and vagabonds, a much higher caste. For the poorest, the cubes produced by the mafia and various experimenters from residues and bio-waste in illegal factories, where quality standards and ISO norms were not complied with, were left. It was just a matter of supplying the wretched with calories for a few pennies and making some money on it. However, when you lived in the dark for many generations, drank dirty slush instead of water, and ate such humus, it turned out that evolution could not only be undone, but also pushed in a completely different direction. That's why some sever men didn't look like humans. And this one was one of them.

"Zarchnch," the figure said.

Theoretically, he shouldn't be able to see us, but he must have heard the splash of this glop or sensed us. It seems that despite the two-hour hike in the sewage, we still did not smell as required by the local label - EdDR. Eau de Dead Rat.

"Zarchn. Chrm chrm hrmla strm," it rang out in the dark.

I have unprotected the Bolshevik tool against the counterrevolutionaries.

"Sounds like mine ex after a flask of wine," whispered Belch.

There was no longer any need for "radio silence".

We haven't seen him very well. We slowly got out of the disgusting shit dripping off us.

"Fuck, on the left," said the Pole.

"What?"

"There are more here," he explained.

I looked around but couldn't see or hear anyone, not even with infrared.

"Are you sure?"

"I can bet on the left testicle."

"And you didn't sell it for half a cow to the Russians?"

"Shut up," Belch growled harshly as he pulled out the American delicacy.

And although he was plagued by the storms of this stupidest war - right after the three-day slaughter between the Kosice Federation and the Žilina Empire - the dangerous situation was on his nerves. He has become lazy.

We took a few more steps and all I could hear was a sound in front of me.

"Over there." The Pole pointed at 3 o'clock.

And he was right. Something moved there.

We emerged from the slush onto a stable concrete surface. I unzipped the double-shielded rubber zipper and pulled the signal flare from my side pocket.

"Lower the contrast," I whispered, unlocked it, and tossed it to the right.

Red light illuminated the space.

Fuck.

Well, fuck.

* * *

At least fifteen figures scattered in front of the red light. All I could see was their outlines and flickering shadows, but they were terrifying. Some in ruffled dirty rags, others completely naked.

"That should scare them off," I smiled.

"I hope so."

"No gloom-mongering," I growled, and as long as the flare was pointing the way, I was able to follow from the swampy dung in the direction from which came a voice similar to that of the ex of Belch.

"I hear him."

And not only him. I, too, instead of snorting and grunting, suddenly registered a baby crying. I sped up and climbed through the rusty iron doorway into what was once a service room, but now looked more like a cave. Old garbage, rags, electronic components and rusty tinned food were everywhere. The last of the light from the dying flare allowed me to see it in perfectly outlined contours.

"Brum," I heard from a pile of old newspapers.

"Zarchn," the voice on the left countered.

There was a guy who looked like a cross between Jiřina Bohdalova[1], the famous avatar from the evening TV cartoon for children Wodnik Szuwarek, and the robots attack from the Cat's Eye nebula or Żwirek and Muchomorek are building a 7G network and a hippo.

"Stop, fucko," I shouted to the sever man and pointed my gun at him.

"Shit," swore the Pole standing next to him. His hands were shaking.

---

[1] Jiřina Bohdalová – popular Czech actress and TV presenter, known in Poland, among others from the series The Cottagers (cz. Chalupáři) as Mrs. Fuchsová [translator´s note].

"When was the last time you shot?" I asked. His obvious fear made me pissed.

"Last week... To the sparrows. Never to a man."

"Fuck."

"Fuck."

* * *

The sever man stood hunched over less than two meters from me.

"Zarchn?"

"Well, he doesn't have a rich vocabulary," Belch observed.

I ignored him. The child we had been looking for in this shit and its surroundings for two days cried out somewhere against the wall to my right.

"It's impossible for you to misunderstand me, sever man," I said slowly and loudly, and at the same time made my way to the body lying in a pile of crumpled newspapers and old leaflets. Belch was holding onto me. The flare was dying, and the contours slowly lost their sharpness.

"I'm taking that bastard and gone. Nothing will happen to you," I continued.

"Zarachan?!"

The same word, slightly modified, sounded more threatening.

"Wojciech, give me gifts."

The owner of the best Polish restaurant in all of Prague - and admittedly the only one - opened his sack again and took out two packages of protein bars.

"It's more nutritious than that bastard. The whole family will eat well. Half of it is Christmas dog flavor, you'll like it. And if you roll it in mud, it will taste like homemade food," I continued in a calm voice and took a few more steps towards the baby.

"No. Child mine. He Zarachan. Me Zarchn," he surprised me.

He didn't look very much like his kind, but as he spoke, a shiver ran down my spine. Instead of a bizarre monstrosity, I saw a caricature of broken humanity pushed to the bottom, and at once something squeezed me down. His hunched shape seemed to straighten. He had a deformed spine and face. He looked like one old politician from the beginning of the last century, whose name I was desperately trying to remember, but otherwise human. Fortunately, the baby started crying louder and my sympathy was gone.

"It's not Zarachan. It's a bastard from Cursed Whore Teresa's Orphanage. And that's where we have to return it," I replied, taking another step towards the rustling pile of neonatal tenderness.

We were already close to the baby. Zarchn still stood and did not move. I reached down for the toddler. It was lying naked among the newspapers, a small circle painted on its stomach with some greasy black substance. On one of the leaflets I noticed an inscription: "Retro week in Lidl". I thought it was about some porn, but I didn't feel like wasting my time on dirty archives.

"Not bastard. Sacrifice to the Ascender," Zarachan objected.

"What the fuck?" the Pole did not understand.

His sharp turn caught my attention and I followed his gaze - sever men began to gather at the entrance. They were boys and girls like oak trees. That is, as far as we mean oaks covered with mold, which, twisted, grow into the world through the sewer grate. Some looked very young, others old and withered. Most were wearing nothing - nothing at all. Others only dirty scraps. Despite the nano-carbon filter mask, my nostrils were struck by a thickening, disgusting stench that was not even matched by the stench of sewage, the remnants of which still dripped from our pants. The filter protected against viruses and bacteria, but it turned out to be too thin for the molecules of this abomination. The sever men were not identical. A few of them looked deformed with strangely processed tissues. In one woman's face, pieces of skin were hanging down to the nipples of small breasts. Another guy had a similarly stretched belly, dotted with dozens of ulcers. He tied pieces of some kind of plastic tape around him to keep them from tangling between his legs. Others had growths or purulent rashes all over their faces, but some of them looked like if they took a proper shower, they could come to the surface without anyone noticing.

I grabbed the crying bastard with my left hand. The sever men didn't like it. They started to hiss and growl, and some of them even said some words, but they sounded so many at once that I couldn't understand them.

Crunch.

At first, I didn't pay attention to the sound under my feet, but then, despite the solid soles, I realized that there are more crunchy things. I risked a glance down and for a few seconds I had no idea what the hell I was going to do. In the end I got pissed, opened the zipper on my left thigh and fished out the flashlight.

Click - I heard, and the sharp flash of the mask blinded me for a moment. Immediately after that it switched to light and I saw a pile of baby bones on the ground. Some looked quite fresh. What I was crushing with my heel now were the bones of the chest of about a six-month-old toddler.

When I tried to shift, a pair of ribs made a strong crunch. I turned furiously and shone my flashlight on Zarchn and his guests. The light was not working well on them. They growled and groaned and shielded their eyes from the beam of brightness. Now I could get a better look at their bodies. A strangely yellowed and gray skin appeared to the eyes. I also noticed that some were holding iron bars, hooks, and rusty homemade machetes.

"Man, I'll be drinking vodka all week," Belch said, swallowing loudly.

Probably trying to suppress the vomiting. And not only him. But puking into your own mask is not a very good idea.

The baby's cry intensified.

I shone Zachrn in the eyes. His yellow-gray face twisted and he muttered something.

"Let us go," I said firmly.

But the mass of sever men took a step forward.

"You have no hearing among your relatives," Belch shook his head.

Despite the situation, I laughed.

However, the sever men had no sense of humor.

"They will leave a sacrifice for the Ascendant here. They will go away," said the woman with white hair covered with bits of mud, who stood in a tangle around the entrance, decisively.

Zarchn nodded approvingly.

I looked at the woman with parched breasts. Her eyes were hazy and her ribs showed through her skin. Even so, I could bet she wasn't over thirty. There is no room for a good and long life in the sewers.

I think I instinctively shook my head, which the sever men logically took as a clear gesture that there is no point in negotiating with us.

* * *

The barrier of bodies moved. The sever men moved forward like a solid mass, regardless of who had iron in their hands and who only had dirt behind their fingernails.

Boom!

A Bolshevik drill against the counterrevolutionaries rocked space, and Zarchn fell to the ground.

"It wouldn't be too smart to shoot his knee," Belch muttered, and of course he was right.

As the kid tore to the max at the sound of the gunshot, the sever men started running towards us. The Pole sprinkled them with a series from his Thompson. Since he had a hundred rounds in a ammunition drum, he could do it. 45 ACP ammunition decently reduced their ranks. The sever men were bleeding and screaming and falling to the ground, but the gunshots and roar of the baby drowned out the screams. We didn't even have time to shout our obligatory "fuck". The guy with his belly wrapped in tape pierced his jaw and barely escaped the rusty wrench that the bony woman was waving next to me. I kicked her left knee and then, twenty centimeters away, shot between the eyes of some guy with a toothless mouth full of saliva. His blood, bits of brain, and chunks of his skull splashed around us. I was protected by a mask, but the child took on a new red color.

"Aaaa!"

The scream was mine. A gray sewer freak with a broken knee bit into my calf. Probably in agony, she managed to chew through the protective suit just above the shoe. I kicked her in the head. It hurt like hell. Good thing I did all the vaccinations at a time when it didn't cost a fortune.

The uncertainty left the Pole, he changed the machine into firing single bullets and pounded the mass in front of us, surely worthy of a guy from an amusement park, mowing perfumed roses with a well-calibrated airgun.

That is, until one of the guys stabbed him in the stomach with an iron rod. He bent and the thompson fell from his hand.

We were flooded with incoming support. Probably all the inhabitants of the underworld were rushing towards us, judging from the roar of the muddy slush.

* * *

I kicked the closest guy in the weirdly swaying yellowed cock. He cringed, and at that moment I hit him with my knee on the head. While he whined in pain, I grabbed him from the side and used to ram two women standing with wrenches between us and the exit of the Zarchn cave. At the same time, I tried to protect the screaming and throwing child with my own body. One of the women fell to the ground on impact, and the other hit me on the shoulder. I noticed the ancient logo of the Transport Company of the Capital City of Prague on the tool.

"Bitch!" Was the last word she heard.

A Makarov shot stuck in her ribs. She stumbled and gasped for air. Gunshot lung wounds will soon kill her. I shot the other one between the eyes. Her suffering lasted much less. About one and a half picoseconds.

"Shit!"

I turned towards the cave and saw the Pole thrashing under the flood of bodies. Women and men beat him with their primitive and blunt, but no less effective weapons, or only with their hands, biting their teeth and scratching their nails. he twisted beneath them. Someone ripped off his mask.

I shot two attackers and kicked the others away. Finally, he could get up. Blood ran down his face. Probably not only his. May he also have all possible vaccinations, because there must have been more bacteria in the nails and teeth of the sever men than were left in Kim Jong Trump's bunker.

Boom - I killed a smudged boy in work pants who was running to us through the slush with his screwdriver pulled out. After a while, he plunged into it up to the protruding ears.

"Here you go." I handed Belch a Makarov and a teasing kid.

"Here's the last bullet. Keep it to yourself," I muttered, and moved between the wounded and dying sewers. I picked up the Thompson from the dirty, bloody ground. I estimated there were at least fifty rounds left in it. However, the smile that this discovery brought on my face soon faded away. Even if I had hit everyone with precision, it wouldn't have been enough for the surrounding horde.

* * *

The row of compact bodies stood in a semicircle about ten yards from us. The baby roared, but no one cared. The wounded and the dying around also howled. This cavalry, which arrived too late for Zarchn, and too early for us, was not a rabble of sewer. These guys and women were kind of like the local Praetorian Guard. Not only were they wearing pants and some of them even wearing shoes, they also looked reasonably well fed and decently muscled.

"How many are there?" Belch asked.

After losing his mask, all he could see was what my flashlight beams shining on the ground behind him in the hole where Zarchn was bleeding.

"About a hundred, maybe more," I replied truthfully.

They lined up one by one, holding in their hands not only pipes and various menacing-looking tools, but also long rods with sharp ends. Just damn effective spears. They stood shoulder to shoulder, several rows from the edge of the flowing slurry to the wall on the opposite side. Most of them had exposed torsos, but it was not as terrible a sight as Zachran's friends and colleagues.

"Do you have a spare magazine for this American?" I tapped on the Thompson.

Belch shook his head as the baby bew mud. I wasn't surprised. I was close to that too.

"Okay, if I say "Christ", we run! Ultimately, we will meet either in Slavic hell or in your pub."

"I'm Silesian and therefore I'm half German and one quarter Jewish. I don't think I will end up in Slavic hell. I can't even squat. My heels are always up." He smiled crookedly and wiped the trickle of blood that ran down his eyes.

The kid started to pee. Only now did I realize it was a boy. He made a really nice fountain.

"Christ!"

* * *

Just before that, I pulled four flares from my pocket, fired them, and threw them at the sewers. Right after that, I started shooting. Vintage weapons shot as reliably and elegantly as any modern gun. I could smell old machine oil and burnt gunpowder, and everything looked like crossing the Acheron. The flares blinded the dark-accustomed sever men, disorienting them perfectly. The shooting introduced real chaos. Belch ran into the smelly sewer with the baby in his arms. And I followed him, shooting anyone who figured out where we were going. It was a massacre. A fucking underground safari. One wounded or dead for two or three rounds. The crowded people rushed forward, bleeding, falling, screaming and wailing - and I was shooting like at an illegal street fair.

Until I ran out of ammo. Not a single cartridge left, not even for me. When Wojciech pulls the Makarov trigger at the last moment, we will probably have to hug our heads.

* * *

There was a splash of water around us. After a while I caught up with the Pole, grabbed his free hand and tried to show him the way. Without the night vision mask, he was practically blind. Unlike the sever men who followed us. Besides, in this slush they felt at home. Those who realized immediately and were the first to follow us, I ruthlessly shot, but now others were catching up. I held the submachine gun like a club, trying not to get lost in the few turns and confluences of one smelly slurry sewage with another. While there was little on the surface of the liquid, here we got a good swallow of it. Unfortunately, it looks more like the contents of a septic tank. The sewage splashed, stalkers screamed and the kid roared. I admit he deserved admiration. I would have run out of breath after the first ten minutes, but this brat was screaming incessantly, like some VEP Christmas electronic toy for spoiled bastards. Although this one is certainly not. I suspect that if he survives this, he will be more traumatized than any N-level lady who saw a homeless man pissing in the street and felt sick.

28

They were catching up with us. Some skinny boy came the closest. He had long hair in a ponytail and he was wearing some strange raincoat. In his hand he held a piece of plate shaped like an arrowhead. I could see he was right behind me. He was approaching centimeter by centimeter until, supported by the screams of others, he was within reach.

Loot! I swung the Thompson. In the role of a club, he turned out to be great. I hit the sever man on the head. He lost his balance and slid under the water. I tried to speed up but we were out of breath.

"Left!" I shouted to Belch.

After less than a kilometer of crazy escape, we managed to reach the stairs leading out of the shitty slush. We got them here less than two hours ago. I helped him climb a two-meter-long concrete overhang covered with a thick layer of something slippery. I had to push my back, grab his leg and lift him up.

The Pole and the child fell to the concrete.

"Iaaaaaaa!" Someone yelled behind me, and a slush-stained figure jumped on my back.

* * *

I dove all the way to the bottom of that shit. Someone was holding me by the throat and was hitting my head with a piece of iron. I was partially protected by a mask, but mostly by the smelly slush that dampened the force of the blows. I have not seen anything. Impenetrable darkness. I held my breath, trying to find support for my feet. It was not very successful, especially since the sewer clerk hung around my neck like a tick. I tried to lean against the bottom and raise my head to gasp, but to no avail. Another blow pushed me back under the surface again. A hand ripped off my mask and I sucked the humus with my nose. I felt as if I was inhaling a burning napalm. Another attempt to get up was unsuccessful, so I did the opposite - slipped to the right where the iron pipes ended and dived deep.

Legs plunged into unstable mud, but the attackers lost their balance as well. One of them let me go, the other was still holding my neck. Only now did I drop the reliable Thompson and feel the sever man's body. I ran my fingers down his ribs and made it to... well, hooray, he's a guy, I thought, and with a squeeze I crushed his unexpectedly huge balls.

He let go of me, but I was still holding his tortured organ. I am like a sewer rat when I need to. I bite and won't let go.

* * *

Finally, I surfaced. I let go of his balls and grabbed the sever man by the hair, immediately dragging him under the water. Deliberately. Let's see how long he stays in this shit.

* * *

At last I was able to wipe the greasy disgust from my eyes and saw that everything around me was bathed in the pink glow that radiated from the fairy.

Then I'm probably dead, I thought.

* * *

I shook off the first shock thanks to a few things. First, the sever men. The one I was holding below the surface was still trying to get out. The other one I shook off by the jump suddenly surfaced and lunged after me. In the glow of the pink light, I also saw a group of other people wading after me through the slurry. And most importantly - the fairy was actually a foreteller.

Although he had long, shimmering wings that shone into space, his beard was so huge that he could keep bees in it. I noticed he had straps on the wings that fastened them over a pink quilted jumpsuit. His fuchsia antigravity boots held him a meter and a half above the surface, forming circles on the lazily flowing slurry. Though he was five feet and with heels that looked strange on the anti-gravity heavy boots, he was certainly human.

"Who the hell are you?" I asked.

I wasn't just surprised by this floating creature. Even the pursuers stopped and stared at him.

I am a rainbow fairy

I have the sun in your gaze

I am already carrying the cloud

I am pink and white

I dance, look how![2]

The foreteller finished rapping in a sonorous voice. It sounded just as menacing as the retro hits that were now on N-level street teens.

"Could you please help me?" I blurted out desperately and punched the face of the sever man who had approached a dangerous distance.

Finally, I had both my hands free, because when the foreteller was rapping, the guy I was holding under the water drowned. Wherever he went, it was definitely a better place than the one he lived in.

"Of course, Mr. Vachten. Perhaps you should plunge into the arms of this coffee river again," said the foreteller, and at that

---

[2] This and other unmarked fragments come from the song "Duhová víla" by Hana Zagorova - a popular Czech singer [translator's note].

moment I noticed that there was a black metal-plastic container between his flapping wings. He pulled a tube from behind a blue band, and when there was a "click", a small flame of fire appeared at the end of it.

"A fairy with a flamethrower," I whispered, took a deep breath, and plunged into the slush again. I still managed to hear:

Look, look, the rainbow hall!

Look, look, the rainbow ball!

And where is the king at this ball??

The world above me changed from pink to red-yellow. I had to hold my breath for more than two minutes, but couldn't hold it any longer and had to surface. I didn't think there could be an even bigger stench in the sewers than when I lost my mask, but the combination of burned bodies and shit evaporating from the surface of the sewage showed it was possible.

I will throw myself into the slaughter

Your burning temples

I give the rainbow guard

What smells like chamomile

"I don't want to argue with the flamethrower guy, but chamomile doesn't smell like it here," I said, drawing saliva all the way from my heels to remove any slurry from my mouth.

"Of course, I can feel it too. Even Unicorn Perfume cannot cope with it," said the foreteller sadly.

I appreciated that he gave up the crap rapping people listened to a hundred years ago, and worse, which was becoming fashionable again. I did not react to the remark about Unicorn Perfume.

"Could you please help me out of here before the other sever men get here?" I asked, in spite of the situation, quite matter-of-factly and calmly.

"Other? My refill to the flamethrower has run out," the foreteller was scared.

"Another reason to get out of here."

"Please, without embarrassment, it was heard from the magic receiver," the guy replied and shook my hand.

I had no idea what he was talking about, but I squeezed the provided hand, and after a while we were both upstairs. The shoes had to work at full power, because it was quite slow. But it's always better than nothing. Reinforcements of the Praetorian sewer guards broke through the slurry towards us. I landed on a concrete surface and heard a baby chattering softly.

"What the fuck is this?" The terrified Belch pointed at the foreteller.

He could barely catch his breath. The memory of the good old days gave him a real blast. Despite everything, he managed to make the child not only alive, but also stop roaring and choking on the foul air.

"Rainbow fairy," the guy explained, flapping his wings about two feet from us.

"We have to go, asap." I ignored both, grabbed the kid and ran up the stairs.

The bastard began to roar immediately.

...to the clouds...

Half an hour later we managed to reach the service shaft of the U metro line, which was still in use. It wasn't that easy, because we had to crawl through a narrow hole that the sever men had dug here with primitive tools. The foreteller helped carry the child upstairs, and Belch and I, despite being exhausted, broke through that narrow opening into the shaft. Immediately thereafter, we secured it with a solid steel cover that subway maintenance workers installed last week in a futile struggle with the ever-emerging new passage of sever men to the surface. We only opened it because of the search for an orphan.

The sounds of the pursuers following us had stopped about a good ten minutes ago, but I could still feel their odor lingering behind me. Most likely, however, it was us, and I, and the Pole, that stank so much.

Through the shaft we got to the Veleslavín station. It's probably rush hour again, but the U-meter underground was still overcrowded. People not only moved from place to place, but traded and lived here. Two dirty guys with a naked child and a fortune teller... Well, we still didn't get much attention. For example, an Easter bunny stood nearby. According to tradition, she was completely naked, only the plush tail was sticking out of her anal opening. In one hand she held a traditional Czech Easter rod made of eight wires, and in the other a plastic basket. People came over to feel her breasts and be whipped with a rod for good luck. The stronger the stripes, the greater the promise of happiness throughout the year. Then they threw small coins or caloric bars into the basket.

"Hey you, come to the Security. You will get health insurance. Great recruitment for men with a future." The information drone caught us practically right after entering the station. A moment ago it was buzzing by the bunny, but she chased him away with her tail.

We ignored it, as did City News reports of the upcoming mayoral elections. It was only Belch that caught his attention to them.

"This is your boss, isn't it?" He nudged me with his elbow.

He was holding the toddler again. Somehow he was able to calm him down. But I took the pistol with the last round.

Above our heads, the foreteller flapped his wings, obscuring the screen in front of us. However, it was enough to tilt your head to see the holographic transmission of City News over the passing subway train. He was right. Right now Mina was talking about her ambitious plans to run for mayor.

"She fired me," I growled and quickened my pace.

"And are you surprised at her?" the Pole smiled maliciously.

As for the fact that less than an hour ago he had almost die and had a crust of his own blood on his face in addition to a pile of mud and grease, he looked quite pleased.

We passed another Easter bunny - which probably had a one-meter tail, looked at least two hundred kilos and was just whipping a family with three children with a rod - and we left the station onto the street. The air quality did not change much, but two more foretellers were waiting for us. One was smoking a huge cigar and sending pink smoke rings up towards the tops of skyscrapers.

Tired, I sat down on a rickety bench with a double swastika, the symbol of the Black Rebirth, and finally tucked the gun under my jacket. Belch, the original owner, did not protest.

"Well, you elven freaks. Who are you and why did you save our butts?" I asked, resigned. Not that I am not grateful to the rainbow creature and his flame thrower, but what's there to talk about? I could get out of the sewers somehow, but when you are among the sever men and a bearded foreteller shining pink comes for you, it becomes known that you will soon get into some serious trouble.

And as always, I was right.

* * *

"We have a job for you, Lieutenant Vachten," said the cigar-smoking foreteller, and released another pink puff.

"I'm not anyone's lieutenant for a long time," I sighed, and the Pole nodded.

"Yes, he washes dishes at my place and sleeps in a three-shift hotel," he added.

"Madame Lota wants to talk to you. Immediately. She doesn't like to wait. She has it after her grandfather," finally explained the foreteller with the flamethrower.

"What Lota?" I raised a sullen eyebrow.

"There is only one Lota, Mr. Vachten," smiled the rainbow foreteller, and at that moment a pack of cheerful youth stopped a short distance from us. Two girls and three boys, all in pink sweatshirts.

"Look, the drops are rolling, I have more of them in my hand than you!" One of the boys started shouting.

The foretellers waved at them enthusiastically.

"OK, I'm going. Anything but listening to this stupid song," I gave in and winked at the Pole because of the gun.

He nodded that I could leave her alone. I preferred not to think about how much I owe him already. My guns - my favorite K22 - had to be stuffed to pay for the rent at a three-shift hotel. It functioned according to the principle stated in the name. The human had exactly eight hours to get enough sleep before being replaced by another tenant. Once a week it was possible to take an ion shower which was included in the price. I shared the bed with a whore and one guy who was acting as a security guard at DEZATEG. The whore turned out fine. Sometimes she left candy on my pillow. The dude smelled of oil, and the bitch and I caught fleas once. But it took a pinch of salt.

"I'll take the bastard to Cursed Bitch Teresa," Belch said.

"Don't forget to charge them. Hope the guys don't charge me. I would not like to suck them in exchange for magic dust."

"Lick," corrected me the rainbow foreteller with the flamethrower and huge beard.

Seriously, I wouldn't have figured it out. Mentally, I prayed to the Easter Bunny that last year's flogging would be useful.

* * *

I couldn't get rid of this stupid song. The foretellers loaded me into the hovercraft, and as soon as we got off the ground, they played a song in a half-hour, remixed version. The original, archaic performance was gradually joined by all current performers known from the City News Show tits or cock and sing music program. Earlier, one of the foretellers took a blanket from the trunk and put it on the back seat. I think when I get off they ritually burn it. Actually, it didn't surprise me at all. I was all sticky with crap sewage, and the stench of crust drying on every part of my body and clothes didn't make me unconscious just because fresh air began pouring into the open hovercraft.

After a while we found ourselves above the skyscrapers. The sun began to set over the queen of cities and it made an incredibly romantic impression. If I hadn't experienced what was happening down there, I might have got the impression that I live in the happiest city in the world. This was probably what the people below thought, who were now boarding the fragrant express train at the Košíře N-metro station.

Soon we reached the new center all the way to the VEP-tower, the headquarters of the VEP Corporation, one of the five most powerful companies that practically controlled all life in Prague. I had a few hot moments here on Christmas, but it felt like it happened in the last century. We have just rubbed against one of the balconies on which Caucasian firs grew, hung with shells from real hens, painted in traditional Easter diamonds, and I found myself singing wearily with the hovercraft player: In your gaze I have the sun... I hit my head prophylactically and right now we landed on a small heliport about a tenth floor from the summit.

I jumped out and a few pieces of dried shit fell off me. I looked up at the sky and saw a flock of hovercraft coming in from all directions. The foretellers led me across the adjoining terrace to a small room. It looked like a greenhouse. It was filled with strange plants that I had never seen live. Some of them smelled so intensely that they might even outshine my odor. The two foretellers disappeared somewhere between the trees, leaving a lonely rainbow fairy with an empty flamethrower. She led me down a tiled corridor to the bathroom. Water bathroom to be clear. I mean bathrooms with real water.

"Have you ever washed yourself with water?" She asked me from behind a huge chin.

"Fire up, Maya bee," I growled, closing the plastic door between me and the flying monster.

I desecrated the space in front of the contactless sensor with a dirty paw and turned on the cold water with a finger gesture. I tilted my mouth towards her and started drinking heavily.

* * *

The water in Prague is not the same everywhere. Most importantly, not equally accessible. Getting one liter of drink each day was often a more important expense for a person than, for example, a night. Most of all, the water that was sold downstairs turned out to be smelly shit. This one here was of the highest quality. Real clear water that you didn't have to jump on one leg for ten minutes to stop the bubbling in your stomach. I finished drinking and took off my clothes. On the floor of the clean white bathroom, a pile of tattered rags looked like a corpse in a monthly schedule. I got in the shower, set a pleasant temperature, and immediately began to be massaged by water from six different jets. I was fucking having fun. I soaped myself with perfumed purple mucus from a glass bottle and rinsed. And so three times.

"Mr. Lieutenant?" A woman's voice came from behind the glass partition.

I pushed her back and saw a young brunette in an ankle-length red dress. Her hair was braided into two braids tied with long brown pins. Her gown was embroidered with oriental dragons biting each other's tails. Slits on either side were waist-deep, revealing that he wasn't wearing any underwear. I myself stood completely naked in front of her. Sharing your bed with a prostitute will deprive you of all your inhibitions, not to mention the worker with fleas.

"I'm not…"

"I brought clean clothes," she interrupted me.

There was indeed some black cloth in her hand. I went outside and turned on the body dryer. After a while, there was not a drop of moisture left on me. I resisted the urge to go back to the shower and reluctantly took clothes from her. The material was incredibly light, thin and pleasant to the touch. I put on the pants and tried on the top.

"In this way." She helped me.

It was some complicated shirt or what the hell it was. All strewn with silver flowers. It looked like something out of some historical movie - no buttons, just cords that need to be knotted and tied together. She finally handed me the leather sandals. I looked like a porn eunuch. She herself was standing in black high heels.

"Ivana," she said.

"I didn't ask."

"I noticed. I'm not stupid, Mr. Lieutenant."

"I'm not…" I growled.

I found it pointless to finish this sentence. Suddenly I missed the foretellers.

"The celebrations have long started. If you don't want to miss the most beautiful performance, we should go," she said after a moment and smiled.

She had such an indulgent, slightly contemptuous, omniscient look. It was annoying.

I walked through the pile of dirty rags from which I fished a gun and stuffed it into my pants. It was worth more than my kidneys. Especially for a Pole.

* * *

We took the stairs to the third floor and found ourselves in a room I already knew. Huge space that could be accessed from outside from a large hovercraft heliport. The whole place has changed since my last visit. And it is thorough. Music greeted us at the entrance. No remixes of Hana Zagorova, which would be appreciated, but music coming from real musical instruments. It had nothing to do with the neophytes that can sometimes be heard on the street. At the edge of a hall full of marble columns decorated with living flowers, garlands and draperies, several musicians lay on carpets. They played harps, lutes, flutes and other instruments that I had never seen in my life, let alone know the names. Little fairies and foretellers floated in the air, and they wore only togas instead of leather clothes and flamethrowers. They looked like they were out of some medieval movie. Or rather like from some pseudo-historical fairy tale. Women in long dresses, men in something like me, some even wore some kind of armor. There were even a few swords at the waist. Young girls held trays with glass cups filled with...

"Wait a minute, isn't that mead?" The nose registered a characteristic smell that I have not felt since the war.

Ivana smiled pityingly, but I kept one girl anyway and drained a glass from her tray. The drink struck me.

Meanwhile, the music fell silent and the muffled sound of a harp rang out in the silence. The hall lights went out. Now only real candles were lit in the chandeliers hanging from the ceiling.

"Come on, the show begins," Ivana whispered, leading me a few meters away.

Lota Dejčerová sat on a stylized throne in an azure dress. Two foretellers with huge daggers at their belts huddled at her feet. Several young men and women crowded under the throne.

I sat down on a fluffy, brocade pillow. One of the musicians started playing the Pan flute and the elves ran into the center of the hall. Naked. They only had flower wreaths in their hair. Of course they weren't real elves, but that was what the dancers looked like. Perfect young, athletic bodies, ears made by a plastic surgeon, and their faces with long hair full of flowers gave the illusion incredible strength. They danced for a moment, then intertwined for a while, and finally a fire-breathing dragon ran between them. It was a realistic leather suit, covered with scales, which masked several men. After a while of dancing, running, and even singing, the elves defeated him and began kissing on his lifeless body. There was applause and ovation in the room. I joined it, although for this type of fairy tale, seriously, I was too old.

"Mr. Lieutenant?"

"That idiot word again."

Lota was sticking out above me. I remembered her younger. Now her recently twenty-year-old face showed two deep lines around her mouth and one on her forehead. Nowadays, inheriting a business and technological empire would bring many problems. It's not like killing a dragon, I thought and stood up.

At this point, she left the hall, and the foretellers followed her. Ivana and I walked past the room where Lota's grandpa was murdered - the door was sealed - and we got into a smaller room where a fire was burning in the fireplace. For no practical reason. Outside, a typical Prague spring was raging, with 40 degrees temperatures and an air as dry as the jokes of the homeless. But I understand that it gave the space an atmosphere. Lota sat down on a wooden chair covered with red velvet, and the companions flew away, closing the door behind them. I sat down across from her and Ivana stood.

"I'm surprised by your carefree attitude," I said, trying to find a comfortable position.

"Why?" She asked.

"You're not afraid of me?"

Lota just smiled.

"You don't even have a decent gun with you. Unlike Ivana," she replied.

I looked at the brunette with braids.

"Does she have a submachine gun in the ass?"

Ivana reached out and a laser bow about a meter long extended. I think it could be used to weld pipes and cut hovercraft in half.

"Her family came to Prague from somewhere in North Bohemia. However, on the outskirts of the city, they were shot by automatic systems. She survived because she was a child. But no limbs. My grandfather gave the smugglers two crowns for her and improved her over time. The beautiful legs you see are artificial. Better you don't know what's in them."

I swallowed loudly.

"Besides... somehow I'm not afraid of you. I know who you are, Mr. Vachten. I know you wanted to save my grandfather and stopped Albert Viktor. Do you know he's called Jack the Ripper today?"

I shook my head. I didn't care. Because of this bastard, I lost my flat and livelihood, but I did not complain.

"His death set many things in motion..." She hung an unfinished sentence in the air. I guess she learned it from her ancestor.

"That's not why I'm here. I'm not interested in politics. I guess you know about me," I said. I know what she meant - mayoral election.

While in recent years corporations have become content with the avatar of a once elected but long-dead mayor who maintains the semblance of democracy, they are now embarking on an enterprise called elections. A dangerous thing. The elections never did any good. Always only loss of hope and disappointment.

"You may not be interested in politics, but politics is interested in you. It'll get any of us in the end anyway." She shrugged.

"My grandfather used to say that politics is like a whore - you have to know when to get on it and when to get off it, so you don't catch anything."

"Then he would get along with my grandfather," smiled Lota.

"I doubt it. My grandfather was an alcoholic. He had nothing. Just like me. He was just a cop."

"Just like you."

"I'm not a cop anymore."

"But I need a cop," Lota replied.

It surprised me a lot.

"There are plenty of them in the Security."

She shook her head.

"The Security is full of people who can get someone off the street who creates problems. They can also obey orders and, if necessary, clean up someone on their basis. But there's no decent cop out there. The cops are gone. You are the last."

I couldn't help but huff.

"Hmm. That's nice of you, miss, but no matter what you need a cop for, I'm not anymore. I'm fed up with my own work," I said, and stood up.

If that fairy with the flamethrower hadn't saved my ass, I wouldn't have bothered to come here.

"You mean the job that Fairy Fay comes up with to keep you from starving, and you pay for it with your savings from better times?"

"What?" I frowned. But I didn't move.

"At Cursed Whore Teresa, they are grateful for every child that dies, because it will leave more food for the others. I know this because it is one of the places where I load my money. In life, they could not pay anyone twenty crowns to find a baby. Nobody wanted to burn down the dog meat sausage stand either. Fay paid them to give you food and money to stare at the suspects hanging around all day long. Nobody else in this city will make you earn, and certainly not for a real job. Mina already took care of it. You betrayed her trust, you are already dead to this city. Without your... ex...?" She frowned, as if searching for the right word to describe our brief relationship with the cybersorceress, and continued. "Without Fay, you would have starved to death."

"If you know Mina killed me for the city, why do you want to hire me?"

I capitulated. Sure Fay had her hands on those last picks. She got it all over this idiot Belch. They had a deal. Shit, what a moron I am! My fingers tightened on the back of the chair until it hurt.

"I don't care about Mina. She does not interest me, although she is very interested in me, it does not matter. In this city, someone is committing crimes worse than politics. After the fall of DEZATEG, I am the owner of Praga's Security. I am restoring your old position and rank, plus your salary and account. Ivana will take care of it..." "There is no crime worse than politics, miss," I growled, but wasn't sure.

"Someone killed Petlán. Today at noon. He was not first and probably not the last..."

"Who carried out the crime scene investigation?" I interrupted her.

I didn't realize how quickly and instinctively I jumped on this case, and yet if someone overthrew the owner of PRAGUETECH, one of the most powerful corporations controlling the city, it smelled of politics per kilometer.

"Nobody yet. I had them secured. It's waiting for you."

"How can I be sure that I will take care of this matter?" I asked finally.

"Because you're the last cop in this fucking town. These are your words, aren't they?" she smiled.

And she was right. I guess for real I was the last cop in this fucking town.

...and back

Dusk has fallen. As Ivana and I were getting ready to leave, the party was entering a new phase. The naked elves began to copulate with each other, and their sexual party was immediately attacked by the dwarves with helmets and axes. Real sex - I understand that, but I didn't like all this weird theatrical fantasy. But that's how it worked. While one could not get enough of the technical innovations, another escaped into the world of dreams and fantasies. Reality as such is always too frightening for man to resist the temptation to run away from it. Everyone did, rich and poor. Except the rich could afford it in a little more style than by inhaling the fumes of cheap glue.

I grabbed one of the foretellers who hadn't turned into an armored dwarf and grabbed my coffee. Real coffee. I almost burned myself, I drank it so greedily. I stained my weird, fantastic clothes a bit, but I didn't care. I was used to dirt. Only Ivana gave me a grudging look. She had put on a leather jacket over her oriental dress. She looked like... well, just fucking sexy. I remembered what Lota had said about her origins. I looked at her legs and found nothing that indicated that they were artificial. But that's how the technology worked, the more money, the better the effect.

At first I thought we would go to the headquarters of PRAGUETECH, a two-story monster glowing orange all over the area. Instead, we got to the old center to the Staromiejska metro station. Here the N line did not arrive. The old center did not attract the rich. What was outside turned out to be better, more fragrant and crazier. While the artificial prostitutes had four vaginas here, the whores at Kolbenov's station were able to offer six fully functional holes of this type, plus some anal. (Likke real! Try it, you will not regret it! Under the Fragrant Pussy with a Monday discount of 30%!). I couldn't understand what could be attractive about it, but there were people who tried everything out of boredom.

The hovercraft descended from the darkness over the city into the night glow under the pillars supporting the S. metro line, Ivana for a moment as if searching for something, then navigation led it through old tenement houses to a place where a hundred onlookers and ten the Security officers stood.

"Kotrman cocoa in a thousand ways!" Proclaimed the neon sign above the booth that someone had constructed from an old electric bus permanently attached to the wall of the tenement house. The original paint of the body was peeled off by rust, then the body was covered with bright colors. It looked like it was taken out of a documentary about an ancient hippie movement. Blacks, whites, Romas, Indians, Asians and God knows who else - sat together and drank cocoa. Above them was the inscription: I drink cocoa, so that nothing bad happens.

"I think someone got fucked by a muse with ten condoms," I sighed as I tried to read the faded text.

"Mr. Lieutenant?" Ivana said, smoothly landing in front of a line of well-armed safes, in a place separate from the crowd of onlookers. To my surprise, most of them wore bulletproof vests, helmets, and shields. I have not yet seen a crime scene secured by the armed forces. Besides, at least ten Security drones, armed with rotary machine guns, were snarling above us. If someone were crazy enough to spy a drone here, they would probably turn it into a pile of shredded scrap in a second.

"Oh, yes," I growled, ignoring the inscription and the bizarre paintings.

We approached the two navy security guards who were guarding the body. A square barrier made of white sheets hung on a simple plastic structure was installed around the corpse. I pushed one of them aside and went inside.

Ivana waited outside.

"Fuck, you can't..." said Major Karel Adam, my former police colleague, now newly appointed the Security Commander.

"You talk faster than you think. Always the same, right?" I smiled crookedly.

He waved his hand resignedly, as if chasing away an obtrusive advertising mini-drone.

"I should have known when I got the news that a new detective would take over the investigation, that they would send the biggest asshole in all of Prague," he replied and added, "I thought you were enjoying your luxurious who..." that word left unsaid.

This is probably some new trend among people - I thought.

"A whore, a bitch, a cyberhooker, a trans-bitch, go ahead," I dispelled his embarrassment.

"...the love of your life?" He said sarcastically.

"It's complicated. Life is complicated." I sighed and started examining the body.

"Is that why you look like a male prostitute in those velvet pajamas?"

"It's complicated too." I rolled my eyes.

"Nothing is complicated. Only you are the idiot who absolutely has to crush your life into atoms. It's always been like that," he growled, but when he saw that I was taking care of a dead Petlán, he quieted.

"Were the technicians here?"

"A whole army. They scanned what they could, every fold, every atom strained through contraptions, but the murderer had cleaned everything up with an ozone chloride solution."

"What?"

"This is some kind of brutal disinfection. Coats the surface with an ozone film that destroys the smallest biological traces. There is no complete DNA left to indicate the culprit, no strand or pubic hair. Nothing. Just a corpse and this." He handed me a bag of small, hard pieces of something black.

"Couldn't it have been here earlier?" I grimaced.

"Apparently not. It's a piece of clay. It is not found in this area. This could have fallen off the killer's shoe or other garment. This contains clay, silt, and traces of many different chemicals. Most likely from some factory or warehouse. Quite possibly belonging to PRAGUETECH," the Security man explained.

Traces. I hated them. They rarely helped, and most of all, they distracted me from what was most important - the story that unfolded here.

"How was he unprotected?... He has... He had a lot of money. He was the master of a quarter of the city. He was your master. Without his permission, you couldn't even whack off."

"Says the guy who's doing the same job now..."

"Fuck off."

"No, you fuck off," retorted Adam, but then took me by the screen. Twenty meters away was another one with two dead bodies.

I asked Karel to leave me alone for a while and try to calm the crowd as they chanted something I didn't understand. When he was gone, I put on the rubber gloves I took from him and unbuttoned the jacket of the first bodyguard. There wasn't much left of it. The perpetrator inflicted six stab wounds on him with a blade at least twenty centimeters long, and perhaps longer. His friend looked similar. He picked up five stab wounds - one more fatal than the other. He was probably the first to get hit. Someone surprised them. The first was attacked from behind and struck in the kidneys, and the second in the abdomen. They hadn't even had time to get their pistols - a serrated chrome PR 05 with a twenty-five round magazine. For a while I struggled with the urge to appropriate them, but I realized that I am actually a cop now, and cops don't do things like that.

Contrary to the mercenary necks from dirty work, which I was also this morning.

As a reasonable compromise, I commandeered nine millimeter bullets from the magazines that fit my Makarov.

I returned to Petlán. He ended up worse than his security. Someone made chaff from his lungs with a blade. He not only stabbed, but also slashed. And it's fucking deep. The entire brocade shirt was soaked in blood, but it didn't stop there. The murderer went to a lot of trouble and drew a circle on the victim's body with a black felt-tip pen, through which two crossed lines ran. I rummaged in Petlan's pockets, but found nothing but twenty crowns bills, and turned the corpse on its side. I noticed a tattoo. It looked like the italicized numbers 6 and 9.

I ran a gloved hand over them and they blurred. So it wasn't a tattoo but a drawing - just like this weird circle. If I hated anything more than clues, it was the clue-leaving killer. It's that fucking tip from the murderer.

"Exhibitionist prick," I sighed and walked out from behind the screen. I looked around the area. The crowd in front of the police barrier on both sides of the street was thickening. I swung the fly and, unexpectedly, perhaps for the first time, managed to knock it to the ground. She quickly embraced herself and joined her friends who were already using them in the drying bloody pool from Petlán's corpse. There was a plastic plate with the number 14 near the screen. It indicated a possible trace. Next to it, on the ground in a puddle of brown slush, was a large plastic cup.

I headed towards the booth.

* * *

There was a real cocoa scent in the old electric bus. However, I doubted that such a booth had access to real milk or cocoa beans. The price range on the drinks card confirmed my reasoning. The woman behind the counter was over sixty, which did not stop her from wearing an Easter Bunny costume with a long plush tail tucked between her buttocks. Her long, stretched breasts fluttered between the leather straps. She washed the plastic cups and then wiped them with a damp cloth. It didn't look very appetizing, as she was constantly sniffing and wiping the snot off her nose with the cloth at the same time.

"Would you like to drink something?" She asked.

"Cocoa."

"But what? We are famous for the fact that we really have many kinds," she sobbed through her tears and icicles.

"Maybe Playful Cocoa according to Bohdalka, or Jiřina Bohdalova?" I read the first name that caught the eye.

"It's from our retro collection. But it is not as popular as Zagorka Cocoa, which is according to Hana Zagorova's recipe. Mr Petlán liked that very much. He always waited for a decent sheepskin coat to get on. He loved sheepskin coats, you know?" And she started crying again.

I made sure she poured into a mug that hadn't survived the last wash and tried it. Zagorka Cocoa, which I finally ordered because of Petlán, turned out to be so sweet that it made my tongue go numb.

"Why?" I smiled at the bunny.

I think she guessed from my expression that I was interested in why someone who could afford real cocoa made of genuine milk would come to such a kennel to drink something like this...

Uhhh - my sip of cocoa receded. I used my best to swallow it again and not ask if they were preparing it from the boiled icicles of the local staff.

"He said that as a boy he used to come here with his mother, apparently he had memories of happy moments coming back here," she explained, blowing her nose on a cup-wiping cloth.

I watched with fascination at her drenched, dry breasts, and when I finally managed to tear myself away from them, I looked towards the screen. It never occurred to me that this man was not born into luxury. Sometimes things are just too complicated.

"I whipped him fortunately," she said after sniffing out her nose. Her interrogation was practically the same.

"It didn't do much, did it?" I wiped the cocoa mustache off my upper lip. My proverbial tact produced a powerful stream of tears, accompanied by a sniffle.

"Did you see what happened here?"

"I already told the Security," she sobbed.

"Maybe, but they're a little idiotic. Did you see the killer?" my tact and empathy reached its zenith.

"Only after it was over. Mr Petlán was carrying his Zagorka with a double sprinkle when suddenly he ran up to him. He had a knife in his hand and..."

More streams of tears.

"Did you see the face?"

She shook her head.

"He had this long black hoodie over his head. But he wore large black glasses under the hood."

"How did Petlán react?"

"He got into a conversation with him."

"About what?"

The waitress shrugged.

"They talked for a while. A few sentences. I thought it was a joke or that they knew each other from the old days, but then..."

"They had fun with stabbing?"

Today I was the king of empathy.

During this time, she blew out some big snot. I preferred to look away to the enormous City News projection hitting the side of her booth. There was no escaping this television. There were screens or projectors at every corner.

A man could walk halfway through the city without missing a second of the program. The Corporate Council was also trying to do this by installing the ubiquitous receivers. If you want to control the ten-millionth mass crammed among concrete and scabies, then you can't let it think too much. At most, whether the poor flower seller - Marika, will finally win the heart of a rich guy Pijer, a Polish cabbage trader, who got rich in Prague and became an idol of women, girls and virgins. At least that was the plot of the hundred-episode series Pijer and Marik, which was just passing before your eyes. Marika enlarged her breasts because of Pijer. However, the insidious surgeon Dorian Svoboda - convinced that Pijer was responsible for the death of his fiancée Jana - put plastic explosives in them instead of nanosilicon. The moment Pijer touches her tits and does "here, here, here", they will both explode. Only Pijer is a gentleman and he doesn't touch Marika's breast...

"God, what a shit that is," I spoke to the smell of cocoa and went back to watching my constant sobbing and sniffling. Due to the show and the sobbing waitress, I didn't even notice that the atmosphere around me was starting to thicken.

"We're falling," said Karel, standing behind my squares.

"If someone is screwing on it, just call Lota." I waved my free hand, wanting to continue with the questioning of the snotty queen of chocolate substitute.

"Dude, they want to massacre us!"

I turned and saw the police special units give way to the billowing crowd. While I was petting dead bodies and conducting a teary audition, the crowd thickened.

"The Security is tyranny! Freedom for People! Food for everyone!" finally, the chanting of the crowd reached me in an understandable form.

"You have drones and an armed army. Do something about it," I said to Adam.

"What about this?" He pointed to the other side.

Twelve hovercraft bearing the PRAGUETECH logo arrived from the new center. They did not look like ordinary cars, nor in a deluxe version for the rich. The black color was aggressive, as were the machines themselves, which - as you can see at first glance - had a coating of nano-steel. PRAGUETECH is a producer of a good half of the combat drones that protected the borders of Prague from the outside, and it looked like the famous armored division of the corporation. The hovercraft circled the Security drones for a while, but then fell to the ground. Five armed men in bulletproof suits and black helmets with bulletproof lenses jumped out of each of them. The Security could only dream of something like that. Meanwhile, members of the Security Corps began to retreat dangerously towards the black cavalry.

"New world! New world!" The crowd chanted again.

A mass of heads loomed from behind the police cordon.

"How much do I owe?" I asked the saleswoman.

"Five."

"Karel, pay for me. This shit has no pockets for change." I winked at Adam and headed for the crowd.

Of course, even if my suit had pockets, I wouldn't find a heller in them. There was also a zero on my e-account. In addition, I made an exchange trade - I gave a cell band for five cans of ultraprotein lunch.

The chief of The Security officers caught up with me when armed with PRAGUETECH caught the body of their former boss. Two of them put automatic rifles back on their shoulders and pounced on the corpse.

"You're obstructing the police investigation," I interrupted them.

I think they were surprised. They looked at each other, then one of them lifted the lens of his helmet.

"What?" He asked surprised.

The guy was nearly two meters. I noticed the green eyes staring at me in amazement.

"That's the law you are breaking now. You can go to jail. Obstructing an investigation is a serious crime." I shrugged.

"Dude, you must be fucked up," Adam growled in my ear.

He looked as if he was about to shake with a force of at least five on the Richter scale.

"Who the hell do you think you are?" The guy huffed.

The others aimed their guns at me. These were the PRT-99 double-barreled jointed cholers. He spits not only with nine-millimeter bullets, but also with decent laser shots.

"I'm investigating a crime and you're spoiling my job," I replied, sipping cocoa casually. Surprisingly, it didn't taste so bad anymore. The feeling of nausea was suppressed within seconds.

"You're Karel Adam, aren't you?" The man turned to the Security Commander. The man just nodded, so the armed man added:

"Who is this idiot?" he meant me, of course.

"Responsible for the investigation into the murder of Mr. Petlán. VEP hired him," he explained.

The guy choked for a moment.

"Don't let that bitch from VEP screw up with PRAGUETECH affairs. The body of our CEO will be taken by..."

Pride comes before a fall. Or it leads to a lack of vigilance, and a lack of vigilance can cause someone like me to suddenly pick an old Soviet gun out of his comfy velvet suit and stick it through the helmet's opening right between the eyes. As soon as I did that, all the guys in black had the deadly slot machines unlocked. It was enough for one of them to pull the trigger and I would be turned into scorched greaves with minimal nutritional value.

"You make the work of the police difficult," I repeated in a calm voice.

I think the commando chief was surprised that someone could point a gun at him as well.

"My God," Adam sighed, terrified, and looked at the two approaching safety cordons.

The distance between them narrowed rapidly as the righteous people gave way to the thickening crowd. Soon it will be crowded in front of Petlán's body.

"But," gasped the guy with the gun stuck to the bridge of his nose.

"There is not any "but". Someone killed your boss. I understand some people might not have a shit for it, but I do my job here, so don't pump your ego, just get out of the fucking crime scene," I said as calmly as possible and drank cocoa.

I felt a disgusting lump in my mouth. I quickly spat it on the street dust and, in order not to empty my stomach, I tried not to look at what bounced off the ground and, making a humming noise, disappeared into the distance.

We stood facing each other for about twenty seconds. Neither twitched. I mean, neither I nor any of the armed men of PRAGUETECH. Meanwhile, the police force behind me approached me dangerously. I even felt the stench of bodies, huddled together, chanting strange slogans. But seeing the unusual scene in which we acted as living statues gradually silenced them. They moved another tens of centimeters closer to the guys in black, and they moved back to me. Drones, controlled by someone from security outside our street idyll, growled overhead. We were now like Pijer. It was enough to do the indecent "here, here, here" and those tits laden with explosives will cause a street massacre.

"We want the truth!" Someone shouted behind me in a familiar voice.

* * *

70

I turned towards the crowd with the gun still pointed at the guy. A familiar face emerged from between the bodies of the two officers.

"Hi Caesar," I grumbled, still watching my target.

I had to stick the barrel a little harder on his forehead. Hectoliters of sweat were dripping off him.

"Are you working for the Council again?" Caesar muttered.

"I'm investigating a homicide again," I replied.

Surprisingly, the crowd was still silent. Caesar climbed onto some giant's back. He has aged since I saw him in a tent town on Pod Lipami Street, where the poor lived, who still hadn't fallen across the U-line to the level of the sewers. He still had a few teeth missing, but he looked not only more mature but also more confident. He was wearing an old tweed jacket with no buttons. In this heat of Easter it would be madness to button it up anyway. Plus, worn-out corduroy pants, sandals, and a white T-shirt. A cap on the head.

"What are you doing here? Did you go with your buddies for cocoa?" I asked after a moment, shaking the leftovers at the bottom of the cup.

At any moment, I could die trampled on by a human herd, so it was time to wonder if I wanted to do it with that nasty slush in my mouth. But I finally drank.

It was definitely not one of the best decisions of my life.

"Apparently Petlán is here, everyone says that. We demand our rights!" Caesar shouted, and the crowd chanted in a multi-voice:

"Yes! Yes!"

"Someone bumped Petlán off. And that's why we are fighting a war with his friend here over the nerves about who will take his body."

I almost had to scream for the words to reach Caesar.

He, with the help of two young girls, climbed up the back of his saddled giant and stood on his shoulders, silencing the crowd with a few firm gestures.

"You're kidding?" he blurted out.

I nodded at Adam to reveal a nearby screen. He lunged at him with such force that he smashed the structure, revealing the sight of the dead body to everyone.

* * *

My hand started to ache. I kept it pulled out for so long that in the meantime Pijer forced the sneaky Dr. Dorian to pull the explosives out of his beloved's chest. Then everyone started singing and dancing. It looked quite scary, because Dr. Dorian was holding a bloody scalpel in his hand, but it still bothered me less than the announced next show, Paint Pictures Again, in which City News celebrities were to sing re-arranged hits by Hana Zagorova.

I finished my cocoa and slowly lowered my gun, secured it, and tucked it back into the waistband of the fancy suit. But the guys kept pointing at me.

"We'll get your body back tomorrow morning. We have to take them to the police lab," I finally said amicably.

The armed guy slid the glass closed, which made him invulnerable. And inaudible. From the way his helmet moved, I figured he was talking to someone.

Then he turned without a word, as did his companions. They jumped into the hovercraft and disappeared.

However, I had no doubts that tomorrow the entire team, along with a lot of PRAGUETECH lawyers, would appear at the Security Headquarters. And PRAGUETECH's lawyers are much smarter and ruthless boys and girls than gunmen with guns.

I felt relieved. Probably too much, because I lost my vigilance and vomited half of the cocoa in a fit of nausea. Meanwhile, the crowd behind me said that someone had already lynched the powerful businessman for them and started singing I am a rainbow fairy... Coupled with the sounds my stomach made, it sounded fine.

This is what my beloved city looked like in a nutshell. It was like that lame dog with scabs - it smelled, fell apart, only acted sporadically, but still had something about it that made you pet the mutt anyway while holding your breath. Of course, you had to disinfect your hands afterwards, but it's still your beloved pooch.

"One more cocoa?" She asked amused Ivana, who had somehow reached us, breaking through the demonstrators.

Instead of answering, I chucked up one more time.

Zodiac

As the individual demonstrators and onlookers split into several groups arguing with each other on departure, it took a good half an hour before I got to the hovercraft with Ivana. Meanwhile, the safety officers loaded the dead bodies and, with all traces of the crime scene, brought them back to headquarters.

"Lota said you were going to pay me three hundred in advance," I said when Adam finally disappeared with the rest of his men.

"She didn't say anything like that," Ivana smiled.

"Okay, she didn't say, but I should probably get an advance." I winked at her in a way I thought was mischievous, but I guess I just scared her.

She shook her head and headed for the hovercraft.

I ran after her like a dog and sat on the edge of the back seat. It was a good decision because after its dramatic acceleration during take-off, my stomach twisted again and the demonstrators below us were sprinkled with the rest of cocoa.

We reached one of the residential skyscrapers that grew on the rocks of Dzika Šárka during the Bavarian crisis in the middle of the last century. We circled the thirtieth floor, about a third of the older but well-preserved building, and flew into a small indoor heliport next to an antiquated VEP 77 hovercraft. Ivana approached the door, which swung open on command. I figured he had all the necessary hardware in his limbs instead of the cellular band.

"Where are we?" I asked.

She pulled a cellular wristband out of her pocket.

"Here is your business apartment. This will give you access to everything. Also to the account. You can take your advance as well." Ivana smiled slyly and threw the band at me.

I grabbed it and squeezed it tight.

"I'll pick you up at nine tomorrow," she said after a moment of silence, and without further explanation, got into the hovercraft and disappeared.

* * *

I felt a slight musty smell. This surprised me as the air conditioning was clearly working before our arrival. Otherwise, the apartment could suffocate. But after walking from the corridor to the first room, I understood why. The bookcase was to blame. The huge real wood structure contained hundreds of volumes. Real paper books. I have never understood this fetish, but my boss had a soft spot for it too. Besides, such antiques represented real wealth. At least for those who could, above all, want to afford something like that.

Sun Tzu, The Art of War - I read on one of the books and looked at the footer. It was published in 1949.

"Shit, a lot of money," I said appreciatively, and put it on top of the others.

The rest of the room looked old-fashioned as well: a large bed with a meter-high mattress, a wicker rocking chair, and a wooden chess table. The living room, which also served as a bedroom, led directly to the bathroom. In addition to the enormous tub, there was also an ion shower. One of the first of its kind. Someone had arranged the flat right after the district was established and no one has renovated it afterwards. I opened one of the built-in wardrobes and found various pieces of clothing in it. I pulled out black pants, shorts, socks, and a white T-shirt. Everything smelled a bit musty, but it had not been twenty hours since I'd been swimming in the town's fermented shit, so I waved my hand and picked up the one that suited me best, navy blue. Considering the material, it was a good fit for snobbish retroparts, but the style basically matched the current trends.

And even if not. In this crazy city, everyone assumed what they wanted. Preferably nothing. Everyone does not care.

I stripped off the clothes I had gotten from Lota and just fell on an incredibly comfortable bed. I felt as if I was sinking into foam. I just wanted to close my eyes for a moment and then settle my old debts, but I zonked out completely. I didn't wake up until dawn.

* * *

"You have an erection, sir."

I narrowed my eyes and looked around. I haven't slept in a few days and this bed really put me down. Confused, I quickly summarized the memories of the last several dozen hours and tried to figure out where I was. Consciousness reluctantly woke up from the coma after an exhausting day. Somehow I wrapped myself up and I noticed Ivana. I was surprised she was dressed differently, but then realized I had slept all night and she mentioned something about arriving at nine in the morning. Just like yesterday's dress, this one also had a slit up to the waist. But this time it turned out to be green with familiar oriental motifs.

78

Finally, I caught up and looked at the subject of her interest.

"You see something like this for the first time?"

"No, but at your age and after what I've heard about you, I'm surprised you are still capable of something like this." She shrugged.

I looked deep into her eyes. I didn't know if she was really surprised or just making fun of me. I got up and walked over to the pile of clothes I discovered yesterday. Thanks to the fact that I have lost a lot of weight in the last months, everything fits like a glove. From the closet I dug up a belt for which I put the gun.

In the meantime, Ivana sat down on the bed and intuitively reached for the book that I had carelessly put aside yesterday.

"If the advantage increases, take action; if there is no hope of success, stay where you are," she recited from over the open page.

"What does it mean?" I asked.

"That we have a job, Lieutenant." She slammed the volume shut and got up from the bed I had been on all night.

"Mr. Lieutenant" I said.

"What?"

"Well, you are my assistant, aren't you? So the dynamics of our relationship should change a bit," I said, taking the book from her hand.

"The leader is captivating by example, not by force."

"What?"

"It's also from this book... Lieutenant, sir. I read it here after all my surgeries. And the rest, too," she explained.

"This is your apartment?"

"No... Mr. Lieutenant, this apartment belonged to Mr. Dejčer. His old student nest, as he used to say. Here he educated me in many areas of my life. In this one, for example," she said, pulling out a book called Kamasutra.

"Saw it on City News. Mice and gerbils played there, and every third joke was about farting."

"Eh, some casual variation, I guess." She shrugged.

"More like idiocy. All City News does is shit. Or propaganda."

"You can talk it over with them, because the director himself is waiting for us at ten."

"Reason?"

"The murder of one of their employees was the first reason Mrs. Lota called you. Nobody expected Mr. Petlán to die," she explained.

* * *

I pulled my sturdy black shoes from the closet, put them on, and allowed myself to be driven to the City News building. As our hovercraft approached it, I thought once again how it was possible that people living and moving around it did not get acute seizures. The entire CN skyscraper shone and flashed like a crazy Christmas tree.

From the entrance from the U level to the Dejvická metro station up to the 130th floor - CN transmission attacked from everywhere. The series "Young ladies" from the Střížkov station was just playing. One of the characters was banging on the head with the other feather duster, gesturing wildly at the same time. We landed at the highest heliport, where we were greeted by security in bulletproof vests and automatic machines in their hands. In addition, a concrete air raid shelter with machine guns was located a short distance from the landing field. Probably no one had such protection. Only the fourth authority, the media.

"We have a pass..." Ivana reported as some bodyguards approached us after the engine was turned off.

"We didn't shoot you down a hundred meters from the skyscraper, where the forbidden zone begins, so we're probably informed about it," the security chief interrupted sharply and helped out of the hovercraft with gallantry.

His boys searched us. They found a gun with me that I had to put in the backseat. It was only then that we were taken over by a lady in her fifties in a disposable black jumpsuit covered with glittering sequins.

"Director Král doesn't like to wait, we should hurry up," she said after the search was over.

I looked at my new cellular wristband. Debates about erections and the shoe hunt made us late. The display read five minutes past ten. Ivana sped up and I brushed her hand lightly to make her look at me. As soon as our eyes met, I discreetly shook my head. She understood and slowed her pace. The woman in black was slightly irritated by this, but she couldn't help it. As soon as she was a few meters ahead, she just had to stop and wait for us to approach the walking patients.

The office of Václav Král, the CEO of City News, occupied at least half a floor of the skyscraper. We couldn't really see where it ended because there was a small jungle in the middle of it, from which the sounds of parrots could be heard. On the other side, the air shuddered over the ten-meter pool. The CEO himself looked like a donut. He lost his neck somewhere, probably along with his spine, and decided to keep his stomach at least a meter in front of

82

the rest of his body. He sat behind an enormous desk that an average U-level family could use as an apartment, and with a massive gold signet ring, he tapped nervously on the wood.

The lady in black announced us and immediately disappeared. Apparently she was afraid of the penalty for bringing us late.

"I have no time. I have an important meeting in ten minutes," he said in greeting, and he tapped the ring hard on the table top.

I looked at this place and saw dozens of different indentations. He'd probably been discharging his nerves like this for a long time.

"You don't have. Please cancel them. This is a priority," Ivana said firmly.

I had to appreciate her tactics.

Král smirked as he continued to mutilate the desk top.

"I'm just listening to the Corporate Council, and that's not you, madame... miss...?" He shrugged in a questioning gesture.

"I'm an assistant to this lieutenant here. The Corporation Council has separated the spheres of influence, as you well know. City News belongs to VEP, and so is the Security, so you have to cooperate if you don't want that lady in black to sit in this chair tomorrow and your name is gone forever." Ivana smiled at him.

"Fuck..."

"Neither am I, Mr. Král. Just please show us everything we need. You know what," she said, and snapped her fingers.

Fluffy got up from behind his desk and slammed his signet ring once more on the table with fury. At that moment, as if on cue, a naked female figure emerged from among the vines. I recognized her small breasts immediately, as any inhabitant of Prague would know them immediately. It was the actress who played Doña Pipa in the soap opera Dirty Lopez. She wore only a black stripe that cut into her little "doña pipa."

"Er, I thought we had a meeting," she said nervously at the sight of us.

The Director just rolled his eyes and followed us. I couldn't take my eyes off the naked soap opera star.

"You want an autograph, *Mr.* Lieutenant?" Ivana stuck an elbow to my.

"For God's sake, stop saying "Mr." to me. It sounds like fucking rats in your mouth," I whispered, leaving Pipa alone and following Král.

* * *

We descended thirty floors in his personal elevator and found ourselves in a corridor labeled Service Floor III. There were two necks with automatic machines by the elevator. Král winked at them and they got out of our way.

The door swung open and we climbed into a huge refrigerator, five by ten meters in size.

"We usually keep champagnes and cakes with whipped cream here, of course for the show Lick the cream off me, you Prague stud, but now we have something like this," Král said and pointed to the corpse on the ground.

I looked questioningly at Ivana.

"Why aren't the Security technicians here?"

"They were here with Adam. They found nothing. Just like yesterday with Petlán," she explained, pointing to me that the body now belongs to me.

"I'd like some warm cocoa," I sighed, rubbing my hands together to ward off the cold. But it didn't do much.

* * *

The body had much in common with Petlán's corpse. Especially a large number of stab wounds in the chest. And a painted picture around his neck - two wavy lines with a trickle of dried blood

85

running through them. It came from a wound in the face. The killer also delivered two blows to the face - stabbed his left cheek and right eye.

"Who is this?" I asked.

The man must have been around seventy. Unlike Král, he did not have access to excess calories. The ribs literally shone through the emaciated body. I mean, before the murder, they showed symbolically, and now a few ribs were actually visible through an stabbed chest.

"His name was Lukáš Pajac. Watchman. Night watchman," said the television director.

"Where did you find him?"

"Downstairs, in the entrance hall. The killer entered there using a stolen chip in an armband. Judging by the camera footage, he appropriated the identity of one of the directors of the show Fuck or Die."

"And where was that director?"

"He was fucking. He has six witnesses," replied the director.

"I get it. And this guy in the meantime died. So classic, show must go on," I sighed and added: "his name tells me something."

The Director just shrugged.

"I hope the Security has downloaded all the security camera footage?" I said after a moment of silence.

"The security cameras? We don't have such. There is television here. Actresses don't like being shot by someone before they are painted," Král explained.

"Or they won't dress," I recalled Pipa.

"There is one more important matter on which we included you in this, M... Lieutenant," Ivana interrupted and nodded at Král. I ignored the fact that this "M..." she's mocking me.

The Dircetor tapped his cellular band, and a moment later a hologram of his virtual surroundings appeared. He had the newest generation of cool PRAGUETECH toy that reacted to even the most delicate gestures.

"Immediately after the murder, all workers received it on their cellular bands. We were very surprised. We have the best security of all. We are the ones who guide the world..."

"And the world is not supposed to screw you with this. I get it." I cut him off, but paused.

There was an image of some white puff of smoke or cotton wool, which spoke in an electronically altered voice.

"The Zodiac is talking to you. I like killing people because it's great fun. That girl on the N subway last week. She was young and beautiful, but now she's disfigured and dead. It is not the first and it will not be the last. I stay awake all night thinking about my next victim. Maybe it will be the beautiful blonde who watches the children in the house next to the little grocery store and returns home down the dark alley every night around seven. Or would it be that beautifully shaped blue-eyed brunette who said no to me when I asked her on a date in high school? Or maybe it won't be her at all. But I'm going to cut out her female organs and display them so that the whole town can see them. I will kill the powerful and the insignificant. Just because it amuses me. And I will kill until you let me speak to the whole city."

* * *

I hated them. Freaks. The history of criminology is full of them. I understood normal killers. Most of them, at least. A murder during an argument, a persecuted wife who kills her husband with a tofu beater, revenge for infidelity, an attempt to hide the fraud by killing the victim, all of this is understandable. The extreme situation could lead even perfectly normal people to the brink of the abyss and in one stupid second cause a twist that took them to places where there was no return. I understood the same as mercenary killers. They got assignments and they did them to get whores, drugs and drinks, or a few ampoules of insulin for Grandma.

But this one was one of a special kind of bastard. Motherfuckers who were amused by the death of strangers and wanted everyone to know. They didn't kill for lust, lust, revenge, money, but simply because they thought it was so much fun and a way to stand out from the crowd. Most of them said something about wanting revenge on society for all the humiliations they experienced, which usually meant that some girl in third grade refused to show them her tits or they pissed in a coding lesson and their classmates were laughing at them. It doesn't matter what actually happened. These guys nurtured their hatred and then felt their strength for the innocent. And they thought they were smart and charming, and the whole world would go crazy over them.

* * *

From the City News building we were transported to the Security Headquarters. I took over one of the many vacant offices. As the former Prague police transformed into Security, tasked with carrying out the will of the Corporate Council, its staffing base also shrunk. The office had a couch, a desk, and a stack of dusty shelves with plastic binders.

I asked for coffee, of course I got an instant coffee product, pulled the blinds on the windows and turned off the light. Immediately after that, the projector on the desk switched on. There were three other Security guards around him - Karel Adam and two technicians. Ivana, standing by my side, had a neutral expression, while the others showed a lot of commitment. It is clear. Nobody has done any proper police work here for many years. I was wondering when was the last time I experienced something like this myself, but that was a long time ago. Even before the war with Poland.

"Give me a close-up of this girl," I asked the technicians, and a life-size puffy body hovered over the couch. The knife wounds were exactly the same as those of Petlán and Pajac.

"Daughter of an accountant from ARKAS. She studied food technology at Charles University. She was just coming back from some student party. Until that guy on TV died, we thought that some jealous friend of the year killed her," explained one of the technicians, a long, skinny blonde man.

"Why?" I asked.

"Because it happened on the N line. And on the N line you don't kill. Only decent people use it," he explained.

"Rich, I mean decent?"

90

"Well, yes," he nodded simply.

There was something about this girl that did not suit me. She had a torn shirt, the same stab wounds as the others, but it was missing something. I tripled the entire holographic image and examined her body millimeter by millimeter.

"There's no sign. He didn't mark her. Neither the wave nor the sixty-nine," I finally figured it out.

It didn't add up. Even the victims. They had nothing to do with each other. Except for stab wounds. A watchman, one of the most powerful people in the city and a student. For this without painting. If this breach had not confessed to the murder, no one would have thought of counting her among his victims.

"Maybe the Zodiac was in a hurry. Someone interrupted him and didn't have time to tag her?" Adam suggested after a moment of silence.

"Don't call him that."

"What?" Not understanding, he frowned.

"This is a bastard. You have to use that as an official term. I don't care what name he gave himself, but he certainly chose it because he feels it gives him strength, and we won't let him, at least at first. This is a prick, okay?" I said, and the security guys grunted in agreement.

Only Ivana smiled and nodded.

"Zodiac, you'd like that, son of a bitch," I growled after a moment and ordered the holographic projection to move closer to the darkened windows to project the bodies of Pajac and Petlán next to it.

"Show me that knife," I said.

"It wasn't one knife," replied the technician, waving his hands over the hologram, and two knives appeared over the corpses: one massive with a smooth blade and one with a serrated one. That son of a bitch was stabbing with both hands."

"We can reconstruct them in a 3D printer if..."

"I don't want to," I interrupted him, "no need. These are military knives. One is Czech, produced in České Budějovice, and the other is from Germany. It was delivered to NATO troops," I explained and sat down in my chair.

"Everything's OK?" Karel Adam asked.

I appreciated his concern, but it was useless. I felt that my head was about to burst, I tried so hard to get all the unknowns into a specific equation. Nothing made sense. I forgot that this was the beginning of every major case. Building a story is the key, but when a person doesn't know how to build it, no story makes sense.

I ended the conference and let the technicians go. Then I asked Karel to gather as much information as possible about the victims, and to look at all those who died in recent years who might resemble ours in something.

"There will be thousands of them. Lots of people die violently every day in this goddamn city," he said.

I just shrugged. He didn't seem happy with the answer, but he finally left too.

We were left alone with Ivana.

"Why?" I asked.

"What?"

"You heard it. In this city, many people die violently every day. There are at least a hundred freaks like this. A few streets away, an old lady is cooking a stew from two students who owed her rent. Today at least three prostitutes will be shot by some wreckers, and another ten people will be stabbed on the street for drugs or a glass of artificial milk. Why is this psycho so important that a rich girl obsessed with elves, leprechauns and fairies told me to get out of the sewers? Is it about this TV?"

Ivana nodded thoughtfully.

"DEZATEG broke up. Their activities are to be taken over by four or three other corporations. VEP resigned from DEZATEG factories, and in return gained control over the Security and City News. We are afraid that the Zodiac will undermine our fragile influence. No matter what the format the freak is, it could create political instability. The equilibrium achieved is fragile and the people in the city have sensed it. You saw it in the streets yesterday," she explained.

"Politics," I growled.

"Aren't this pose of yours a little annoying, Lieutenant?" A woman with the most beautiful artificial legs I have ever seen winked at me.

I did not answer. Instead, I looked at the corpse again. I had a case to resolve, and that was important. I'm a cop again, and the cop has to find the culprit. If only for this unfortunate girl who got in the way of this break at the wrong hour. The fact that this city has recently turned into a pressurized boiler that can explode at any moment was not my problem at the moment. My job was to catch the murderer.

But before that, I had to settle an old score.

* * *

Ivana wasn't happy with it, but I needed a ride and she's my assistant, though I'd say she was more like a guard and a nanny rolled into one. So she dropped me off at the place Under the Drank Payoff. As always, there were two thugs standing in front of the entrance, submachine guns elegantly slung over their shoulders. They both pulled out the plastic boxes and reset them. I spat on one and put my finger on the other until I felt a needle prick.

"Clean," said one of the guys boredom.

The needle retracted and there was a hiss of sterilization.

Ivana went through the same procedure. Under the Drank Payoff was a noble place whose motto was: no problems, no consequences. Therefore, each visitor was tested for all known diseases. This gave him twelve hours of absolute freedom in a place where he could enjoy himself with unrestricted fun. Before entering, I still had to put the gun in the safe. Another important measures. Safety first and foremost.

"I'm a rainbow fairy!" we were greeted by the remixed song after the entry.

Ivana started rocking to the beat.

"Do you like it?"

"No." She shook her head. "But I know it pisses you off, so I enjoy it," she smiled at me.

I waved my hand, gesturing her to follow me. She looked around curiously. After all, this is a completely different party than the ones organized by its boss. Several frames shone above our heads, in which naked, mostly teenage models curled up to the rhythm of a prehistoric song. The owner of the place, Neny Nenutil, also owned rare goods. An eighteen-year-old black girl was hanging above us, and I saw two Asian girls in the back. Considering how incredible their bodies were, and with what recent plastic surgery has made, they might have been sixteen or eighty years old with equal success. Despite the early hour, many bodies were huddling in the place.

"Vermouth and tonic twice," I said to the bartender.

She was not only topless, she had nothing down either. She nodded and held her armband out towards me. I gave her mine. The payment was processed and she started to prepare the order.

"I'd bet you'd order a double vodka mixed with a triple whiskey," said Ivana.

"Yes, but not right now. I need a clean head," I explained and handed her one of the glasses. On the other, I drank half. In fact,

96

even such a small amount of alcohol hit my head. I should have eaten something before.

"Finally," I was relieved as the ten-minute remix of Rainbow Fairy finished and there was silence in the bar. But not for long.

The owner of the tabernacle himself - Neny - appeared on the scene. Like other men of his caliber - I mean those who were called gangsters - he called himself "uncle." When it came down to it, people would sometimes say to him too, "Please don't kill me, I'll give you my daughter and business!", but still "uncle" can be heard more often. Neny was from the same cloth as his Mafia competitor, Bowler. Except more sophisticated and elegant, and his homes had more pussies than employees. He did business in show business and related industries. These related industries are mostly drugs. After the cyberwomen had to withdraw from public life and luxury events, they found refuge with him. It was one of the arguments we had with Fay until she let go and finally I had no one to drag him with.

Neny wore a jacket embroidered with gold coins. Someone had to polish them every day, probably as a punishment, so they gleamed and flickered in the light, tossing bunnies over the silhouettes of the good three hundred attendees. Besides, he looked like an ordinary obese man in his fifties - with a novice baldness, a perfectly trimmed beard, and black hair somehow long between a hedgehog and a comb, the tips of which gleamed with silver.

In one of the booths there was Bowler alone, accompanied by two thugs with arms like a construction crane and three beauties with implants. They were - like Fay - cybernetic trannies, but they did not have such an adventure that people would make them an object of religious worship.

"Welcome to the big party today. You already know that this night will be..." He dragged the pause as long as he could, until he finally exclaimed. "Looooooong!"

And at that moment a song even worse than the Rainbow Fairy started to fly. Some guy was singing it in a squeaking voice, and there was the moaning of children who were clearly being tortured. I suspected it was again some trendy cover of a prehistoric song that ancestors probably recalled the spirit of Mother Earth or something similar.

You know, I'm also sad

And that's probably the reason to meet again

And it's not a joke, I feel that today will be ahead of us

Long night

Long night

Long night [3]

Along with the first words of this terrible song, amid the exuberant shouts and howls of the crowd, who were playing today in the Under the Drank Payoff, Women with a Thousand Pussy burst onto the stage with impetus. There were five girls, they didn't have a thousand pussies, but had too much of them anyway. There was also a group of Men with a Thousand Cocks, but they performed elsewhere. Plastic surgery to add breasts or an additional genitalia is relatively popular with cheaper prostitutes, but this is really cool. The girls were led by Erika, known as the Seven Brave. That's because she had seven vaginas and made the movie Erika and the Seven Brave. Needless to say, what the brave ones did, in any case, you have to pay dearly for a movie distributed via secret disks. Erika spoke with a Slovak accent and who knows why she called everyone "lover". Fat Tom made me watch parts of this movie once. I haven't been able to get an erection for a week.

It flashes so close

---

[3] Fragment of the song "Dlouha noc" by Helena Vondráčkováá, which she also sang in Polish as "Long Night". Quotes from the Polish version of the piece [translator´s note].

It's like a current piercing your heart

You've had enough of this, you've been all alone for too long

Or perhaps this spark has kindled a flame in my heart today

I want you again

Let the heat of the night light us up

It's gonna be a long night - so let's play va banque

It's gonna be a long night - no one is going to sleep tonight

I patted Ivana on the shoulder and showed her the empty glass.

"It's time for a double," I said, resigned.

She smiled and walked with me to the bar. Whatever the bartender poured out for us cost more money than I needed for a month at the bottom of society, but I didn't care now. The account has been linked to VEP. I was going to use it properly. Like Erika, I didn't plan on doing for a whore.

I recognized Fay right away. She sat in one of the booths with her inseparable partners Long Liz, Kelly and Kuka. They were all prepared for the show. Fairy Fay wore phosphorescent panties and an unbuttoned white shirt. The loose material lightly touched both breasts, tattooed ones and zeros forming the image of a butterfly.

There were implants on the temples, between the breasts and on the strong hips. Others glowed inconspicuously between the fingers of her hands.

When she noticed me, her eyes narrowed with anger. Interestingly, almost all of my ex-girlfriends reacted this way to me. I was just carrying a piece of a motherfucker capable of arousing the worst instincts in women.

"Did you come show me your new whore?" She snapped.

The other sorceresses put their hands on their hips in a gesture of female solidarity. The fact that I saved all of their asses didn't matter now - women's solidarity first!

"I'm the lieutenant's assistant," Ivana grinned at her.

The hell was deliberately making me angry. The word assistant uttered the same as the lover would have spoken.

"I came to pay you back," I ignored the tension and the scary intrusive song.

"You don't owe me." Fay lowered her eyes. She could never lie.

"I am. I don't know how many, but I don't need you to look after me, I'll be fine," I said.

Contrary to her, I lied perfectly.

"Belch said you didn't have even a heller," she retorted.

"Belch says whatever came into his head." I waved my hand.

"You can't lie," she said.

"I don't want to interrupt your pre-copulation reconciliation, Mr. Lieutenant, but something seems to have interrupted the show," Ivana said loudly, pointing to the stage.

The Thousand Pussy Women Group finished shaking and opening their collection of artificial and real pussies, as Uncle Neny preached into the microphone during the song.

What was rolling on the scene now were the heads of two security guys. They were kicked there by someone who was following them in black boots and a black coat. He wore a mask over his face similar to the one I used in the sewers.

The music stopped playing. At least something positive.

* * *

Erika screamed but stayed standing bravely on the stage while the stranger approached her. Heads rolled down to her legs. The pussies on her body shrank so much that not one of the Seven Brave could penetrate them.

"He has a sword," Fay gasped.

"What the fuck is this? Anyone from you again?" I turned to Ivana.

She shook her head.

The guy really had a long, narrow sword in his hand, and he wasn't the only one. More and more the same dressed people, all in black, entered the bar through the open main entrance. Each of them had a white mark on their arm. Kind of a dotted circle with eight lugs bent to the left. I didn't know what it was, but one thing was clear to me - anyone who bore a sign in this town was just a dangerous asshole.

And again it turned out that I was right.

* * *

The dude grabbed Erika's hand and then...

"Fuck," Liz cursed.

"No, not that," I sighed.

And I was right again.

The sword cut off Erika's head, the only place she hadn't had the implants that made her so famous. You could say that seven pussies died in one blow for the homeland. Quite skillfully, he grabbed Erika by the hair and yanked the implanted microphone from her forehead. Apparently she was going to sing after the dance performance. Although the guy shortened her life, he certainly spared all of us suffering.

I watched both mafia bosses winking at their gorillas and at each other. I assumed that the "zero weapons, no syphilis" rule applied only to the club's regular customers. I would be surprised if Bowler would allow himself to be disarmed during a courtesy visit to competitors. But that was not enough. There were at least fifty masked freaks with swords in the clubhouse. Another thing was, were they only carrying these swords? Their rifles were easy to hide under their coats. I believe that Uncle Melonik and Neny thought the same thing.

"I called the Security," Ivana whispered.

It was enough that she thought about it. She must have had a pretty decent set of chips in her head to control her bionic limbs and implants. A very practical thing. I figured she was more equipped than all the trannies at the club put together.

"We don't care about your useless lives. We want sinful whores worthy of the death of the high priest, the Sun. We want cybersorceresses," the sword-wielding freak declared.

I turned to face Fay.

"What did you guys screw up again?"

104

"Nothing, fucking nothing."

* * *

There was a murmur in the place, and that wasn't cool. Many people instinctively looked at the booth where the sorceresses were sitting. I grabbed Fay by the shirt.

"A bunch of freaks want to get you. They don't carry these swords to pick in their teeth. You had to get up to something. I thought you were done with those committed performances, that now you are just fucking with Neny."

I was shaking her more than I should, but I was furious. Not even for her, but for the freaks who marched like that, rolling the heads of those guilty gorillas in front of them, and just like that, they got a girl who did not have any taste and needed a psychotherapist rather than another pussy, but she certainly did not deserve death, like a genetically mutated pig at the DEZATEG factory.

"Nothing, damn it, nothing. We only work here. Only here. You know Neny has synthesized a new drug. E-snow. Everyone is crazy about it. We smash three hundred people here every other day. The raid was terrible. That's it," Liz said.

She wasn't lying. I would recognize it. Her buddies looked terrified.

"Fuck," I cursed.

Sword-carrying freaks rushed at us.

"What now?" Ivana asked.

Judging by the fact that she wasn't talking to me, 'Mr'. or 'Lieutenant', she must have seen the situation as bloody serious. And it was so.

"In addition to the laser, do you have a rotary machine gun?" I asked hopefully.

She shook her head.

"Then please stop them. I have a plan," I muttered.

"What, for God's sake?" She shouted incredulously.

"Prepare the bait to lure the enemy. Pretend confusion in your ranks and crush it."

"Have you read The Art of War?" She said, surprised, as if the very fact that I could read seemed strange to her.

"On the toilet, before sleeping. I was constipated," so I calmed her down and ran towards the bar.

* * *

This place is well known to me. Before I left Fay, I spent a lot of time here. I watched their every performance and what happened to people then. I knew that transwhores - as girls with implanted gadgets were called - were simply prostitutes. Actually, that's how Fay and I got to know each other, but the level of e-snow boosting their art is crazy. And I'm an old school boy. I was jealous like an idiot.

The sword freaks took the grounds quite professionally to be able to observe the entire place and every movement of the crowd, and then six of them headed for the sorceresses. These had nowhere to run away.

I started to run, which caught the attention of one of the freaks. He followed me. As he ran, he jumped over the skinny boy who had something flowing between his legs that was definitely not a genie. Fortunately, a human obstacle stopped him.

I ran behind the bar. On one of the lower shelves there was a bartender who had managed to get among the beer cans. Only one leg was sticking out. It's weird that it can fit in there.

Crash!

The sword stuck in the bar a good five centimeters.

"Neny will castrate you, dude," I sighed.

Uncle Neny was damn proud of the old wooden bar that had allegedly been the private property of the ancient gangster Don Mrázek. The one who had inflicted such a scar on him did not have a good end. But neither do I.

I reached for the closest standing bottle on the shelf - Real Slivovitz from Žižkov. The vintage bottle from 2090 looked pretty decent. But compared to the freak's sword, it's still not enough.

The next blow nearly grazed me. The masked guy jumped over the bar and hit just few centimeters from my left arm. Several bottles fell from the shelves. He swung again, trying to stab me. To my surprise, it was probably not the first time he had held a sword in his hand. Sword. O. What kind of motherfuckers sre they?

I jumped and threw the bottle at him. But it's hard to aim the bottle. It slapped his shoulder, which only stopped him for a moment. He took a step, and I barely managed to dodge another blow. He aimed at my chest. The tip passed right past my stomach. I sucked it on instinctively, although there was no reason to do so. Several months of being at the bottom of the social lowlands wiped out all fat stores. I made two quick forward leaps and hit the bastard on the head with the first bottle that fell into my hand. It broke, and the rest of the golden liquid poured over his head.

'Doorly's - Barbados Rum', I ran my eyes over the torn label.

Well now we were in deep shit. A bottle from the legendary island must have cost more than a whole fucking Řeporyje, including the golden statue of the prophet Paweł Novotny, who was worshiped there, rubbed with honey and the blood of children.

The guy with the sword swayed slightly, but remained on his feet.

And he stabbed me with that goddamn sword.

* * *

The blade passed through my left side. I crumpled up in pain. I did not know how deep the wound was, what it damaged me and how many seconds I had left to live, but I stuck that broken bottle from Barbados in his neck. The protruding debris pierced his throat, so I pulled my hand and ripped open his carotid.

I mean her.

As I tugged and the blood sprayed straight onto my face, I tore the mask off. Now the twisted face of a twenty-year-old brunette was staring at me.

"Fuck," I cursed, releasing the neck of the bottle stuck in her throat.

She let me go as well, and in the last, futile surge of strength, she tried to snatch the Barbados rarity. She failed to do so and fell to the ground.

The sword, however, remained in me. The blade went almost right through. I leaned over to the bartender. It hurt like hell.

"E-snow... How do you run it?" I gasped.

I painfully tried to capture the necessary dose of oxygen.

I must have looked terrible with the blade in the puddle because she came out of her hiding place, walked through the corpse barefoot, staining her feet with blood, and pushed the mirror aside between the bottles behind the bar. She typed a five-digit sequence. One, two, three, four, five. Neny didn't care much about security, he probably counted no one would dare to stick his nose in his affairs, because whoever did this would cut off his nose, have it stuffed, and put it on the bar Under the Drank Payoff tab. Access to the small control panel has been opened.

"It gives ten in a half an hour," she pointed at the display.

It was probably supposed to be the beginning of a long lecture, but I didn't have time. Firstly, I was shivering strong, and secondly, three armed guys screamed at me. I reached for the display, leaving a bloody streak on it, and set it to the maximum value of 100/5, whatever that meant.

110

It started to snow in the bar.

Actually, e-snow started to fall.

* * *

E-snow is perhaps the most fascinating drug ever. It was the highest stage of drug intoxication. The nanoparticles that were formed from the breakdown of snowflakes penetrated the body not only through the nose and mouth, but also through the skin. The whole body went into a trance, much like good old LSD, but at the same time the nanoparticles in e-snow stimulated neurotransmitters, especially in the central nervous system. The human body pulsed on waves of oxytocin and dopamine. And something else stimulated the whole thing - anyone who had implants aimed at sexual arousal experienced it even more. Moreover, those who had implants were able to drag those who did not have them with them. History did not record the orgies that had occurred in Nene's tabernacle in the past few months.

Transwhores, thanks to technological improvements, were able to intensify and control everything. I saw how at first they were completely surprised and upset when they realized what - thanks to e-snow - they can do. They were like a conductor who determined the intensity of human bliss with a wave of his hand. A gesture accompanied by a specific thought was enough, and the person's excitement increased or decreased. Sometimes they deliberately pumped up the excitement to the breaking point, then lowered it - only one single person felt nothing, while everyone around them squirmed and groped and copulated as if it were a fight to the death. And when his excitement peaked and the lock released, he melted into the delight of everyone else.

I turned and felt the e-snow flowing through me. At first, my skin tingled slightly, and my nose felt a tingling sensation as if I was about to sneeze. I shifted discreetly to the bottle shelf as a sword freak jumped onto the bar. Two more rushed after him.

"Ah, my lord, yes…" exclaimed one of them in a woman's voice.

The sword fell from her hand. She started groping herself. I was already thinking that there were only women behind the masks when the guy at the bar discovered his face and suddenly started moaning.

The e-snow apparently kept me on my feet. The pain was subsiding, but I was starting to feel dizzy and had a terrible erection.

"Fuck, I need that blood elsewhere," I sighed despairingly.

* * *

The bartender turned to me. The e-snow seemed to have no effect on her. Angrily, she kicked a guy from behind the bar, who didn't seem to mind at all, then walked over to me. She pulled a

112

clean cloth from one of the shelves, grasped the hilt of the sword in my kidney, and yanked. It didn't reach me at all. The blade just slipped, and to me it seemed the sexiest thing in the universe.

Then she did do one sexy thing: she turned to the nearest jerk, who was salivating through the mask, and plunged her sword between his ribs. He was dying and he hadn't noticed it at all. The moment she splashed me with some cheap plum brandy, I felt a tingling sensation, but then I helped her stop the bleeding with a cloth. She bent over the shelves, took out a sterile bandage and wrapped it three times over the cloth, which in the meantime had soaked my blood.

"It's gonna hurt now, okay?" She looked me straight in the eyes.

I was convinced that these were the most beautiful eyes I had ever seen.

"I love you, yes please," I sighed. "Ow! Fucking hell!"

* * *

"You're a cyber...?" I said after a moment, when this hellish erection was finally starting to subside. The brain was now functioning relatively normally, and pain was slowly taking the place of pleasure in the body.

The others didn't do that well.

I watched a group of masked swordsmen writhing in paroxysms of ecstasy. Two were still trying to approach us, but their bodies trembled with waves of orgasms, and their eyes were cloudy.

But worst of all, horrible remixes of out-of-date hits started playing again in the bar.

Cold, cold, cold everywhere

Snow everywhere, locked down tight by ice

The houses are like a cake, white sweets everywhere

The north wind drew his sword, ready to attack

"I'm a cyberhooker," the bartender replied to my query. She had to break out to shout over the music. "I just have implants hidden under my skin, sweetheart!" She explained.

She turned and pulled her sword from the dead man's body, only to stab the writhing woman with it. I think she realized at the last minute that the excitement would probably end soon, and she herself would go into the other world.

"Oh Perun," she said, then the blade pierced her throat.

I grabbed one of the moonshine bottles from Stara Praga and poured the contents into myself. I did not get it sober. The massacre is still bearable, but not the music.

"Are you having a good time, Mr.?" Ivana said from behind the bar.

* * *

They were all there. All cybernetic sorceresses. They deprived some of their attackers of swords, and probably of their lives, which was revealed by bloody hands and shoes.

Fay had a large, drying trickle of blood on her chest. She looked terrified.

"Your hands." I stared at Ivana.

There were deep scars on them, and two fingers were missing.

"I have a spare." She shrugged, pointing to what was happening in the room.

People rolled on the ground, trembling and experiencing successive waves of orgasms. Some appeared to be experiencing an epileptic fit. Freaks with swords were still trying to get us and keep the weapons, but the oxytocin waves caused by the joint cyber-indulgence prevented them from doing so.

"How much did you let it out?" Fay asked.

"Everything. Ten times the dose. It could kill them, including Neny," the bartender replied, drilling her sword into the body of the guy she had thrown from the bar. While she was pricking him, he was rubbing his wet crotch. In my life, I would never have thought that a guy could get so much cum.

"Neny's fine. And Bowler, too," Fay smirked.

She was right. Both gangsters gathered cyber prostitutes to protect them from overdosing. Now Neny was gesturing wildly in our direction. I don't think he saw who smashed his precious bottle of Doorly's. I'm gonna try to blame it on a medieval fetish freak.

"We have to stop this quickly. Half of them may have a heart attack, and it won't be good for business," the bartender said, lunging at the controls.

Blood was dripping from her sword. She tapped something and there was a humming noise all over the bar. I think they started an e-snow vacuum cleaner in such situations. Because what else.

But the music continued.

Cold, cold, cold everywhere

Who is not warmed by laughter, will pay with a runny nose

Those who are not singing now warm their hands in vain

Now I come to you, and with me sleep, white wind, white day

"Fay, take the girls and save these people. Let them not die seriously from this la petite mort, and we'll take care of those jerks," I said and bent down to get one of the abandoned blades.

I stumbled and didn't fall just because of Ivana. She grabbed me with her torn hands. I appreciated that at least now she had kept the comments about the Mr. Lieutenant to herself.

I smiled at the sorceresses, acting out their cheek so that they would ignore me and finally take care of these people.

"If the advantage increases, take action; if there is no hope of success, stay where you are." Ivana quoted Master Sun.

"It's been a long time," I shook them off and took a deep breath.

The bartender disappeared with the sorceresses, so I was able to drink from another bottle without fear. This time it was Gin from Old Praga. It was something better.

* * *

Cybernetic priestesses of love rushed into the crowd. They disarmed intruders and reduced the level of oxytocin for visitors. Probably at the last minute, as some were fainting and others were convulsing. In order not to pass out, I threw myself on the panel on which I had previously launched e-snow and turned off this terrible music.

"Do you realize that if your organ has been damaged, you must report to the hospital as soon as possible, otherwise you will be killed?" Ivana said.

I shrugged my shoulders. I licked the worse. It didn't seem so bad. A sword pierced a few centimeters from the left hip, and the bleeding quickly stopped. Admittedly, I needed medications, even painkillers, but it looked like gin could replace them.

"I'm missing everything. I have no idea what's going on. Nothing makes sense here." I sighed and, with Ivana's help, moved into the crowd.

Of course, I got rid of the alcohol bottle before that. After all, Uncle Neny kept his sane mind. It's a pity, I'd like to kick his and Bowler's ass, and the thought that they might not remember it was more than tempting.

Cavalry burst through the main door.

* * *

It was headed by an old friend of mine. Before he knew what had happened here, he was drenched in sweat. He and ten more fighter flew in, armed to the teeth. I appreciated it. But they underestimated the fact that microscopic e-snow particles were still floating in the air and penetrating their nose and mouth into their mucous membranes. I walked too slowly and carefully, so I didn't have time to warn them. We met somewhere in the middle of the room where hundreds of people were trying to recover.

Ivana also braved them.

"What the hell is going on fucking me!" The new Security chief was shuffling on the dance floor hit by e-snow. He was lucky the ventilation system had already filtered out most of the drugs.

"I have to..."

"Come on, let he has fun for a while." I squeezed Ivana's hand knowingly before realizing that she probably didn't feel it.

"Are you okay, Karel?" I asked while he and the other Security guys looked surprised. After all, they all had a really mega-erection.

"What's up...?" Karel sighed with delight.

The sight of me combined with what all this e-snow chemistry was doing to his body put him in a difficult position.

"Treat your people as your beloved sons and they will follow you into the deepest valley, Lieutenant." Ivana shook her head as she walked over to Adam and took his hand.

119

Apparently he was relieved.

"What is going on for the all Easter bunnies?" He said angrily, but with obvious relief in his voice.

I wasn't going to explain the know-how of the place to him, especially when Neny himself came towards us.

"What kind of motherfuckers are these?" He growled.

He was followed by heavies and two cyber prostitutes who were most likely supposed to add to his enjoyment at tonight's party, and instead tried to keep him on his feet. Bowler was in a similar situation, but he and his entourage kept his distance. He probably assumed it was none of his business, but he was curious as to how the situation would develop.

"Perun," I said.

"What?" Neny snapped.

Like other gangsters, he also tried to stay in shape among all circumstances and situations and played an elegant tough guy that nothing can affect him. Just not to show weakness. But the crumbling business and shattered e-snow resources of several weeks turned him into a furious madman. I was glad he didn't take his anger out on me.

"She was talking about Perun. Before she died. One of them," I explained and looked over to the other side of the bar, where the naked bartender was hanging around with other cyber prostitutes.

Neny looked at Bowler, who shrugged innocently. I think they just made it clear to themselves that it was not Bowler thing.

"They said Fay and those bitches of hers screwed up," he retorted after a moment and looked at me. He knew I had something in common with her.

"We have to check that. We'll lock them all up..."

"Shit. These bastards will stay here. My people will take these fucking toys of theirs and we'll cut them piece by piece until they shit, pee, and finally die. I have one such drug that will make their suffering brush against the land of death. They will get tired and will not be allowed to faint or lose track of what is happening, and the drug will intensify the pain as much as possible. I call it Amateur Poetry." He smirked at the mere thought of what awaited the non-paying guests at his bar.

"Let me guess, are these really remixed songs by Helena Vondráčková?"

He just shot an angry glare at me.

"I'm afraid I can't let you do that. They committed a crime..." Shit, I couldn't remember which crimes are still regulated by the law. Hasn't the Corporation Council annulled the entire penal code one day, with the exception of "Who doesn't listen to us, will be abolished"?

"Disturbing public order, assault with lethal weapons, holding hostages," Karel Adam rushed to help me.

"I have more people in this neighborhood than you do. You want war, you motherfuckers? You, who jump, how will the Council play?" Neny looked at us menacingly.

Bowler appeared behind him. It was a battle as old as the world - cops versus criminals. So it is clear which side he is on.

I staggered. I wasn't feeling well. My whole body tingled and it felt like I was getting a fever.

Neny was on my nerves.

"You can even breed puppies with them, but only after I'm finished with them. And if you want to tease me, you better consult with your buddy Bowler who has tried to kill me a couple of times. But he only suffered losses in people and equipment," I shook him.

Bowler looked offended.

"It was obviously a misunderstanding," he smiled.

"Which happens at least once a week, I know, I know," I replied and added, "We take our perpetrators and you take care of the rest of the people. That's all."

"Not everything. Get these bitches out of here too. They have nothing to do here anymore. Not in any other business in this fucking city," Neny growled, and turned on his heel.

Our lovely conversation came to an end.

* * *

Medic from the Security injected me with some energy and antibiotics. I had a serious discussion with him that I didn't want to go to the VEP hospital and that I knew what I was doing - so he just rolled his eyes and gave me a handful of pills that should get me on my feet as soon as possible.

"If you have no internal injuries, because then..."

"Yes, I know, I will die. You're very nice," I cut him off as I watched the fuses load the surviving attackers.

Ivana brought me a gun confiscated from a dead bodyguard. Just in time, because Fay just ran over to me.

"They fired us, idiot. Is it because we broke up?" She stuck a finger in my chest. She tried to be furious, but it didn't quite work out.

"It's not my fault. These freaks are here for you. What have you gotten into?" I replied calmly.

"I already told you, nothing. We stay away from that goddamn sorceress cult. You fucking know it!" A tear rolled from the corner of her eye.

I carefully wiped it off.

"I'll find out what happened and..."

"Shit in the lamp. I won't wait for some fucker to start chasing me again," Fay said.

Behind her, Ivana stood elegantly.

"Erm," Adam coughed after me. "We can interview them tomorrow, they don't look very good now."

"Tomorrow may be too late," I smiled wryly.

"I agree," Ivana agreed. "I was browsing the database of the VEP security service. Perun's cult seat is about ten kilometers from the Kolbenova metro station. It is called the Temple of the Sun of the ancient Slavs."

124

"Temple of the Sun? Okay, let's go have a look over there. It sounds like the name of the place where they will pour us grain coffee and serve us bread with salt. If something is called the Temple of the Sun, it can't be a bad place," I said with a smile.

I preferred those medicated drugs that were just starting to work to all of Neny's inventions.

Mina

Prague never fell asleep. I know so many cities have been called that way in the past, but Prague really was like a three-shift hotel. But each of its three layers operated in a different mode. I knew little about the highest one, because my living space was at the bottom of the social pyramid, where people slept and lived shifts. It was approaching midnight, which meant that those who went to work in the morning were trying to put their heads to sleep somewhere, and those whose work was based on other business principles or was related to the night work of factories, factories or plantations, were just giving themselves up to waking up coffee substitutes. With the unmarked Security hovercraft, we stumbled into the traffic between the pillars of the S-line, and finally we climbed up, where, instead of ordinary people, we were passed by road drones, information drones and other hovercraft. And where we could see a kind of darkness above our heads. Because there was never any darkness down there. If, however, someone turned off all the lights, deep darkness would ensue there too. A darkness so final and infinite that U-level humans would probably go crazy. I think that was the reason Prague was never allowed to sleep. And to think too much. Wherever we went, we were haunted by the next episode of Dirty Lopez. Now, for example, he was chasing Adolf Hitler dressed as a burlesque singer.

"Wasn't Lopez Mexican?" I asked when my eyes caught a frame from the show.

Karel just shrugged.

"Every two hundred episodes the whole story is changed. Only Lopez and Doña Pipa remain. Eh, now rather Fräulein Pipa," he corrected himself, looking at the screen we were just passing by.

Pipa just had sex with Winston Churchill. I just missed the plot.

And that wasn't the only thing I was missing with. Like I said in the bar, nothing made sense.

"This whole city doesn't make sense," I sighed.

"Are you feeling sick?" The frightened Security officer asked.

I shook my head resolutely and focused again on observing the skyscrapers I passed, with ten million people living around and under them. Some twenty-five years have passed since the city closed in on itself and sheltered itself from the outside world. Previously, it was similar. The last century saw the depopulation of the countryside. Large agglomerations grew larger and larger, and as technological advances reached a stage where anything could be produced, the world simply plunged into total regionalization instead of globalization. To this day, I remember watching the mass suicides of Chinese workers who had just closed their factories on TV. I also remember how the mayor of the city solemnly closed the defensive wall with the shooting circuit around Prague. He then said that Prague was not Rome and that its gates would not be captured by any barbarians. Politicians never know history. In fact, at the end of the Roman Empire, the townspeople themselves opened the gates to the barbarians and helped them plunder both the city's former wealth and pride. No one could bear the burden of the crumbling empire. The truth is that senators, who had practically no power for several hundred years in the shadow of the emperors, discussed at the time how high the tax on olive oil should be.

I wondered what the Corporation Council was doing now. It was the five largest companies that in practice formed an oligarchy led by a puppet mayor. But he was long dead, and so were the representatives of the two most powerful interests. DEZATEG broke up under pressure from inheritance disputes and corporations taking over its factories. The weakened Council has promised that new mayoral elections will be held after Christmas. Last month, perhaps ten parties were formed, whose leaders will start running for the highest office in the city in two months, and the pre-election debates have even entered the CN agenda. I don't think ordinary people will notice any changes. Once in five years, they went to the elections to vote over and over again for the same man who had in fact died a long time ago, and his function as well, if not better, was performed by a virtual avatar. His competitors were chosen identically, but that didn't matter. The elections still had the result that the Council wanted. Now it looked as if it would be a similar modus operandi too, and all the four corporations were interested in was choosing the name of the new puppet.

"Who will take command of PRAGUETECH after Petlán?" I asked.

Karel, without considering the stream of my thoughts, replied:

"Petlán."

"What?"

"His younger brother, Oscar," he explained.

"Oh," I muttered.

I was interested in whether he also liked milk skin.

* * *

We landed three blocks - about half a kilometer - from the sanctuary. This part of Prague is so boring it couldn't possibly be more boring. Neither rich nor poor lived here. It was inhabited by those who could afford to rent, but for nothing else - in short: the golden middle class, the people who were the backbone of society. Responsible enough and too frightened to take drugs and commit crimes other than domestic violence, while also seeking to amass as much material goods as possible. Honestly, of course - so no chance. People every cop liked, even if their way of life made them go crazy and kill their neighbor because he was playing Mutated Earthworms too loud. These people did not try to cover their tracks, lie in their vivid eyes and construct wild excuses and complicated alibis. Such a man prepared you a coffee-like drink, confessed to everything and asked if there was a toilet in the prison with a toilet seat, or just a box with a chemical cartridge into which you crush a squat.

Here, among the skyscrapers, there was one that had a decent underground passage, in which a virtual porn cinema advertisement was flashed (3D Dáda Patrasová in fifteen versions, now also as a 200 kilograms black woman!), and right next to it was a lonely black door with a strange wheel, that those sword freaks wore on their clothes.

Before we left the locked hovercraft, Karel pulled two bulletproof vests and DEZA02 shotguns from the trunk - a former security gift from Albert Viktor. We loaded seven bullets into each.

"I don't see the bell," Karel whispered.

He did not have to. There were incessant groans from the porn cinema that echoed through the entire underpass. There, the sighing and the smell of piss mixed with the smell of sausages sold 24 hours a day in the booth Tomia. An Arab singer yelled from there. Even if she called for the slaughter of all unbelievers, I was eager to listen to incomprehensible, frighteningly high-pitched tones.

Karel knocked on the door, and then again and again. Only after the tenth attempt, when he started banging on the door with the butt, did the golden mark shift and a crack appeared.

"Leave it to me, I have a plan," I said.

"Who comes in this hour dedicated to Moran?" A male voice asked.

"I'm Dirty Lopez and I came to avenge my father's death," I said.

"Was that supposed to be the plan?" Karel looked at me curiously.

"Well, that's the plan." I shrugged and looked into the eyes located behind the crack.

"We're from Security. You are surrounded. Immediately open the door and..."

The rift disappeared with a crackling sound and the golden mark reappeared.

"And now?" The Security chief smiled crookedly.

Quite right, because the door didn't budge.

"Now this plan. Stand back," I asked him and fired three times at the door. The third shot breached the lock and I was able to kick it open.

Behind them was a guy with a crossbow. He shot and the arrow stuck into my bulletproof vest.

I put lead into him. He fell to the ground and started bleeding from the colander I made from his legs.

I bent down and looked at the arrow.

"I must admit, they have their own style, but crossbows?" I frowned.

He surprised me. If he aimed thirty centimeters higher, it would have pierced my throat. I would not heal that. But as the horse's dose of painkillers was circulating through my body, I found it quite a joke.

A long corridor led from the door which ended in a huge hall. And by "huge", I mean - monstrous. I would bet it used to be a theater or something like that. But the last theater was closed thirty years ago when it was discovered that it only served as a cover for human trafficking. It made sense, because in ancient Rome, actresses were considered equal to prostitutes...

I shook my head. Pain-relieving drugs were tearing my mind in different directions, and I had to focus. Especially since there were about twenty people in the room.

Stop, foot of the stranger, holy are the places you enter!" A wailing female voice sounded.

"Yup, the people in this town are totally crazy," Karel sighed.

* * *

There was something like an altar in the center of the room. It was an enormous slab, maybe marble, or maybe plastic marble's imitation. There were twenty naked women walking around. They all held twigs and waved them. They were led by a woman who had shouted at us earlier. They stopped after our entry.

"I wouldn't kill these young people," suggested Karel.

"You ageist," I sighed and, despite the woman's warnings, I walked closer.

Only then did I notice that a man's body was lying on the marble altar. It smelled of some herbal essences, ointments, oils, to put it simply, something from this assortment.

I loaded the shotgun so that the woman would understand that the situation was serious.

"All those who were Under th Drank Payoff Bar today are either dead or under arrest, and you look like a group of partners in crime. Admittedly, sexy partners in crime, but fuck, enough for today. They wanted to kill me, I had a sword stuck in my body, they drugged me with a cyber drug, reset me, cheered me up and finally got an arrow in the chest. I'd like to know what the hell is going here!" I screamed.

The opiates from the medic apparently stopped working. And worst of all - my heart-touching speech failed because the old woman threw herself at me and tried to flog me with a twig. Birch, which I noticed only now. I knocked her to the ground with a shotgun. It didn't take strength to do this. She might have been fifty kilos with shoes. And now she was barefoot.

"You," I growled, pointing the gun at the busty redhead. A gold pendant with a familiar shape swung around her neck.

"They killed the high priest, our prophet, the one who talked to Perun. Sorceresses," she explained.

Her companions frowned. At the one that wrinkled them the most, I aimed my gun.

"Any problem, miss?"

She shook her head.

"Come see something," Commander Adam snapped me out of my role as an enraged PE teacher at a girls' boarding school.

I turned and strode among the naked women to the altar. I figured the guy was probably only dead for a day. He wore a long white caftan soaked in various fragrant ointments and lotions that women rubbed into him. And bloody stains showed through the fabric.

"Stab wounds," Karel observed the obvious, then pointed to the man's neck. It had a black streak there - as if the original painting had been smeared with oil - but it looked like a fountain or something. Just two arcs coming out of one line.

"Why do the ladies say they were sorceresses?" I turned to the bewildered women.

"He left a message it's their fault," the old woman croaked.

* * *

Reinforcements arrived within half an hour, which made Perun's followers a little pissed off. Not enough to encourage them to dress, but the fact that we had the body of the high priest taken away caused much roar, spitting, biting and scratching. We left the pacification of the last members of the Old Slavonic cult to the young men and girls who had gained experience in the street, and we preferred to focus on extracting this message from the priestess. She wanted to eat the corpse, but a blow to her stomach made her for a moment lose her appetite. In addition, we promised her that we would return the body the next day. We just didn't know what to do with her sword-wielding companions. Especially since the fear grew in me that in these holy places the armed commando of Uncle Neny would soon be standing by the foot.

The Zodiac is talking to you. I'm leaving another dead body behind because it's super fun. That idiot that went to the slaughter smelled like a pig. The first time I saw him, I imagined myself stabbing him. But it's not his fault. It was all because of cybersorceresses, lustful whores who wanted to take for themselves what he wanted to do - a faith that did not belong to them. They made me kill that stinky hog. And others will join him. The one who makes political plans to rule my city, the one who walks in white, the messiah bringing love, the virgin who hides in her tower, the toothless from the street who stirs up the crowd, and a relic of the old days who, like me - wants to destroy everything cybernetic. I will kill them and no one will stop me. I will bring death to all who deserve it and for those who get in my way. For example, these twins lying in the sewer under the porncinema. I was walking by and I didn't like their laughter.

Yours Zodiac

"Zodiac," Karel read aloud.

"Don't call him that. He's a shithead. Maybe a sick freak, a motherfucker, a fucking psychopathic bitch or a gross loogie, but that's all. We will not call him any other name!" I exhaled and handed the paper to Karel.

We put on sterile gloves, but probably unnecessarily, the bastard did not leave any traces.

We walked outside, heading towards a noisy porn movie. In front of him, we actually found a manhole cover about a meter long. I ordered Karel to open the hatch and one Security girl shone her flashlight. Two rattled bodies of women were lying there. It has already exceeded my patience.

"Take them out, find out who they were and if they have any marks left. I'm out of here," I said, and without waiting for Karel's reaction, I just walked away.

* * *

There was a dive on the ground floor of the house opposite. It is difficult to say otherwise. A few shops around have already closed, but this conglomerate of beer, buffet and night shop was bustling. There were several huge rotten tires on the sidewalk, strewn around plastic crates that served as tables. Somewhere in the new center, from about the twentieth floor upwards, or in the student district around U-metro Staromiejska, it could be considered a cool, modern, but sloppy decoration. The one that flashed three times a day on Dickpicgram, a popular social networking site of the Prague Internet, where users shared tips about illegal pubs. But in this neighborhood it was just a dive. A subway train passed over our heads. It was as silent as the snap of a law school prom, but its passage through the structure towering high above our heads brought a bit of refreshing breeze in the still stuffiness that even now reached a thirty degrees after midnight. The concrete was just radiating heat all the time. But the occasional blast of air thanks to the metro turned out to be beneficial. That's probably why it was crowded in the dive.

Under the Smelly Pole - I read it and immediately thought that I had to take Belch here. He liked these frustrating symbols of a lost war. But at this point the name made sense. An old military uniform and a velvet pillow with the order For Courage III degree, were displayed in a dirty glass case. I remember that at the beginning of the war I arrested a former physical education teacher from Karviná, who was selling this kind of crap - one for canning beans. But the host of the place must have obtained them, and he was ostentatiously proud of it.

"Veterans for half price, Poles drink piss" - said the inscription above the bar. Yes, Belch is sure to love this dive. They poured beer here, of course, from hops grown in laboratories and from concentrates. The Zlatopramen brand. It sounded patriotic enough, so I ordered one.

"I'm a veteran," I winked at the guy behind the bar.

It appeared to be the owner himself. He had a huge black beard with silver thread and one glass eye. Probably the army could not afford an expensive implant. Or maybe he only lost them in a pub fight. The bald head was adorned with a small but boldly exposed bush of black hair that curled around the ears and back of the head. He weighed maybe a hundred kilos, which was emphasized only by the tucked-up apron that barely covered his massive beer belly.

"And you have a veteran ID, homie?" The bartender asked.

"God, I haven't heard the word "homie" since the war."

"You served in the Brno Airborne Unit, right?" I asked, tossing my bionic denture onto the counter and tapping it with my toe. I mean... the denture was permanently in place, so I just lifted my leg up on the counter next to the paper tip box, which was desperately empty.

"Fuck, another wounded Pole killer, okay, you have it for half the price," he said appreciatively and poured me an oversized beer.

I winked conspiratorially at him and walked away with my beer to take a seat on one of the empty tires. A pack of six guys sat next to me. Two were dozing, four were playing cards. I figured they were playing "ten". The last time I fucked this card game was in the war. I couldn't remember the rules for anything.

I drank some beers and was surprised it didn't taste as bad as cocoa. Given the origin of the owner of the place, they might have had Starobrno here, but I don't think the bartender will be such an idiot to want to deprive the regulars of their lives and himself of the livelihood.

"You're not a local, are you?"

It was the bartender. He brought me a glass of clear liquid.

"I'm wandering here and there," I explained.

The tire swayed slightly as he sat on it.

I withstood the rubber tsunami and clinked my glass with it. In recent years, I didn't expect much from people. It was enough that they didn't want to kill me.

"This town is fucked up, let me tell you, homie. Nobody respects us, but what can young people know about the world, huh? We were as far as Karviná, Český Těšín, and I was even outside Poland, and they?" He waved his hand as if Prague youth were running around, singing Hana Zagorova's remixed hits.

At the same time, someone at the next table announced that they had won, causing a murmur of dissatisfaction among their teammates.

I just shrugged. That was a rhetorical question.

"It needs to be changed, you know, change. Everything smells musty here," he winded himself up.

"You think so?" I drank a sip of a beer.

"Definitely. What the hell is out there? Well, what exactly is there? We should pick it up, right?"

I had another sip. My side ached. The medications stopped working. I had the doctor's pills in my pocket, but I couldn't remember what he told me about dosage.

"Where did you actually serve?" He asked after a moment, seeing that I had neither nodded nor objected to him.

"In the third Zbraslav Infantry Regiment," I replied. This wasn't the first time I lied. This unit was almost completely wiped out by the Polish bombers Chłodnik while they were traveling by train, so the likelihood of encountering someone who fought in it was minimal. Soldiers, and especially veterans, hated members of the military police, so I did not admit that I was serving in this formation.

The bartender just nodded. But before he gave another wisdom, a group of several workers appeared on the horizon. They were all wearing green DEZATEG coveralls with the GEZ logo on them.

"Sorry, homie, customers are coming, nice chat," said the bartender.

I finished my drink quickly and let the chip on the table take two hellers off the account. I left my mug on the table, walked past the workers and went out into the street.

"Don't be a prick and get in, I'll take you home," Karel's voice said from behind me.

* * *

He drove me to my rented apartment. He dropped off at a private heliport, and I sluggishly headed for my apartment. Fay was waiting for me there. She didn't need to explain anything, Ivana let her in and disappeared. I didn't explain anything either. I just fell on the bed and fell asleep.

* * *

In the morning the sun woke me up. Real sun, not artificial light. The apartment was high enough for the morning rays to fall in through the window. Fay had to pull the blinds open. I opened my eyes and felt the wound. It hurt, but I was glad I didn't die. I swallowed the medic pills and went to the ion shower. At first it sparked a little, but finally it started to work. This apartment could use a plumber and a decent upgrade.

I took off all my clothes and bandage from the bar. The wound under the rag looked nasty, but the antibiotics worked, so no smelly crater was looking at me. I silently thanked the bartender and Sir Alexander Fleming and washed myself thoroughly in the ionic shower. I recovered enough to manage to throw yesterday's clothes into the washing machine. At least the parts of it that had no holes. I took a new one from the wardrobe, quite similar to the one I had put on recently. It seems that young Dejčer had a fairly simple style - black underwear and pants, a white T-shirt and a dark shirt. I took this set and went to the living room.

The music struck me. I knew it. What's Your Story, Morning Glory by Julie London. It came from a record that turned on a real turntable. It really amazed me. I was used to antiques, but this taste in music... Julie London had a velvety hoarseness that could rival even the best black singers of the golden age such as Ella Fitzgerald and Nina Simone. I walked behind the bookcase and saw Fay on the bed. She was lying there naked, with one leg bent and slightly tilted so that I could easily see what she was hiding between her thighs.

"I was worried about you," she said, shaking her hair slightly shining in the sunlight.

Her implants also gleamed with reflected light in the flood of sunlight. Several visible electrical impulses passed through her body, revealing just how aroused she was.

What's your story, morning glory?

What makes you look so blue?

She surprised me. Our breakup was not filled with quarrels and insults, but the silence was even more painful. Especially, when I felt it was my fault while Fay was secretly giving me money through Belch.

I walked over to the bed and just looking at her was enough to put my morning glory on alert. I knelt carefully on the bed, so as not to irritate the wound, and grabbed Fay's legs. I started kissing them slowly, gradually getting closer to her pussy. I dipped my mouth and tongue into it as deeply as possible. Fay was trembling all over, but soon allowed her body to experience her first orgasm. Maybe yesterday's e-snow helped, but soon she started to sigh deeply and tremble again. She probably turned on her cyber spells.

I circled her pussy once more, leaned on my hands and entered her. Slowly and carefully at first, but when I was somewhere in the middle, I pushed with all my strength.

The way that you've been acting

I don't know what to do

For I love you, sure as one and one make two

What's your story, morning glory?

Fay was groaning, and I tried my best not to end up in her right away. She sensed it - she came to meet me a few times with her hips, then let me set my own pace. She was just sighing, and her implants glowed faintly. They couldn't compete with the sun.

Julie London was singing "The postman came this morning" when Ivana entered the room instead of the postman. It was completely unexpected, but at my age I wasn't going to make nudity or sex any scandal.

"Sorry," she smiled.

I looked at her. There was shyness and cunning on her face. As usual, she wore a dress with oriental motifs. Light purple this time. The dragons that I already know bit each other's tails. She had cut-outs up to the hips. A gust of wind would suffice to...

Fay looked at her. It lasted for maybe a few seconds, and I felt another shiver run through her body. They somehow communicated with each other on their own wavelengths. The connection that cybernetic prostitutes could make was in many ways magic. Maybe that's why Fay and her companions came to be called sorceresses.

Ivana walked over to the bed, taking off her shoes on the way.

Then she rolled up her dress and pulled it over her head.

* * *

Julia London's voice was no longer heard from the crackling record. I was looking at Ivana's beautiful body, perfect in many ways, without any imperfections. Somewhere in the back of my head was the thought that it was the work of the magnate's Lota grandfather, who had perfected her. I remembered saying something about how they were interpreting the Kama Sutra together in this apartment. She must have had new hands because after yesterday's scars there were no traces left. It was not known where her biological body began and ended, or what was left of it. But these thoughts only flashed through my mind and vanished the

146

moment Ivana's implants connected to Fay's implants and I was between them. Ivana started stroking my back and ass while I pushed harder and harder.

I couldn't stand it anymore and ejaculated in Fay.

I pulled away slowly, but the two cyber prostitutes, each different, though alike in many respects, didn't even notice. Ivana leaned down between Fay's legs and pressed her tongue to where I left off. I carefully stroked her breasts and ass, then slipped between her legs. She just sighed. Fay gripped my hand tightly and a fantastic energy shot through me. My penis did an amazing maneuver and stood at attention again. Fay just nodded, and I penetrated Ivana. As soon as I walked in, I started pushing furiously. Whatever happened next, I was too unconscious to remember it.

* * *

Naked, Ivana played Dooley Wilson on the turntable. As he sang As Time Goes By, a song that made Casablanca's ancient movie famous, I breathed a sigh of relief that this apartment had been inhabited recently, even before the horrible retro style had hit the ground. Knowing her perversity, she would probably have let go of the Rainbow Fairy without blinking an eye. In her hand she held a glass of Mackmyr whiskey, filled from a freshly opened bottle, and stretched like a kitty.

Fay stroked my hair. I reached for the bottle and drank from the bittle. I looked at the clock. It was close to noon. The morning glory time is over.

"We have to go," I said, looking at Ivana and Fay again.

They were so different and yet so incredibly beautiful in their own mature way.

"Where are we going?" Fay asked.

"Eh, what?"

"I'm unemployed because of you, remember? And you said something you'd give me the money I put into you, you fool," she said and winked at me.

"The latter is true, but the former is not. It's not because of me, it's because of those Perun's fuckers. And the Zodi... freak for freaks, turned them against you," I replied.

"Who?" She asked, not understanding.

"One punk we're looking for. Lota was right..."

"Me," Ivana said, sniffing the whiskey.

"What?"

"I was right."

"You wanted to say something about him not being an ordinary killer, what's happening is a bigger deal. Sure, this is driven by a psychopath, but this psychopath has a plan. Lota was right when she said these words when she hired you. Only, in fact, I informed her about it and that's why I'm taking part in the investigation," she said with amusement.

"Sexy and intelligent." Fay winked at her fondly.

I was starting to get lost in it.

"You can't come with us, Fay. Sorceresses are not affected by this. He doesn't like you and most people do. Even Neny can't protect you anymore. There is only one place where you can hide with the rest of the girls."

"No, I won't go to the pirates," she moaned.

"There is a better place, the kingdom of indigestion and bison grass vodka. Since you are friends, he will definitely give you his best hunter's stew." I laughed and stood up, then retrieved Claire Klingenberg's book The History and the Essence of Illusions in Astrology from the library.

* * *

On my way from Belch, where we left Fay, I called Adam and explained where we were going.

"Did those sewer girls have any sign?" I asked.

"If you shake your head, I can't see it, man," I said after a moment's pause.

"They didn't. Not one," he replied.

It was a mystery. Some got a stamp, others didn't. But discovering what they mean was easy. Zodiac referred to the heavenly zoo - a system of astrological signs. It is an ancient system that tried to find similarities between people born in one of the twelve periods and predict what awaits each of us. And, of course, get the money out of the desperate who believed it.

The high priest of the cult of Perun wore the sign of Aries, we know from a letter written by this bastard. Petlán was given the Mark of Cancer, and the guardian who started it all - Aquarius. The rest of the dead, finished with the same manuscript, that is, with the same knives - and according to Karel, Security man brought out a total of thirty of them - they had no marks. These three were essential, the others were just meat that got in his way. At least that is how Zodiac wanted to convey it to us.

"You think he believes in horoscopes?" Karel's voice came from my cellular band after a moment.

Ivana and I both shook our heads.

"No. He's a freak, but it's just fun. Or a way to sort the victims," I replied.

There was only a grunt in the armband.

"We've got a trace, anyway. A fragment of DNA was found on the paper on which he wrote this letter. He is not part of any of this crazy cult, nor is he in the database. But we have a trace, at least something," he said cheerfully, as if I could get DNA samples from over ten million inhabitants of this filthy metropolis.

But that wasn't the only clue the fucker left. In the letter he made it quite clear who, apart from the sorceresses, he wanted to hunt down. All too clearly as if he wanted us to know. Karel and I discussed this last night, and we couldn't agree on whether he wanted to lead us by the nose or show us how stupid we were and take them out in front of us. Anyway, he was playing with us. He knew we were chasing him, as if he were watching, following, and throwing crumbs at us like blunt chickens that would spit. The way he challenged the sorceresses of Perun's followers, as well as what he wrote in the note, was deliberately synchronized so that we would find him. Two important events are scheduled for today. The first legal political gathering in about thirty years, which will also be attended by Mina, followed by a large Cybernetic Messiah Mass. Both were identified by Zodiac as the next victims, and Karel sent his men to both events, so Ivana and I went there too.

We landed quite far from Palacky Square and covered the remaining distance of one station by the S-metro. Of course, there had been no square for a long time. The river disappeared, and the original square, which must have been there since the Middle Ages, was built up with an endless mass of fifty-story gigantic buildings that housed ARKAS factories and laboratories, constantly spewing tons of artificial meat every hour - the highest and the lowest quality. It was not enough for this voracious and always hungry city. A new square named after the original was built on the roofs of the complex. Once upon a time, this was the only place in Prague where political rallies could be held without announcement or permission. You just can't hail on it. That is, from 1945 to 2036. After the Great Irish Pandemic, everyone had a kick in the ass, and what's more, Professor Hnízdil showed that regularly raising your hands up and down increases the volume of the lungs. Only then did they take him to the madhouse for good. At least, from then until the collapse of the republic, it was Czech Hyde Park, whatever that meant.

Rough boys with no markings were protection here now. Only on their sleeves they wore blue bands with the word "Rebirth" written on them. The same word was on the digital banner that flashed fifty meters above the square. There were similar devices on the other side as well, about a kilometer from here. This was probably how the space for the demonstration was designated.

People used to come here. There was one of the exits from the S - Palacky metro station nearby, so we were quite close. People from Security were also hanging around among the guards with armbands. Everyone looked at them with surprise. They probably waited for the safes to take out the clubs and chase the whole circus out. I also carried this feeling, although now I was one of them. Ivana even brought me an ID today. Politics is a tricky business. Ever since Prague was established as a city-state that broke away from a crumbling republic, politics had only been practiced virtually, and now someone wanted to talk to people in person and wished they would click on his name online afterwards. I think most of it brought curiosity here.

The Renaissance was the first to do so. There were also politicians from other parties in the discussions that took place in the CN in recent weeks, but they didn't get my attention too much, and I think most people shared my feelings. They treated it as just another TV show, a little more boring than Dirty Lopez, Pijer and Marika, or the hotseries of Lola, the queen of the landfill, starring the same actress as in Lopez. I didn't know her real name, and I only remembered her small, plump breasts anyway.

There was a large tent at the edge of the square. To get to it, we had to get through not only the security, but also a group of onlookers and young volunteers wearing blue armbands. Politics seemed to be just as exciting new to young people as another new remix of the Rainbow Fairy.

"I follow you, Mr. Lieutenant." Ivana winked at me.

Even though I loaded her with my male ammunition an hour ago, she still called me Mr.

"Sex is fun and you can even do it with strangers if they shower first," Ivana explained, as I looked a little embarrassed after all the cybernetic bitches had done to me.

I showed the ID to two polite gentlemen with armbands and guns in their belts and swam towards the group standing around Mina. I knew many of them. I saw there, for example...

"What do you want, prick?"

The voice belonged to Fat Tom. While the others debated something, he was just standing at the edge of the crowd, possibly airing his jewels under the Scottish skirt he was still wearing. I was afraid it was still the same for decades. He even threatened me with a clenched fist in front of my face. But only for a moment, because that got everyone else's attention.

Fat Tom was an old friend of mine. We played online games together and had a beers. But he also belonged to an illegal pirate group that was left over from an old political movement. Pirates, after a series of attacks on technology companies, or - as they themselves said - after the War with Big Brother, plunged into non-existence. Many thought they were just legends, but they still lived outside of official structures, trading information and sniffing around in cyberspace. Their boss, Hynek, collaborated for several decades with Mina, the last head of the republic's secret services, who once handed over power to corporations, but never came to terms with it.

Hynek isn't the only one around her right now. A lot of people standing in the nearest circle could be about a hundred, they were people related to the old republic. I knew a few faces, but not too many of them. They lived on old tales, resentments and struggles that had long interested only them, and now felt the good old days might come back. It has always been so in society that the desire for change and the new conflicted with regular bouts of longing for the good old days. Because the old days are always good. Somehow it was like that. Like a hard erection, young people who respect the old, and bread that is crunchier and more fragrant than what is today. All the hideous corruption, the collapse of the state, people on the margins of society, political struggle that ignores real problems - everything the old republic was known for - it seems as if no one remembered it anymore.

"What are you looking for?" Mina asked after a moment.

She took a step towards me, leaving her companions behind.

"I'm here on business. We have to talk." I showed her the ID.

She casually tossed her blue hair back. She had an amazing charm for her age. Before the closure of Prague, she was one of the most powerful people and could afford a decent dose of gene therapy. But what she had without medical intervention was a charisma that even her worst enemies could not deny her. Therefore, it also became a torch for those who wanted to return to the good old days.

"Security has nothing to do right now," the guy next to her began, but she only raised a fist to her right ear. The gesture worked, and the guy fell silent. And then she just walked with me through the tent to the edge of the parking lot.

The others watched us from a distance.

"Mr. Adam has already informed us about the killer," she said in a calm voice.

She was a statesman. Her whole personality radiated with it, everything - attitude, determination, appearance. She was just born at the wrong time. The businessmen screwed her. But now, years later, fate was rolling them over.

"He's not an ordinary killer," I said.

156

Slowly, calmly, we reached the raised concrete barrier. Mina sat on it and leaned forward, making her look a bit like a majestic sphinx watching the city below. She was silent. She waited for some young man to bring us two cups of coffee. Real coffee! Only Bloody Ali, a Buddhist, who used to add a little pacifist spiritual wisdom to each cup, made this one.

I smelled and drank.

"What do you mean he's not an ordinary killer?" She asked after a moment.

"He wants not only to kill, he wants to wreak havoc. He gets things moving, deliberately and mindfully," I explained what I meant.

"Things have already been set in motion. Look around. This city is run by the Corporation Council, made up of the top five companies that feed and dress the entire agglomeration. When the republic fell apart, they just took the best and made it a haven with a puppet mayor at the helm. But there are only four corporations now. DEZATEG is falling apart and others are scratching it. Lota plays her fantasy games, locked as little Lota in a tower full of elves, dwarfs and fairies. The Petlán family is struggling to control PRAGUETECH, and the only ones who are still in power are the Sejm from ARKAS and Šmídová from GEZ. They enlist in private armies and prepare for what change may bring. And the city feels it. You do not see it? Times changes. It was started by the mayor's fall, but then you just wasted your chance to do something," she said.

At that point, she looked more like a basilisk than a sphinx.

"The city feels its own shit and Happy Sausages rather than change," I snorted.

She was right. Prague is like a pressurized pot that releases steam in an uncontrolled way. All the cults that arose one after the other, the prophets of doom in the streets, and the politics and that bastard with knives.

"This time the elections will be real. The corporations promised it, and I will win it, make the changes, and nothing can stop me. Even Zodiac," she said.

Well, she knew who we warned her about. I think her spies knew the truth and brought her piles of information. After all, Hynek and his boys were able to break in virtually anywhere. For them, the Security database is a children's sandbox, to which it was enough to come, take all the toys, and as a souvenir to clean up there.

"Be careful. You don't know what he's capable of," I said.

I don't know what I promised myself after talking to Mina, but I still tried to protect her. After all, I worked for her for several years and lived with her.

"And he doesn't know what I'm capable of. I will restore to this city its glory and the state. And you and your little police desires and ideals will no longer hold me back. I have enough resources and determination," she said.

There was no anger or resentment in her voice. Mina was just coldly calculating and planning. All this in the name of a vision of some greater good.

"One justice is more powerful than a thousand weapons, Mina," I replied.

"Who said that? Dirty Lopez?" She could be quite sarcastic if she wanted to.

"Sun Tzu, my reading in the toilet. Very informative." I nodded and had a cup of coffee. It was definitely better than cocoa.

I did not say goodbye and did not try to warn her a second time. It would be pointless. She was a sphinx, she had her vision and determination, and I was just a cop.

On the way, I came across Radoslav Sejmen, the owner of ARKAS. Mina seemed to have the power she wanted in her hands.

Cyber Messiah

As we walked back through the tent, Fat Tom shook his fist at me. The worst part, however, was the growing crowds of people who came here. Judging by their appearance, they were residents of the S and N levels. It made sense. U-level residents did not buy tickets for higher routes. Perhaps some could afford it, but those who had resided in U for a long time ten floors up already felt strange.

I understood that very well. It's like being in class with a girl from a wealthy family whose dad is a lawyer and mom wears expensive boots. She looks at you, she likes you, but you still can't imagine that you could ever touch her. Man not only feels out of his league, but just feels like a different species. And at home, you compose some poems, thinking that someday you will read them to her and you will be like Romeo and Juliet. However, if you dare after a few months, you will find that a pack of hockey players who never had this strange impression fucks her.

"What are you thinking about?" Ivana asked.

"About hockey," I said truthfully.

"And what is that?"

She surprised me a bit, but I wasn't astonished. The last hockey stadium in Prague was demolished about thirty years ago. It took up too much space.

We descended to the U level and inhaled the familiar smell of piss, bottom and desperation. In the crowd of people, we came across three Easter bunnies. After all, Easter was approaching.

* * *

Ivana was driving, so to speak. Her hovercraft was a hi-tech toy that, even in the worst traffic jams and chaos, could navigate by itself without any problems. She eventually corrected it mentally through one of her implants.

I pulled out the History and the essence of the astrology illusion.

"Johannes Kepler was to say: 'Where would a reasonable mother of astronomy be if a crazy daughter of astrology earned

162

nothing?' He didn't believe in astrology, but he just earned money so that he could research the planets," I read aloud.

The book seemed interesting, but I didn't learn anything from it that I didn't know before. The key to Zodiac must lie somewhere other than in astrology.

"It's not cool," said Ivana.

I slammed the book shut and looked straight ahead. People were flowing through the streets. Mina could not compete with them. There were thousands of them.

We sent a hovercraft to one of the parking buildings. They functioned in an uncomplicated way - the automatic control led the vehicle to the platform, where the vehicles were stored by type, with an accuracy to the centimeter. Saving space was crucial in Prague. Ivana tapped her cell band to validate the fee, then we were swallowed by the crowd and moved to the Letna Center.

* * *

I knew them. I knew them all too well. Those who worked, and were poor anyway, but somewhere inside believed that it might change someday - and if not, for some reason they believed that they were leading a good life. So, did those who lived similar lives, but inside hated anyone who was doing better. And I also knew those who gave up, labored to survive, and tried to wrest some of that instant happiness for themselves - alcoholics, junkies, street thieves, the homeless, occasional mercenaries, people who bought this and that for a pittance, that they would hold anyone who enjoyed five penises or seven pussies for even meager pennies. And then someone stabbed them and left them like a carcass because he didn't have enough hellers to pay them. These people had almost nothing. The only thing they could give anyone was their faith.

And the crowd carried us like a river to the center of the events that took place at the intersection, where there used to be ordinary cars, but now there were only old buses and some booths and shelters where you could take a nap. There was a pile of old cars in the middle of the old intersection. It was called the Pyramid of Dread. Accurate term. When traffic stopped in Prague, an artist pulled all the parked cars here and stacked them with a crane on top of each other. I think he called this work The Accusation of Consumer Society or The Golgotha of Capitalism - or something like that. For this, the DEZATEG foundation for artists paid him a million dollars, for which he took drugs to death. It seems to me that only this act turned out to be a true artistic accusation of the consumer society. Since then, the Pyramid of Dread has fallen apart a little and stinks. Local residents used it as a garbage can for all kinds of waste, including corpses that need to be disposed of. Some old cars were used as bedrooms. And now thousands of citizens were coming here from all sides.

"Do you have it under control?" I asked Karel over the cellular band.

"Have you lost your mind?" he replied.

I shrugged.

"How the hell can we control anything here? The people I sent here mingle with the crowd, I pull them off. I'll just leave the drones here. I'll take the Security guys to your buddy. Permitting the demonstration was really bullshit. In the old days, drones would have chased it away with rubber balls," replied Karel Adam.

Seriously, the function changed him.

"He's not my friend."

"Whatever, but she has armed guys from ARKAS and GEZ. Nothing's going to happen to her, and I'd rather put someone there. The more the better. We're gonna protect this asshole from the air. It can't be otherwise," he explained, a little calmer.

I nodded and broke the connection. I think he was having me on. Mina pulled the strings for better protection. She might seem inaccessible, but she never underestimated the risks. Adam wouldn't admit it to me, but I didn't care. I knew he was used to hearing his ladies. And I just wanted to get this freak.

As we approached the Pyramid of Dread, the crowd thickened, and we had trouble getting there.

"When I grew up and had to replace artificial limbs and implants with larger ones, I regretted every piece that was missing. What a pity that I didn't lose my sense of smell then too," Ivana shouted in my ear.

She was not used to the smell of bodies that had not been washed for months. There were not only ion showers on top, but plenty of washing water as well. God, in the apartment where she lived, the former creator and ruler of VEP - Dejčer also had a bathtub with a supply of clean water. One filling of it corresponded to the monthly consumption of this liquid by an average family who used water only for drinking. The body can be cleaned with a dry cloth, sand or you can just oil it. The use of water for this appeared to be pure extravagance. This was the reason why, if - once in a blue moon - it rained so much that the water got all the way to level U, most of its inhabitants undressed and reveled in the raindrops. It was caught in every vessel that was at hand. But now something else was falling from the sky - hope.

"A piece of messiah's garment! Fifty hellers for small one, three crowns for big one!" Yelled the guy in a long white jacket.

Hmm, white... a bit yellowed and gray, but the original color can be guessed.

"Hey, I remember you. You have three penises. You walked the streets naked and offered yourself to everyone for an energy bar," I said.

It surprised him a bit. He was holding thin strips of fabric in his hand. People crowded around and haggled. He really valued his stuff.

"Me," the guy turned hesitantly, "that was a long time ago. Now, thanks to Cyber Messiah, I have become a better person."

The others nodded appreciatively.

"You killed a whore. On Christmas. You were high," I said.

Ivana took my hand and squeezed it tightly. She was not afraid, she just wanted to let you know that I was provoking unnecessarily. We are in the middle of the crowd and it will be hard to get out of here in case of any conflict.

"It was a cyber whore," said Three penises.

"Death to ones and zeros!" An old woman threw into space.

"Death to ones and zeros!" The others joined.

Three penises looked at me triumphantly.

Ivana squeezed me even tighter and I sped up.

There was a wave of screams in the crowd, but after a while people returned to discussing the business with the relics.

Many of the arrivals wore coveralls bearing the logo of one of the five corporations. However, most of them stuck to the uncrossed pieces of tape with the rotated numbers 1 and 0 underneath them - in such a position that they looked like they were lying down.

"Hey, where are you going?" The tall man in GEZ coveralls growled at me.

"Security. We're going to... protect Cyber Messiah," I hesitated for a moment, and fished my pass out of my shirt.

He grimaced but let us go. People were afraid of Security. I hadn't surprised them, and now it even suited me. We continued our way to the edge of the Pyramid of Dread. At the wreckage of škoda karoq, from where a birch was growing right through its center, covered with lots of crumpled plastic packaging and dried human excrement, we were stopped by a kind of protection. They were women who wore caftans like the one that adorned Mr. Three penises, but this time really white. They were adamant.

"You serve the dark," the girl said with a smile.

She could be about seventeen years old. She had long white hair down and sparkling blue eyes. She was barefoot.

"What?" I shook my head.

"Your drones circling in the holy heavens and your ubiquitous technology plunges the inhabitants of this city into darkness. The time has come to throw it all away and save the soul of this city, brother," she explained.

Giving me a smile again. And it's not crooked at all.

"Yeah, dark, sure. Seriously, I need to talk to the guy who drives this," I growled.

Fighting through the crowd did not have a good effect on my mental balance.

"He'll talk to you. With all of us." She pointed to the top of the pyramid.

He was standing there. He looked, how to say, like a real Polish cabbage trader. He had short black hair, a mustache, and was wearing a straitjacket. He could be either forty or sixty. Somehow, he climbed barefoot on a pyramid of cars and apparently never stepped into a rotting corpse or a rusty sheet metal. He raised his hand above his head, and everyone fell silent. All. It was amazing. I looked around the crowd - no one even flinched. Then he spoke. Calmly and carefully.

"My heart is overjoyed today," he rumbled.

His voice barely reached those standing in the front rows, but those who heard him repeated the sentence, followed by others. His speech flowed like a surfer on a wave - carried all the way to the end of the crowd.

"You came because you long for a better world. And it will come. We will be free, brothers and sisters, we will be free from everything that troubles and torments us. From technology, from rulers, from killers of our bodies and souls..."

"I would have smoke," I said as another wave of words flashed past us.

"I didn't think you smoke."

"I don't smoke, but I would smoke now. I don't like that kind of shit. It's always a harbinger of trouble." I sighed, but Cyber Messiah's more phrases continued to flow around me.

"We've reached the end of everything. Next is the wall. They locked us in hell, but I am here to open the gate to a better world for you. I am here to cleanse you and this sinful city. We'll go outside. We will sow the fields again. We will break the cyber shackles!"

The words rang from one listener to the next.

"It's fascinating," said Ivana.

"You think so? In my opinion, this is pointless bullshitting. One bearded man from my street was preaching something similar. Mainly women came to him, before it turned out that he was cleaning their soul with his penis through the anus. Until one day a car ran over him. This is what I call karma," I replied.

It made her laugh.

"Sure it's bullshitting, but it makes sense. Everyone can get what they want from it. And that's the charm of this bullshitting," she explained.

"And where did he even come from?"

She shrugged.

"Nobody knows. I searched the Security databases and those kept by VEP analysts. No one heard of him until he began preaching a year ago. First to a small group, and now..." She looked around meaningfully at the surrounding crowd of people.

A thousand of them might have come here. Others were probably standing in the side streets, where the words of the prophet were carried. Parents put their children on a piggyback so that they would see Cyber Messiah better.

It took an hour, maybe more, before the cabbage merchant, the preacher, carefully stepped down from the Pyramid of Dread.

Women in straitjackets pounced on him and started kissing his hands. Instead, the people around him fell to their knees and stretched out their hands to bless them. They loved him as they had loved cybernetic sorceresses until recently. But while Fay and her buddies were treating it all as a show and their own cult terrified them, this guy was evidently nursing him. He believed what he was saying, he believed he was the new messiah, he just chose to be.

He approached us slowly.

The others fell to their knees, only we stood.

"Need something, brother?" He threw in my direction.

He was probably surprised by my standing posture.

I don't know what it was because of it, but there was a weird smell spreading around it. Pretty provocative. Like a perfume with the scent of flowers.

"Yes, your name and cyber document or print in the web. I'm from Security. You are in danger," I said.

Ivana just smiled. I think she was a bit scared, but more interested in what was going to happen.

"I don't have any papers, no print in Pranet. Not an account. I don't want it and I don't need it. You too, brother," he replied in a very calm voice.

As a result, the closest-standing girl in a straitjacket just got an orgasm.

"At least a name," I did not want to let go.

"What's my name?" He said, turning towards the crowd.

"You are Cyber Messiah, Cyber Messiah, Cyber Messiah," the crowd answered him, the words carrying on and on.

Golden remixes of Rainbow Fairy, golden elves, dwarfs and fairies. I would fucking appreciate it if someone with a flamethrower showed up, I thought, while the guy just turned and walked into the crowd.

As the sea before Moses, so the ocean of human bodies opened before him. They fell at his feet and asked for his blessing, and he just walked slowly, lightly touching their heads and their hands, and blessing. I saw it a couple of times in the church. A few churches survived, but while a handful of old people went there out of habit, those here experienced the mystical touch as something amazing. I was following a group of women who were following him at a decent distance.

"You don't want to arrest him, do you?" Ivana asked with amusement.

"There is no basis, but we should know the identity, and where we can find him. We can't wait until..."

Someone from the crowd surrounding Cyber Messiah fell to the ground. Not ceremoniously and in tribute - but because someone bumped into him, squeezing his way through the crowd. This someone just sneaked past a family with five children. The bearded man was blessing a twelve-year-old girl. Her parents were probably S-level because they dressed her up like they wanted to sell at a market. She wore a blue dress, white pearls around her neck, shiny new navy-blue ballerinas and a pink bow in her hair.

I broke through in front of two young men in straitjackets and saw him.

"Zodiac," I said, even though I had forbidden the name to be spoken aloud myself.

* * *

He matched the description given to me by the Easter bunny, the one for the productive nose and circulation of articles that undoubtedly had little resemblance to cocoa. He was even wearing the same damn hoodie and black glasses, so his face was barely

174

visible. All I could see was a beard with five days of stubble of silver-gray bristles.

I took out the hammer on the imperialists, but - as is usually the case in such situations - everything went very fast.

* * *

"Be careful!" Ivana shouted when she realized what was happening.

People around me clustered confused into one mass of bodies, so I couldn't shoot. There was a risk of killing an outsider, even if I hit Zodiac. The bullet could have passed through or bounced back. I preferred to elbow the woman who was blocking the road and shoot it into the air.

Blood. There was an awful lot of blood spilled all over the place. That son of a bitch had a knife in his hand - one of the military toys I suspected he had. Blood ran down the blade. He looked at me. I aimed it at him and he dove between the failing family and other people. He struggled through the crowd that was closing behind him.

"Vachten!"

I turned to Ivana.

"He runs away!" I screamed furiously.

"But she's dying," she said.

In her arms she held a blonde with a bow in her hair. A red rose bloomed on her breast, as the poet would say. People screamed and wailed around, and the cabbage trader just stood and stared in consternation.

I jumped to the girl and tore her dress. The wound was not too deep. I used a piece of cloth to stop the bleeding, like the waitress at the bar recently. Ivana meanwhile opened her hand. She just opened it. There was something like a first aid kit inside. She took out a few syringes of some liquid.

"Oh, it's the same prosthesis as my leg, but I usually wear a gun there," I appreciated the practical use of the spare limb and the storage capacity, thanks to the excellent technology of Dejčer.

I guess the first shot was antibiotic and the second shot was epinephrine.

"Mommy," the crying girl moaned.

Probably the first aid helped her overcome the shock. I ripped another piece off her dress and bandaged the wound tightly.

"She has to go to the hospital," Ivana tried to reach her terrified mother.

But at that moment the bearded man bent over us.

"Hey," I said, but the dude picked her up.

She didn't weigh very much for her age, but he lifted her easily as if she was a feather. The girl stopped crying. She did not defend herself. She just looked into his eyes with devotion, which she probably learned from her parents. And then he raised her above his head.

"She's alive," said the cabbage trader, and the grease began screaming.

"Miracle! Miracle!" Stormy shouts vibrated through the air.

It didn't work for Ivana. She grabbed the girl's mother's pressed, brooch-embellished shirt, which she repeated like a mantra, "miracle, miracle," staring like a calf at the new line of the ARKAS slaughterhouse.

"Take her to the fucking hospital or I'll find you and kill you!" She was shaking her.

"He ran away," I growled, and Ivana looked at me.

"I called the hovercraft," she replied.

And it was so.

Her car appeared over the heads of the screaming crowd.

Golden implants in the head!

Shadows of War

Due to the crowd around the miraculously healed girl and Cybermesiah, we had trouble getting into the hovercraft. In the last thirty years, obstacle detection systems had been installed in them, and they could not drive into a living person, even if the owner tried his best.

"Jump on me, please," I said to Ivana as the hovercraft growled over our heads for a few seconds and we couldn't get anyone out of the way.

The pilgrims to the Golgotha of Capitalism got their miracle, and the escaping killer did not interest them. My assistant jumped on my arm and I lifted her up. The only thing missing from the perfection of Swan Lake was tip-toe dancing and twine in the air. Instead, she reached out and gripped the edge of the hovercraft door. Luckily, she had folded the roof like a convertible on arrival, so she jumped through the door and into the driver's seat. Her dress torn up, and considering that, as a rule, she was wearing no panties, the whole world could see all of her holes. But no one was looking at it, even though it was a beautiful sight indeed.

She did something for a while, then found a purse that she threw through the door for me. However, despite all my efforts, I could not reach it.

Then I saw him.

* * *

"Hey, Three penises, help me get upstairs!" I shook an old friend who managed to reach us. Apparently, he wanted to steal another piece of the Messiah's robe so that he could offer it to other believers for an appropriate fee. I think he was the only one who understood what all this business was about with faith.

"Fuck you!" He spat.

"You have three seconds before I shoot all three of your cocks off. I'm serious." I waved my gun in front of him and pointed it eloquently below.

He looked at me, the gun, the hovercraft, and the messiah. Maybe he really believed it all and wondered if another miracle could be squeezed out of the shot cock, but then he put the correct unknowns into the equation and did for me what I had just done

180

for Ivana. But the sight of my legs straddling is not so beautiful anymore.

* * *

As soon as I fell into the seat, we rose a few meters higher. I threw the gun into the glove compartment and moved backwards - hence I had a better view of the crowd below us. From this perspective, they looked just like a solid mass, some thousand-headed monster. The hovercraft turned ninety degrees and we headed in the direction Zodiac was going.

"Man, we have a problem!" I yelled at my watch, at Karel Adam.

"I just don't have..."

"I'm chasing that bastard nicknamed with Z. Yes. He was missing a bit before the Pyramid of Dread. Give Ivana control of all drones in the area. We have to find him!" I screamed.

Although there was no such need. A cell band would catch my whisper even from two meters away.

"It can't be so fast..."

"My code is 15487963, I'll take care of the rest," added Ivana.

Karel muttered something and hung up.

I widened my eyes as I looked for Jesus, who decided to return and speak to his 1,853rd follower - but I found neither Jesus nor Zodiac in the crowd.

"We're going into the crowd," Ivana announced, closing her eyes.

Fortunately, the controls of the hovercraft worked quite subconsciously, and most importantly, it had a decent AI that would not let it fall into the crowd below us.

Fay once told me how it works. Thanks to implants, the neural network in the brain becomes a computer that can connect to anything and send data to the subconscious. Such a person closes his eyes and real images begin to press into his mind. This way you can run whole movies into your brain, but after a few episodes you may start to think that you are one of the Dirty Lopezs.

"I have something on the October Agreement Street," she said, and the hovercraft sprang up abruptly.

"Do you see him?" I asked.

I strained my eyes as hard as I could but saw nothing suspicious.

"Some movement among people, a fight, maybe... wait, I got him!"

The hovercraft accelerated. We flew past the subway pillar S and ended up on the side of the street. I haven't seen too many people here anymore, rather a few nervous random passers-by wondering what's going on here. They were still not used to seeing large gatherings not being fired by Security drones.

Finally, I saw him too. He disentangled himself from some cluster and ran across the street. I decided to take a shot. But the missile struck harmlessly into the façade of the old building. It looked like one of those high-rise apartment buildings from the seventies, which was built during the great housing crisis, when Prague welcomed one hundred thousand new residents every year. Zodiac ran through the door and disappeared behind them.

"We should have shot him with a machine gun on this drone," I sighed as we landed nearby and jumped onto the hot asphalt. Security drones, which Ivana had pulled from all over the neighborhood, were hovering around. But now they were useless to us.

"Sorry, but I can't control twenty drones, watch their cameras, steer a hovercraft and shoot. I'm just an ordinary cyborg specializing in Kamasutra," she replied irritably.

I think her brain has overheated.

"All right. Call the special unit and wait for them here," I replied, looking at the copper plate hanging above the entrance to the building. She informed that there was the church of St. James.

* * *

Most of Prague's churches simply disappeared. When the Catholic Church was banned in the 60s, all its property was taken over by the state. And it did what it did best with him - it sold the speculators their fortune at discounted prices, in exchange for a commission for the relevant politicians and officials. St. Vitus became an amusement park, which after bankruptcy turned into a horror house and then a brothel. Some maliciously argued that in this way the cathedral again serves what it had at the beginning. Some churches were razed to the ground by investors, others survived until the accession of Pope Julian, when the Catholic Church experienced a temporary renaissance and some buildings were returned to it. But without the faithful, for those few are left. And the church of St. James survived it. It was built in the 30s, in a style considered to be modern at the time. Then, instead of demolishing it, just around the remains and above it, a skyscraper was erected. Thus, the temple served the residents as a vast park with original decorations.

"Hey, look where..." one of the house's tenants yelled after me.

I ignored him. I ran down a huge corridor that led to a variety of wings, stairs, fire escape corridors and elevators. I felt that the Zodiac did not come to live here. He was headed for the church.

Its massive door swung open. I checked the Makarov button again and ran inside. The humid air of the indoor greenhouse greeted me. Where there used to be church pews, today there were ornamental trees and shrubs. The architect really knew what he was doing. A waterfall roared nearby, and I think I even heard a bird chirping. Only the walls and large stained-glass windows remained from the church. Considering the age of the building, I was not surprised that Jesus, Mark, Matthew, Luke and John were presented in fashionable costumes at the time - with baseball caps and on skateboards. In the next window, Maria Magdalena was rapping, and the Virgin Mary was appearing in some kind of television show.

Yeah. It would be better for this church if it had been torn down, I thought, and at that moment a gunshot was heard from next to me.

I hid behind a tall fir tree, though the moment I heard the boom it was too late to dodge the first bullet. I was just lucky, the next bullets stuck into the tree trunk.

I listened for what was happening. The fire scared only a few of the birds, and they were now hitting the stained-glass windows furiously.

Boom! - I fired at random in the direction from which the shots were fired.

There was no one.

I carefully stepped out from behind the tree and looked at the bark.

Small caliber?

Given the size of the holes, it looked like a small-caliber weapon.

The small caliber ridiculed for centuries could turn out to be deadly, and most importantly, the effectiveness of this weapon was guaranteed by a decent magazine volume.

I heard a branch crunch and I ran between the two birches. Another shot made me fall to the ground.

* * *

The bullets hissed overhead at a dizzying pace. Leaves and pieces of shot twigs fell around me.

"Reinforcements are on the way, nowhere to run, prick started with Z. If you give up I'll get you a decent padded cell and high calorie porridge for you three times a day!" I yelled, but only because I was just crawling, and it frustrated me that I couldn't locate him. But he was silent. And I hated the silence.

Crunch, crunch, said a few stuck-on twigs, and I shot that way and then again.

I ran after him.

* * *

I ran from behind the trees and reached the old altar. There were roses on it. My bullets landed somewhere in it but encountered Zodiac along the way.

Blood - I smiled. A few drops gleamed on the tiles that peeked out from under the carpet of fallen leaves. I crouched down and - fortunately - I noticed movement from behind the altar.

Bang! Bang! Bang! Bang!

* * *

A machine gun fire sounded nearby, and I flew to the ground and rolled out of the shooter's field of view. Dude switched to a heavier caliber. He must have had some fold-out, one-handed bitch that he hid in a holster under his sweatshirt. For a guy who kills victims with a knife, he carried a decent arsenal with him.

I jumped up, and my stomach wound ached. Ideally, I should lie in there about three weeks, but he would probably kill dozens of people during that time. I took a deep breath and slowly made my way to the altar. I watched from the barrel of the Soviet gun if anything would move, so I could fire it right away. I felt a bit of pain and exhaustion, but I was going in the right direction nonetheless. I knew he was on the other side, waiting for me with all his arsenal.

I gathered up, ran and jumped onto the altar. I trampled on a few roses. I was surprised that no one broke them and sold them at the bazaar. These flowers must have cost a fortune. But the locals probably wanted to keep their secrets to themselves. I tried to push aside the thoughts of flower trade that had occurred to my mind under stress and took another step. Two more and I'll see him.

Ding.

The metallic sound snapped me out of my thoughts about flowers.

* * *

I ran with my finger on the trigger. Behind the altar lay an abandoned old Slovak K22 weapon and a pile of empty machine gun shells. There was no Zodiac. I bent down and picked up the iron hatch cover in the ground.

Bang, bang, bang, this time he was firing single bullets. Fortunately, I took that into account.

The metal cover fell to the ground and another projectile bounced back off it. Behind the altar there was a corridor leading to the basement, and maybe even deeper. It was not an ordinary crypt, as underneath medieval churches, but catacombs that led down to the underworld of the city.

I checked the K22. As I thought it was empty. I tossed it to the ground and kicked the lid. Not a living soul.

* * *

I went inside carefully. I was drenched in nervous sweat all the time. It was not a pleasant situation. If it weren't for the fact that he was afraid of reinforcements, he would have just waited here and shot while I was going down. I jumped off the ladder and tried to orient myself in the surrounding darkness. Two corridors diverged from here. I turned on the cellular wristband, which made me an easy target, but without it I would not have seen its marks in the deposited earth. He ran away towards the center. I turned off the device and ran after him.

* * *

After a while I heard the splash of boots wading in the ubiquitous mud. I slowed down. Maybe he was waiting for me, or maybe he was just resting. I pressed as hard as I could to the wall, sliding on a layer of algae, moss and some mucus. Fortunately, I couldn't see anything, and the damn thing that stuck to my clothes and body did not seem so terrible to the touch. It occurred to me that with these developments, I would have to start washing in a rented apartment, and not just throw it into the washing machine, because I will soon run out of clothes. I put my gun out in front of me. I have the last four rounds left. How many did he have? It's hard to tell, but it fired enough.

I was walking as quietly as possible. Little by little, I was holding my breath and trying to catch what was happening in the dark. It was difficult. I couldn't see practically anything, I didn't have any night vision goggles or a protective suit. And no sign of fortune tellers with blasters.

It's a struggle of nerves. Whoever fires first will reveal his location. The second shot will be clear, unless...

I knelt and raised my hand with the gun as high as possible over my head. And I fired.

* * *

A volley sounded. A series of missiles flew overhead. At this point, I had my pistol steady and fired twice at the barrel fire.

I have one last bullet left.

* * *

I heard a scream, but that didn't have to mean anything. The machinegun sounded again in the dark. I crawled on in mud and shit. The stench was awful. A couple of missiles hissed nearby. And then it stopped. All I heard was loud breathing. Maybe I can get him.

I got up and decided to attack. I sensed that it must be just a few meters in front of me.

But he anticipated me.

* * *

Only darkness and mud saved me. He probably stumbled while attacking me, and instead of my heart, his knife stuck into my shirt. He tore it open and I stuck the barrel into his jaw. He grabbed me with his free hand and we hit the ground together.

A shot rang out.

It was the last bullet in my gun. And it went down the drain somewhere!

* * *

I let go of Makarov and left him to his fate. I needed my hands free. Zodiac didn't say a word. He just swung again, but I grabbed his hand with the knife. The other one reached my throat.

I was choking. I was gasping in pain, but I couldn't let him win. I couldn't let my body be found by Security somewhere in this shit, bitten by mutant rats. The blade of the knife rested against the larynx. I hit the bastard on the nose with my free hand. It had no effect. My hand, soaked with the shit here, started to run over his face until I found his eyes and squeezed my fingers into them.

He grunted, gasped, and I followed him. Even so, I heard the splashing of footsteps approaching us.

* * *

I managed to pull the knife blade away from my skin. Pushing my toes into my eyes had an effect.

"Humgans," said someone behind us.

This upset Zodiac.

I lifted my hip, disrupting his mind, and - for a change - now I rolled him over on his back. I twisted the wrist of his knife until it crunched.

He hit me on the jaw. But he released the knife.

I grabbed its hilt.

He released his other hand's grip. He felt around him as if he was looking for something. Until he found.

He stuck the barrel in my ribs.

I strained with all my strength to roll over. While doing so, I slipped the tip of the knife between his ribs.

Humgans!

* * *

The stranger's roar echoed in space, breaking out into the world along with the air escaping from his punctured lungs. Still, the dung had shot out. Bullets rattled against the ceiling, and bouncing spheres whistled around us.

"Taste..." I pushed the knife even harder. "...your own," I pushed the knife as hard as I could. "...medication," I gasped, and when Zodiac stopped moving, I rolled over, exhausted.

"Meat for the Ascendant," a hoarse voice said a short distance away from me.

I had a strong sense of *déjà vu*.

* * *

Only it wasn't some kind of psychological hiccup in the brain. I just climbed into the sewer again and, as was to be expected, ran into a sever man. I turned on the flashlight in the cellular band. I lit the faces of the three men in torn rags who stood about two meters from me, and put my fingers to Zodiac's carotid - he was dead.

The sever men took a step back, but they didn't seem particularly afraid of the light. I grabbed the machine gun that was lying next to the body. It was a type of weapon the type of which from time immemorial was referred to as "Uzi". But it wasn't an Uzi. On the hilt I read: "Twardowski 07".

"Hey, I have a gun. Stay away from me or I'll shoot you. You better go chew on your rat or whatever you usually do!" I yelled at the sever men as I unbuttoned the dead guy's sweatshirt.

I had to pull the knife out of his chest. I put it in my pocket and with my free hand continued to feel over the dead body. I found that I had managed to graze him lightly twice. One time in the chapel and another time here in the sewers. That's why he attacked me so thoughtlessly - he was afraid that he would bleed out over time and lose his strength. I have noticed that my cell band is reporting missed calls. I presumably turned off the sound, and Ivana was probably trying to call me. But you can rarely catch a signal in the channels. Anyway, what would the sewers need?

194

I felt the corpse with one hand as carefully as possible. On my left bicep I found a tattoo of an open parachute with the words "3. Commando Company of the 51st Airborne Battalion".

Blue Company - I nodded.

I grabbed his forearm but pulled him only a meter. I needed help.

"Stop! Meat for the Ascendant!" One of the sever men shouted.

There were more and more of them.

"How the fuck you guys still living here?" I growled.

I had to make a quick decision.

"What would Master Sun say now?" I tossed at the sever men.

"Only the one who can act without claiming glory, and similarly withdraw without fear of punishment, only for the safety of the people, only for the sake of the ruler, is the jewel of his country!"

Ivana! I didn't look back. I had the sever men at gunpoint.

"What are you doing here? Where are the Security guys?"

"It took them a while, and I was already worried about you. Everything's all right?"

Phew, she surprised me a lot. Entering the sewer for me was quite risky. I could be dead, and she would be the next victim of Zodiac.

"Yes, but, well... we have company. With this withdrawal... Well, I guess we'll have to," I said, sighing.

"Is that him?" She didn't have to specify who she was talking about.

"Yes," I agreed.

"Really, he's dead?"

Good question. I loaded a bullet into his head. It went through the nasal septum and got stuck in the brain. It was then that the gun made such a nasty noise that you can tell it's the last round.

"As Sun Tzu would say, we have to forge ahead!" I said.

"He would never..." Ivana protested, but she realized what was going on quickly and we rushed to leave. Fortunately, the sever men did not follow us. They got their meat.

* * *

We made it back to the church where relief has just arrived. And as is the custom of succor - it came too late, but Karel Adam showed up personally, which I appreciated.

"What are you...?" He began, but I handed him the bloodied knife.

He recognized him. It looked exactly like the virtual models prepared by his technicians.

"That blood is his. He's dead. The sever men came, so I had to leave the body, but I shot him in the head. With this, even theoretically, there was nothing he could do. His brain is a pulp," I explained and sat down on the altar.

I fucking wanted to pee. After such effort, it's normal. But I didn't want to pee in the church. Especially with all these people.

"This gun is yours?" He nodded at the toy I had slung over my shoulder.

"His. It must be a war booty. Soldier, paratrooper. He would not be the first or the last to lose his head in the war," I replied.

"I'll let the Council know," Karel said after a moment, looking at me as if waiting for me to tell him what I thought of all this.

But I thought nothing. The case has been closed. And what was left of the Council, I really didn't care. I needed a bathtub, clean clothes (again!) And a hunter's stew.

Pipa

I was pleased to note that my VEP account armband was up to six hours after Karel announced the news. However, Lota did not contact me or Ivana, and my virtual fingerprint, as a Prague Security Lieutenant, has not been deactivated either. I was looking forward to spending her money on charity. Of course, I would be the beneficiary myself. Who needed real meat, potatoes and cabbage stew more than a hard-working hired law enforcement officer? Or what is left in the city by law.

On the door of the only Polish restaurant in the whole of Prague, I and Ivana were greeted by a sign saying "Locked up, dicks". Belch was simply the king of the anti-customer approach. I was not far from my new home, where I had shower and clean clothes and a nap. The pub was located at the narrow end of Ruzyňska Street. I grabbed the handle, the door unlocked. We walked through the darkened room to the bar, where a complete

198

squad of cyber wizards sat. A Polish veteran was just putting my dream hunter's stew out of a pot. Only Fay was scrubbing something with the nano-cloth at the sink.

"My God, thousands of guys were pouring down on me, but the worst thing a girl can experience is washing the dishes," she said in greeting as she set a few clean ceramic plates on the table. It was truly unique. Belch brought them all the way from Warsaw and allegedly belonged to the Russian Tsar. But considering there was a worn swastika on the bottom of two of them, I knew he was making up.

"Hi, prick," Fat Tom joined the greeting. He had just scrambled out of the kitchen and was walking so fast his apron was literally flying. In his right hand he held a jug of yellowish liquid - Belch's famous moonshine. He placed it on the table and held out his hand in greeting.

Slap! We gave a high five and I immediately sat down behind the bar to join the others. I kissed Fay and a portion of meat, cabbage, and potatoes landed on the plate.

Ivana looked suspiciously at the racket and the things on the porcelain.

"Try it. It's the best food you've ever eaten, trust me," I said, but I guess I was overconfident. After all, I was saying this to a woman who had once been a companion of famous for hedonism, the richest guy in town.

She reached out and carefully put a piece of cabbage in her mouth. I think she liked it, although it felt like she was eating it for the first time in her life. Maybe cabbage is too little of a sophisticated dish for this city's wealthy decadent party cream.

"I thought you hated each other." She pointed at Tom, shoving another bite of her meal into her mouth.

"We've been buddies since time immemorial, but now we have to hide it." I shrugged, and when Tom poured the fucker's brains, we clinked our glasses.

"You have to put everything at once - cabbage, potatoes and sausage. Only then will the hunter's stew taste perfect," explained Blech to Ivana.

It was ages ago the last time I filled my stomach with something so good, and it felt like after an incredibly long time I could finally stop and enjoy that perfect moment. Everything that happened in the sewers began to fade as if it were just a nightmare that melted away with the onset of dawn.

"Clown," Tom said after a moment.

"Who's the clown?" I did not understand.

I put another batch of hunter's stew on. Earlier, Ivana did the same. The joy of a simple combination of the best things in the world has probably never been known at elven-style foretells.

"That was the name of the dead one in City News. He was a war correspondent," explained the pirate.

"I thought he was working there as a security guard or a cleaner," I muttered with my mouth full.

"Yeah, but he was a reporter before. But who needs a reporter when you give the news in the form of a show where the world is beautiful, and everything is going as it should. In the information service, where you do not describe reality, but create it, all you need is a pretty face, which you can make to measure, if necessary," he explained.

"What are you talking about?" Belch joined in.

Our previous trip to the sewers had left a few scars on his face, but otherwise he looked pleased.

"One of the dead was once a real reporter," I explained.

"Embedded reporter. I found some information in the old news and even one video of some old reportage. He worked during the Czech-Polish war," added Tom.

"Poor man, he must have told you how we rubbed your asses back then." The Pole smiled crookedly, but I didn't want to continue the veterans' chatter.

"I guess that's why he seemed familiar to me. The first case on which I worked in the military police was the embezzlement of an ammunition column. I think he did a report on it too," I said and gulped down moonshine.

It did not surprise me that Clown turned out to be more than just a helper on television, because it was this wartime trail that made it all - or so I thought - meaningful.

I took another sip and pulled one of the confiscated weapons from my backpack.

"It still interests me. Zod... the dead bastard, had it," I said, setting the machine gun on the table.

"Heh, Twardowski," laughed Belch.

"Never seen it before," I said.

"Thousands were actually produced, but all ended up on the eastern border. In Silesia only trackers got them..."

"Partisan hunters," I interrupted him.

"Yes, boys from special units," nodded the Pole, looking at the weapon as if it reminded him of something.

"But the corpse in the sewers was not a partisan. He had a tattoo of the 3rd Commando Company of the 51st Airborne Battalion. Their units are color-coded. This one was blue. Can you find out what the psycho's name was? I don't want him to be called Zodiac," I said to Tom a term I had forbidden myself to pronounce.

Tom poured a glass of moonshine into himself, and from one pocket of his apron he pulled out a tablet. While he was rummaging around in it, I walked over to Fay. She got light blushes from alcohol. I hugged her, but my head was full of memories of the war. Many of the veterans who survived never mentally returned from her. It didn't matter that nobody cared about this war, that nobody knew if Poland still existed, and some Ostrava flew around the ass, or God forbid some Havířov - a city that everyone didn't give a shit before the war. I remembered the Under the Smelly Pole buffet. Its owner was still at war. He couldn't stop it. I did not have such problems. Only the city I returned to looked completely different.

"Are you sure it's the 51st Airborne Battalion?" Tom spoke after a moment.

"Yes, absolutely. I locked up one lieutenant who raped recruits. How's his fucking... Novák. Jan Novák," I remembered.

"There was no such battalion. There is no mention of him in old military records or in former government reports," replied Tom.

"You pirate bastard, I remember them. They performed several actions incognito. There was quite a jumble there," protested Belch, who was still dreaming about the Polish weapons.

"I'm not saying that you are lying, but that there is nothing in the file about them. Before Prague was cut off, all data from the Internet and government and public databases were transferred to Pranet. There is nothing about this unit. Maybe some of this prick's reports about them were left in the CN archives," growled Tom.

To calm the situation down, we drank another glass of brainfuck. Fay looked a little drunk now, and I was surprised to find Ivana pouring another glass into herself. I found her more balanced and stylish no matter what the circumstances. Drinking a lot of alcohol somehow did not go hand in hand with it.

"Lota's calling," she said after a moment.

She looked as if she had sobered up instantly.

"Well, I haven't agreed on a solution bonus yet," I smiled happily and picked up the bottle.

At this point, the band vibrated and the connection began. Only Security could do that. They recognized that their calls could not be missed. All cellular bands had a built-in program that would answer the call from the Security, no matter if you don't want to, or, for example, you just shit on the toilet.

"Karel?"

Because who else could call me than the boss himself.

"You must go to CN immediately. Something went wrong, and it was totally wrong. I'm on my way now," he informed me, and without waiting for a reply, he hung up.

"Well, what about Lota?" Stunned I turned to Ivana.

"They say we have to go to CN immediately, that something terrible is going on," she explained.

"It's probably not a coincidence," Belch smirked.

Tom did not pay attention to us at all and continued to rummage in the guts of the Prague Internet and even deeper.

* * *

Five minutes later, Ivana and Fay were flying towards a skyscraper covered with screens and holographic projectors. It was only then that I realized I wasn't armed because the only weapon I hadn't left in the sewers was Belch's on the counter.

"Do you have any guns?" I asked Ivana.

She just shrugged.

"Fighting in a hundred battles and winning a hundred times - is not the highest goal. To subdue the enemy without a fight - this is, in fact, the highest goal."

I didn't even have to ask - she quoted The Art of War.

"On the other hand, Marshal Rommel used to say that in the fight between man and man, the winner will ultimately be the one who has one more round in his magazine," I replied, opening the glove compartment.

"Only Marshal Rommel ran from Africa like a dog with a tucked tail," replied Ivana.

"Like everyone who is not the lioness Elsa," I grumbled, rummaging in the messy hiding place.

Found a comb, an old keychain, and a lipstick. None of it looked like dangerous tools.

* * *

CN was just broadcasting a culinary show, What Can You Eat Up?, which involved people proposing the craziest things they could eat and the audience voting how many points the dish was worth. Last week the guy won ten thousand kronor. He cut off the muscle of his left buttock, threw it in a Teflon pan and ate it with artificial ketchup. Now the next episode was attacking from hundreds of screens. The fat woman was smashing a brick to the skeleton of a rat, which she probably intended to make a topping for the cake. Well, I've eaten worse once myself.

Ivana's hovercraft was certainly not a typical serial product, but an improved machine that was refined by VEP technicians. We soared to a height where there was no risk of collision with any other hovercraft and developed a speed of three hundred kilometers per hour. During the flight, we collided with a swallow, which did not dodge and smashed against the windshield. Red sauce, feathers, and some yellow shit - possibly the contents of bird guts - splattered on the glass. Such an appetizer would be a small beer for the participants of the culinary show. We had no windshield wipers, but something like a sonic blower that made the debris melt into space in a matter of seconds, and the windshield looked perfectly clean and transparent again. Though it wasn't necessary at all, because even at faster speeds, Ivan was still steering with radar and navigation. Everything was displayed on a small screen, which she probably never looked at, because the image was displayed in her head thanks to the implants.

"Hey, pungent lipstick," Fay said, assessing my weapons.

I refrained from commenting and put the beauty tool that was the source of the stains on my shirts and underwear back into the glove box. I tried to call Adam, but as I was not granted instant talk call feature, I had to listen to a dull beep.

* * *

Perfect chaos reigned in the CN main heliport. I saw several Security combat drones, as well as tons of CN logo drones with the barrels of rotating machine guns exposed. Suddenly a warning light came on in the radar display.

"We've been tracked down by stationary defensive fire systems," Ivana said dryly, as if asking if I'd like mild or spicy ketchup with my fries.

"Is that your ride?" Karel's voice finally echoed over the cellular band.

"No, dick, you called the Easter bunny who's going to give you a blowjob," I grumbled, looking at the display.

Through the perfectly cleaned windshield, I also saw several rocket launchers on the CN heliport. Television took protection from intrusive fans and critics of TV programs very seriously.

Karel broke the connection and at the same time the lights stopped flashing. After a while, we stopped at the heliport. I jumped outside. There was a nice wind outside. The same secretary was waiting for us as during the first visit. She looked like someone who hadn't slept in fifty hours and had spent that time testing new synthetic drugs. There was a cordon of security guards around, wielding automatons ready to fire. The weapon looked a bit like from the series Bobo the Slayer, i.e. something supposed to be mega-threatening and mega-deterrent, but not very functional. However, it must be admitted that the grenade launchers placed on the guns looked reliable.

"Is that you again?" She said instead of saying hello.

"It's Easter, you should be dressed up," I replied, embarrassing her, and said no more.

We walked through the building, mostly armed security guards on the way. Television maintained its own small army with the best equipment from tech corporations in the city. Drones buzzed overhead, and ordinary workers stood around with serious expressions.

We finally got to the CEO's office. The secretary didn't come in with us. As soon as we stepped in, she slammed the door guarded by five bodyguards and probably slumped to the ground right away, curled up in the prenatal position and started sobbing loudly.

Václav Král was standing, leaning against the table, so you could finally see a bit of his neck. Adam was standing next to him with one of his technicians. I remembered him from meeting over dead bodies.

"You said you'd call the experts, not this circus," Král snapped as Ivana, Fay, and I stood in the doorway.

He was looking at the cyber sorceresses with his eyes. Girls in recent months have not had the best reputation, and neither has Ivana and I left a good impression at first glance.

"What's happening?" I took the invective into the agenda, trying to get to the bottom of the matter.

However, at that moment I noticed a hologram displayed in the corner of the room - in the place where there used to be a virtual golf course. A set of golf clubs was stuck at the bottom of the picture. A truly Easter scene appeared above it.

* * *

At first I didn't realize what I was staring at, but then I understood. Pipa, or the actress who played her, hung in some empty room on a large wooden cross. Naked. Exactly as I remember from Král's office. But now her hands had been nailed to the beams with large nails, and there were crusts of dried blood around the wounds. Next to it was a digital clock that counted down. 22 minutes and 55 seconds remaining.

"Zodiac," Karel said as I looked at the projection.

"I killed him," I said.

Karel turned to the technician, and the technician flashed another hologram on the digital projector. On it I saw a second actress hanging, the one who was famous for her small breasts, only the clock showed the full hour.

"Zodiac is talking to you. I wish you a Happy Easter. I made myself a new toy for this occasion. I will end her life just like Longinus the life of Jesus Christ. I really like you trying so hard because this is a game and it's great that you play it with me. Hope you have fun trying to catch me because I'm having a lot of fun. I am not afraid of the gas chamber that will send me to paradise ahead of time, as are the slaves who work for me. It made me laugh when you tried to kill me, and because you really made me laugh, I put on an entertaining show for you. This arrogant bitch who would never want anything to do with someone like me is now begging for her life. She begged, kissed my legs, promised me that she would do anything for me. But I only have one wish. When she has ten minutes left to live, I will come and deliver my message. I want everyone to see them, so that CN broadcasts them. Otherwise, I will kill her. You can watch both of us have a good time."

"Dick," I said, spitting on the retained hologram.

The saliva landed on the floor next to the golf clubs.

* * *

"Are you sure you killed this guy?" Karel asked me after a few seconds.

None of us have been able to take our eyes off the actress's online transmission of pain.

"I shot him in the head. A piece of brain leaked through his nose."

"Whoever killed, he definitely did," Ivana replied for me.

I made a mental note to thank her for this. Mainly because she did so without sarcastic remarks about me or quoting a Chinese strategist.

"There had to be more of them," I said, something so obvious it was a pity to talk about it.

"Can you track it? Where is it broadcast from?" I asked right after, and nodded at the holoprojection.

"It broke into internal communication channels. Something like this shouldn't have happened. Nobody should get through to us," said the CEO.

"It's already come to this once. After Prick's death, right?" I said, and Král just frowned.

"We can't track anything. Turns out it's broadcast from Brno," replied the technician.

"What the fuck? It's not there anymore isn't it?" I protested.

"It has some archaic IP address. It looks like it's on some old network that's been hiding in Pranet the whole time. We can't trace it because it works by different principles than Pranet and our communication networks and the modules that build on top of it," the technician explained.

I called Tom and the guy briefly described the situation to him. Five minutes passed. By this time, Král had carved a damn deep diamond on the table top.

Tom mumbled something to himself for a while, and then finally started talking loudly and clearly:

"Internet. It works on the original basis. That is, as it functioned before individual countries cut it open, broke its connections and set boundaries for it. The makers of Pranet took its basic design elements while leaving many things dormant. And now someone has woken them up," he said, and the police technician just nodded as his agreement.

"Will you find him?" Karel and I asked almost at the same time.

"How much time I have?"

"Six minutes?" I suggested.

"I would need a day or two. And help from the rest of the pir... crew members," he corrected at the last minute.

The pirates still lived underground, though there might not be anyone else who want to crush them now.

"Can we talk to him?" I turned to the technician and pointed to the holographic projection. I meant Zodiac.

He shook his head.

* * *

"Who is this maniac?" Fay asked after a moment.

Right now, she and the others were staring at the crucified actress with consternation.

"The madman. Total psycho!" Král shouted and snapped his fingers three times.

A simple gesture triggered some internal communication channel.

"Filčev, directing," a bored voice said.

"Prepare a live broadcast for me. We'll be starting in five minutes," growled Král.

"But boss, live... no one has done it for about thirty years," the director protested.

He only allowed himself to do this because he didn't know how furious his top boss was.

"Did I mention that I want to discuss it? I don't want to discuss it, I want to..." he turned to the projection, where the last moments of Pipa's life were still measured, "...four minutes live broadcast!"

"No way, you're out of here!"

An imperious voice came from the doorway. Radoslav Sejmen stood there with his bodyguards and the ruler of the GEZ corporation - the last two of the original great bosses and members of the Council.

* * *

Sejmen looked exactly like what he was - a powerful man who built an empire without compromising or wasting time. According to official data, he was close to a hundred. However, the latest medicine made that I will give him sixty at most. He walked erect, with great confidence. He was accompanied by two men from his army. Under unbuttoned jackets they wore bulletproof vests and two bulging shoulder holsters, which contained AR6, pistols for 50 rounds, caliber 0.22, with a special multi-purpose magazine. They looked like two massive bricks capable of unleashing a herd of little quick deaths.

A familiar personal assistant came running behind them, followed by eight members of the television security with automatic rifles.

"I only do what the Council says, and you are not the Council - you are only two out of five!" Král shouted to the incoming oligarch, who was surprised by the opposition. He was probably not used to something like that.

"I am speaking for the Council, that is, for most of it. All this fun is financed by our corporations. This is no longer a VEP issue, now ARKAS, GEZ and PRAGUETECH are taking over everything," he stated firmly.

"But she..." He pointed a finger at the crucified actress.

"What's her real name?" I interrupted an exciting debate.

"Well, Pipa," Karel replied.

"Pi..." thought Král, and then he remembered, "Natalia Rambousková."

"Anastazja Rákosová," the assistant corrected him.

"Yes, exactly," agreed Král.

I understood him. The actresses and the characters they played were often confused. And I often didn't even know the name of the girl I slept with. Besides, they were telling me, "Quick, right?" Or something like that.

"Thirteen minutes," Fay said after a moment.

They looked in her direction.

Sejmen looked quite disgusted, but then the crowd turned to the crucified Pipa. I mean, Anastasia, who moved several times and then sobbed softly.

"Will you let her die? People love her. She is the star! We have to do what he demands to save her!" Said Král sharply.

Sejmen barely glanced at Pipa.

"Well, so what. One of many. In a week, you'll create a new star and people won't even notice. You still do that. You remove anyone you don't like. You'll make a celebrity even out of my shit if you need to. You are television. It's your job. You're supposed to keep human minds chained to screens so that people think nonsense and don't jump out. You are to arouse their instincts, desires, and imaginations, and then immediately suppress them with cheap banalities. It has always been the main task of television. Just like that busty junkie from Maidens from Střížkov station. She was stoned during the filming, and with your cum up your ass, she's gonna break, and in a week's time another ambitious bitch was in her role. Nobody even remembers her name anymore." Sejmen got pissed off and stuck a finger in Král's stomach.

For a moment I thought that this terrible mass would suck up the Sejmen's finger and then devour it all. But it didn't. Král only turned red.

"But she..." he replied.

"She's in the past and so are you. This bastard can't come into the vision. Terrible things are happening outside, and that will only make things worse. You have to let go of even more porn and devour your own buttocks. But that's none of your business," growled Sejmen, turning to his assistant. "Now you're the taskmistress of City News. Congratulations. And let this fat bastard be brought out by security."

"Eleven and a half," Fay said icily, as if she hadn't noticed that someone's career had just been broken next door. Anyway, what did it mean in the face of this girl's death?

There was silence for a minute.

Král looked at the assistant, and she looked at him, the bewildered bodyguards at them both, and then everyone at Sejmen.

* * *

"No," Václav Král said finally.

* * *

He said it calmly and firmly. Rage, tense nerves, screaming - these feelings were not in that one "no". But such a "no", when said in the right time and in the right way, can work wonders. This "no" has the strength and perspective to go down in history. Like when French general Pierre Jacques Etienne Cambronne was offered to surrender to the British siege of the Battle of Waterloo. He simply replied "merde" or "shit" and then, in a futile attempt to break through the British ranks, ordered the grenadiers to attack, which made him a hero of France. It's just that Král, instead of "shit", said "no".

Sejmen did not have time to react, and the TV security guards unlocked the guns and aimed them at him and his bodyguards.

The advantage in numbers and fire was clearly on the fat man's side.

"You are the Security, and they are breaking the law," the oligarch asked us, making a desperate attempt to save himself, like the captain of a sinking ship trying to defend himself against the impending catastrophe with a matchbox and a plane from an old newspaper.

"I'm not armed," I shrugged.

I had no doubt that Karel was carrying a gun, but neither did he.

"Prepare the broadcast!" Král, shouting at the control room, he was not so composed.

The countdown indicator showed 10:05.

* * *

He was standing there. He just stood in front of the tortured actress. He looked exactly as the Easter bunny described him. He drink, drink cocoa so that nothing happens. He wore that goddamn hood and sweatshirt and big black glasses. A scarf around the neck. He somehow skillfully covered all parts of his

220

body that might betray him, whether it was the shape of a chin or, for example, the shape of a skull. All this was lost in the shadows cast by garments. He glanced to the side - probably to see if it was indeed live, then turned his gaze contentedly to his camera.

"Zodiac is talking to you," he said.

* * *

His voice was electronically distorted, like the first recording sent to CN.

"Prague is a sinful city. I have come to punish them, to punish you. I kill for pleasure and to purge this place of those who are not worthy to exist. I am Zodiac. I am haunted by so-called Security, but they are only fools, a tool of power, they can oppress you ordinary townspeople, but they won't catch me. I am here to have power over the lives of each of you. I can kill any of you like this woman here. Remember what you see, because it will tell you that I really do have power over everyone. I killed Petlán - yes, the one who controlled your life, the owner of the mighty PRAGUETECH - and I will continue to kill. Nothing can stop me."

Everyone was staring at him. Everybody. Even Sejmen, whose authority in this room was in ruins.

"But... he can't... he promised. He's on a vision. He definitely sees it!" Král stammered.

Zodiac showed his back and took a step towards Pipa. He pulled a military knife from his jacket pocket, exactly like the one I killed the bastard with in the sewers and stabbed her in the stomach. The whole city watched as blood spattered from the TV star's body, screamed in pain and wailed, then began to weaken, and after a while she died. The killer made his mark on her body, and when he finished, he pulled out a black felt-tip pen and painted a symbol of gravity on her forehead.

"Let me in to a vision. Fuck put me on a vision!" I shouted to Král.

He was shaking. In terror, out of terror, out of fear, his hands trembled with a million emotions.

"No... I don't have a camera here," he finally replied.

His eyes were probably three times larger than they were before.

"Sound. All I need is the sound. Come on!" I shook him.

"To the control room! Make a sound from me!" He said, his voice breaking.

* * *

"Hey, motherfucker!" I shouted.

222

Zodiac has turned around. It surprised him. My voice did roar on the air. He and I were broadcast live all over town.

"This is Vachten, Petr Vachten. I'm a cop, and I'll get you sooner or later because I fucking know who you are. I know in your childhood you harassed little critters, that you had a dominant psychopathic mother who never loved you, that you would like to be a cop, but you are so terribly worthless garbage that they wouldn't even take you to make coffee. I know you fuck with dead bodies because you wouldn't be able to stand with the living. I see all the shit you have inside, I can see you imagine yourself killing your mother and then fucking her. I'll get you then tell everyone more about how big zero you are, you bastard!"

Zodiac just stood there. I hit him. And not only him. People around me were silent.

"Now turn it off. Come on!" I ordered Král, and he repeated it to the control room.

Dirty Lopez has returned to CN screens. Pipa was jiggling there happily in a robber dance with some Argentinean pygmy. To achieve the effect of perfect absurdity, it was only necessary for her to start singing *I'm a rainbow* fairy.

It happened exactly five seconds later.

Cezar

They pushed us with the barrels of automatic rifles. Not only us - also Sejmen. He was silent and we were also silent.

Král collapsed on his desk. He just ordered them to get us outside, to secure the building, and to protect every fucking dick and every fucking pussy on that fucking TV with their own body.

They left us alone at the heliport, and we went to the hovercraft.

"You're finished. Both." Sejmen pointed two fingers at me and Karel and got into his luxurious limousine.

* * *

We left the explosion zone around the CN. Karel and the technician went to the Security HQ, and Ivana, Fay, and I went to the VEP-tower.

"You killed him. He definitely didn't survive it," said Ivana after a moment of silence.

I was lying in the back seat, leaning against Fay, my eyes shut tightly. I was recreating the events of the last days, especially hours. From the beginning, I felt that so many important details were missing that I only knew enough to pursue ghosts instead of the real perpetrator. That canal soldier kept me awake at night. He looked like Zodiac, he acted like that, and he died that way. Yet there was some other Zodiac here.

"He was talking about slaves. Who knows how many bastards run around town with knives and the same frenzy," Ivana continued.

And she was right.

I was thinking the same. But it made the situation very complicated. Damn hard.

We landed at the main heliport, VEP-tower. I scrambled out of it and found it looked basically the same here as it does in the TV building. The building of the Dejčer Corporation resembled a gigantic rock, dotted with trees and lights. Now, however, mostly exposed barrels of anti-aircraft guns and missile systems were visible among the plants. At the very top was an enormous automatic laser complex protruding. Hundreds of combat drones were flying out of the building.

"The art of war teaches us not to hope that the enemy will not come, but to rely on the fact that we are ready to welcome him; not to hope he won't attack, but to rely on that we have made our positions impossible to get," Ivana quoted, looking at the streaking weapon.

We passed through security and in ten minutes we were in something like an operating room in the building. It looked like old war movies I watched as a boy. Only instead of RAF and Luftwaffe airplanes models, a holographic model of the city was displayed in a reduced scale. Rival corporations' bases and factories glowed red, VEP buildings glowed blue, and everything else glowed green. I noticed that some of the former DEZATEG sites are also lit up in blue. Apparently, the dismantling of the fifth corporation was proceeding at a rapid pace.

When we entered the room, Karel Adam just appeared on one of the holoprojects. He spoke to Lota, who exchanged fancy clothes for a simple costume. Two guys in jackets were standing next to her. Behind them, three women and two men in bulletproof suits and with automatic rifles. The other people who were hanging around or doing something with the screens and projections were in plain clothes.

"Could you say it again?" Lota, exasperated, raised her voice.

"I am not going to discuss anything with you or any other corporations anymore. Security was established by law as subordinate to the office of the mayor. Nobody holds this office, so Security will be independent until a new mayor is elected," Karel insisted.

He surprised me a bit.

"Isn't it just a trick to raise your price?" Countered Lota. She probably saw Karel right through. Or maybe not entirely.

"When the new mayor comes along, I'll quit, but until then I'll just keep this city alive for a bit. Thanks for your attention," he said, and without saying goodbye, he broke the connection.

"Does that mean I no longer work for the Security?" I said greeting.

Lota turned to me and just shrugged.

"I guess it depends on its commander." She nodded towards the empty space after the projection ended.

"I need you here," she said to Ivana, who just nodded.

"You can stay here. Both of you," the owner of VEP said to us.

"You know I won't," I smiled, and she pursed her lips in understanding.

"You're a cop. You're gonna get out of here and try to catch him, right?" She asked.

"If you leave me an account, I will..."

"Account and whatever you need," she interrupted me.

"Well, that's what I wanted to hear."

* * *

From VEP's fleet of hovercraft, we took one standard, which Fay could easily steer with implants. We stopped somewhere above the N level at the intersection of Kovidowa and Prymulowa streets. Lots of poor people lived in this area. ARKAS had famous skyscrapers here, which were called cellular ones. Practically all the apartments here looked like cells. They were about twenty square meters in size and had ceilings at a height of sixty meters. Even families of seven could fit in them. The locals were called "crabs" because of the unusual step with which they moved around their place. Above the intersection was a huge screen that broadcast CN news.

"What the fuck is this?" I blurted out as Fay stopped the vehicle, so we could have a good look around.

In the TV studio, where the two moderators usually sat, there were now eight people, with Král at the helm. In the background, a photo of the killed actress was displayed, whose real name would probably never be remembered.

"...End of censorship. CN TV will bring you real news about what is happening in the city. About a murderer roaming the streets. About the break-up of the Corporation Council. About the death of the mayor..."

They prepared it quite nicely. Each sentence was spoken by a different moderator. Right next to Král, who strained to finally see his neck, moderator Mirka Divišová stood in a fighting stance. Usually she wore low-key costumes, but today she was proudly buttoned up topless with the words "FREEDOM" written on the chest.

"You think they're gonna do it? That they'll start broadcasting the truth?" Fay asked.

We sat in the back seat while the hovercraft held a stable position in the air. I saw little heads in the crowd on the street. The heads of people who, in the last years of their lives, had learned to ignore the news or to perceive it only a third of their brain's capacity, but now stood and stared at it.

"This is TV, honey. They will not know the truth there, even if it would grab their balls and stick their tongue deep into their anus," I replied.

City News unchained are the last thing this city needs. There is no doubt that they were affected by the death of their friend and they used the collapse of the Corporation Council to gain independence. But the truth is a complicated girl, she has many layers, can be contradictory, casts many shadows and is ambiguous like an 18-year-old art student from a broken family. It is impossible for television to grasp it.

I spat at the screen, even though there was no theoretical possibility of hitting it, and we headed home.

All the way to Wild Šárka we flew over people who were looking at screens and holoprojections. They haven't really watched TV in fifty years, I guess.

It couldn't have ended well.

* * *

Karel Adam woke me up in the morning. The cell band turned on at exactly one minute after seven. Sleepy, I reached out for her.

"Good morning," I growled.

Fay scrambled out from under the covers in which she lay wrapped like a cocoon.

"Eh, I can see your girlfriend's breasts," he said after a moment, extremely embarrassed.

"Welcome to the club. Do you want to see more?" The cyber sorceress sent him a kiss and, naked, she knelt on her knees.

I was still fascinated by how perfectly the implants and tattoos on her body harmonized with what could be described as the original biological basis.

"We know whose DNA is on this Zodiac message to Perun's followers," the security chief said after staring at the pussy of the cybernetic sorceress.

Fay realized it was quite a serious matter and wrapped the covers again.

I think Karel was relieved.

"I thought it wasn't in the database," I replied.

"Because it wasn't there initially, but now that no one is controlling us, I let the sealed DNA files be opened," he explained.

"I understand, you are no longer inviolable in the system. How long will it take you?"

Karel paid no attention to it, and then said:

"DNA belongs to Lota, Lota Dejčerova."

* * *

We left the house quickly. I put on one of the last sets of clean clothes - navy blue pants, a black long-sleeved sweatshirt and a navy-blue shirt. The material was really solid. It made it possible to hide a gun in a holster. During the night I ransacked the weapons depot in the VEP-tower. I found, among other things, a few K100 X-TRIM pistols - which, like my favorite K22, came from pre-war purchases from the Slovak armory GRAND POWER. The 9 mm caliber pistol is a reliable toy. Moreover, I found a lot of spare magazines for it. I attached the other holster to the ankle of my healthy leg and stuffed one 0.22 caliber CP22 into the empty bionic limb compartment. I immediately felt a few kilos heavier - a few kilos of healthy self-confidence.

After what happened yesterday and today, I couldn't find a place for myself. I had to get back into the field. Even the coffee Fay had made while I checked the guns, I took with me to the hovercraft.

"Do you trust her because she gives you money or because she hired you to do the job? Maybe it's a trick from the start to buy you," Fay said after the flying vehicle took off.

She wore black pants and a light white shirt over which she had thrown the hoodie she had taken from her spare suit after being disgracefully fired from a bar job. It showed Hello Kitty fucking Mickey Mouse from behind with a fake cock. And that was what Uncle Scrooge, who was masturbating, was watching. It was another symbol of the retro wave that swept the city along with the spring heatwaves.

"Neither one nor the other. I hate traces. I never liked them. If the traces don't match the story, I don't believe it," I replied, sipping my coffee.

"But you can fit the story to these traces, right?"

"And here's the problem. Occam's razor is called this."

"Is it about how ill-will should not be presumed if something can be satisfactorily explained by stupidity?"

"No, it's Hanlon's razor. Occam's razor Principle says that the least complicated story is true," I explained, sipping my coffee.

I didn't sleep much last night. Admittedly, I went to bed quickly, but then I thought about what had happened. It looked like perfect chaos, but it was not. Or at least I didn't believe it. Too many things fit together. Each flap of a butterfly's wings triggered a reaction that led to another, all of which looked like a carefully planned fall of dominoes. I had to look at each block in turn to find out how it was fitted and why the perpetrator chose this particular one - or did they choose it, if there really are more.

We went to the Pyramid of Dread. The Messiah preached here daily. If the one who tried to kill him is not the real Zodiac, the real one will try to do it again. After all, he suggested it in a message he left with Lota's DNA in the temple of Perun's followers. And even if he didn't want to do it, he wanted us to think so. And that, too, had to be for a reason.

"Fuck, there are probably more of them," Fay said superfluously.

Two kilometers before the pyramid itself, we came across the thickening streets full of people crowding one another. Above them, in several layers, hovercrafts crowded with eager to approach Cyber Messiah. It was partly our fault, but mostly City News.

"Today, as every day in recent months, the faithful gather in the open to listen to the sermons of Cyber Messiah, a man who, unlike everyone else, looks into the hearts and souls of the city's inhabitants..."

The reporter Divišová broadcast live directly from the pyramid of rusty wrecks. She stood on a hovercraft with the CN logo, filmed by several drones equipped with television cameras. She looked terribly excited. I remembered the real journalists from before the war. Most of them were heavy alcoholics who were stuck in twisted relationships and turned out to be more cynical than the guy who volunteered for the concentration camp guards in April 1945, but at least they had gotten used to seeing things from different perspectives. Now they were only fascinated with describing the real world, which they did not understand at all after the curtain of virtual reality fell.

"...and everyone is talking about the miracle. Indeed, this man took the dead child, raised it above his head, and it came to life. People talk about more and more miracles, because all they need to do is touch Cyber Messiah and he heals them. If the faithful give up everything digital. Everyone throws away cellular bands, and PRAGUETECH clinics report that the demand for implant removal surgeries has increased by 1,500 percent..."

We flew a short distance from Divišová. If she still wore the word "FREEDOM" on her chest, now it was hidden by a very decent blouse buttoned up to the neck. It pointed out that despite the heat, the woman had no signs of sweat on her body. She had to wear a dress made of very expensive thermoregulatory fibers.

"Where should I park?" Fay asked.

People crowded around the pyramid shoulder to shoulder, and the security of only women was completely unable to cope with the situation.

"In this junkyard." I pointed to the pyramid.

Since it fell apart over time and, more than a pyramid or an indictment from the consumer society, it was just a pile of wreckage, it all went easily in the end. Nevertheless, our landing was not without consequences. The people in the hovercraft reacted indignantly. Apparently, they thought we were aggressive believers. Two women in white jackets ran up to us immediately.

"Here you can't..."

"Yes, I can, I'm from the Security. Do you remember the guy who recently saved a child, and most likely your guru's life as well?" I replied.

The women looked at each other, and the older one just shrugged.

"But this gun, you can't have a gun here!" Cried the younger one after a moment.

"Seriously? Is there any right to it? Because here I am the law." I winked at her and gave her a provocative kiss.

Right after that, I turned to Fay.

"Take off your hoodie, it's hot," I asked her, helping to pull off the mushy retrocool trend. I started unbuttoning her shirt myself.

"Give the girls some space." I freed her breasts and, jumping from car to car, I landed on the dusty road.

* * *

Cyber Messiah was in a large white tent before the sermon began. He was also protected by a group of women in white jackets. They looked even more inaccessible than the ones the welcoming committee organized for us, but when I waved my security card in front of them, they let me in. Besides, they didn't carry weapons. And I do. But Fay irritated them more than the K100 in the shoulder holster. Her unbuttoned shirt communicated clearly that she was a cybernetic prostitute.

"Master?" One of the women who entered the tent with us said.

Cyber Messiah was on his knees and was clearly praying. Only now it occurred to me that I don't even know what for. Somehow his theology eluded me.

"Is it time to go?" He asked in a low voice, not turning around.

"Security. I have to question you," I replied instead of the white-robed admirer.

"Lieutenant Vachten, right? Is your concubine, that filthy cybernetic whore, here with you?" He said, standing up carefully.

It didn't sound like he hated her. His words flowed so deliberately and without emotion, as if he were saying something like, "Would you like whipped cream or rat puffs with your coffee?"

"In all my glory," Fay said, spreading her hands to the sides and thus parting the flaps of her shirt.

* * *

"My sermon begins in ten minutes," said Cyber Messiah.

He didn't check his watch. He had none. He just wanted to narrow down the audition time. His face had changed since the last meeting, his mustache gone, a few minor razor cuts left.

"How's that girl doing?" I asked.

Cyber Messiah only smiled absently, saying:

"She's in God's hands."

"Which one do you mean? Perun?"

"You know very well which god I mean. The one who is in our hearts. In yours too."

"There is only sadness and pain in my heart that they talk to me like a dick." I looked at his face.

"Maybe Mr. Cyber Messiah thinks you are a dick," Fay smirked, looking sternly at the preacher.

The Messiah was silent.

"You know it was no miracle. We both saw it."

The Messiah smiled again.

It was starting to irritate me.

"People's hearts saw a miracle in it, so maybe it's a miracle. If I wasn't there, maybe she would have died."

"If you weren't there, this guy wouldn't hurt her," I said.

"The Lord works..."

"In mysterious ways. I know it. That's what my grandmother used to say when she couldn't shit properly."

"What exactly do you want? Are you trying to lock me up? Accuse of something?"

He spoke calmly and emotionlessly again. His words were seemingly laced with wholesome rage, adrenaline or arrogance, but he uttered them like a porn chatbot.

"No, I'm really interested in who wants to kill you."

Cyber Messiah only bowed his head.

"Not everyone can open their heart to love. There are many who have been enslaved by the devil of technology." He looked at Fay with pity and shrugged.

"Has anyone threatened you?" I continued.

"Lots of people say bad words, but they don't think so often," he replied and glanced at one of the girls who had just entered the tent.

"Master, the faithful are waiting," she said.

"Let them wait. The master has a private service." With a clear gesture of my right hand, I ordered her to go away.

"Who are you exactly? What is your name, sir?" I asked.

That smirk of self-satisfaction again.

"You asked already, and people answered you."

I looked at Fay. She understood.

She stepped closer and gently ran Cyber Messiah over the back of his hand.

His eyes widened.

He sighed slightly.

His jacket stiffened a little.

"Whore!" He screamed.

* * *

Fay took a step back. Women standing nearby ran up to us, ready to defend their prophet. And he stood breathing fast and looked at Fay. His erection was diminishing very, very slowly. It seemed to me that he hadn't ejaculated in a few weeks because he stood up almost immediately and was as stiff as a ship's mast. And it didn't take much.

"Are you trying to provoke me, Lieutenant? Is that the only thing Security can do? Do you know what people think of you? Do you know this is the end of your reign?"

His calm, blissful smile, avoiding answers - all that was lost.

"I know there's a murderer on the prowl who wants to kill you as well. And I don't want to let him do that, no matter what I think about your campaign against the technology of this city. And I don't like when someone is playing cat and mouse with me. Please answer: has anyone threatened you?"

The Messiah's eyes widened, even though he had calmed down a little.

"Nobody threatened me," he said firmly.

"What is your name, sir?"

"Petr Blažek. I haven't said that name in years." He sighed softly, so softly that neither woman would hear him.

"Thank you for your cooperation. If you are in danger or feel threatened, please notify the Security Center," I recited.

"I will not," replied Cyber Messiah, unmoved.

"You don't have a cell wristband, do you? Technology is a crime, so you and the people of this city will go out into nature, you will sow the land, right?" Fay said, slightly swaying her hips.

"While those who have been desecrated by technology, like you, lady, will perish in devil's slavery here," he drawled, then turned and walked away.

* * *

He climbed the pyramid, and immediately the gathered people burst into joy. I've never heard anything like this in my life. Chanted cries of "Messiah! Messiah! Messiah!" they carried through the streets, bouncing off the walls of skyscrapers and echoing back to the feverish crowd. Then the man raised his hands above his head, and everyone fell silent on this gesture, just not to miss a word.

Human faith is irreducible. He will always find a crack to break into the world. Faith is one of the most powerful forces in the cosmos. And the least durable. Six months ago, the same people would have welcomed Fay this way, but now they had a new savior.

The interrogation of the messiah lasted a long time, while the crowd of followers in the area grew even more dense, and for this reason it took us five minutes to fly to the quieter part of the city. Only then did Fay speak first.

"What was that for?"

I shrugged.

"A clever warrior provokes the enemy, but cannot be provoked himself," I recited.

"Is that the Thai guy? I've never liked their food."

"No, it's a Chinese general. I read it in the toilet."

"I just thought you were hanging out there for too long, but I thought you were masturbating. You men do this all the time, right?"

"Of course. We only take a break to eat and read Chinese strategists, silly." I gave her a kiss.

"Well, really, what was it for?"

"Zodi... you know, our killer. If he's watching the messiah, he must have seen us, too," I replied, then turned on Piglet Racing on my cell band and left a message for Tom in our clan chat.

I was interested in where exactly this messiah-Blažek came from.

* * *

Pod Lipami Street has changed a lot in recent months. The tent town has grown to include a few side alleys. We got there on foot, because the town stretched under the pillars of the metro line S. We would have to fly near them with great care. The problem was that the subway pillars were plastered with fancy hovels that climbed on poor scaffolding all the way to the railroad track. People who could not even afford a three-shift hotel lived here, along with their entire families. The hovercraft flew to the nearest parking lot on autopilot, and we set off on foot into the city.

"It stinks even more in here than before," Fay sighed.

She only buttoned her shirt with a few buttons, but she was sweating as much as I was. The local space has created its own very warm and humid climate. Not only was the heat coming from the surrounding buildings accumulating here, and the breeze from the speeding meter did not reach this place, but also the flames that were used to heat it, burning all the street shit, or with which the rectification columns were saturated, where the water brought was

244

evaporated. from the underground by children. In the columns, the contents of the flowing dirty sewage were distilled into something drinkable, as long as the human retained a little self-denial. The remaining stinking mass could then be used as a mortar to build various barriers, roofs and foundations for tents made of old sheet metal, boards and advertising posters.

"Hey, you guys look like decent people. Maybe we'll do a business?"

A hand pressed against my sweaty back. I hated human touch. I turned, throwing off the intruder's hand. It was a guy who was a hybrid of a prehistoric hippie and a teacher of the Russian language. He wore the characteristic red lipstick and wig on his head, but at the same time the fly was so stuffed that if it did not hide a snake at least thirty centimeters long, it must have stocked up with socks for all the slum dwellers.

"You're looking for a baby, aren't you? Newborn? I can arrange whatever you want: blonde, brunette, boy, girl, I also have a half-Asian, but it's for an extra charge. Do you want healthy or crippled? Everything can be arranged," with the old type cellular band he started to display a whole galaxy of various kids. It was his offer.

"I can get the older ones too, if you're interested. Some are already trained. They can handle anything if you understand what

I mean." He swayed his hips as he spoke, mimicking his copulatory movements.

But on the second move he finished the pantomime. Fay swung and kicked him between his legs. And she was wearing her favorite heavy lace-up boots today.

"Gee," the guy squealed, "either trans... or... something..." And he curled up on the ground.

"Fuck off, you prick, if you understand what I mean," Fay snapped.

At the sight of this, other traders, or those who looked like traders, suddenly turned back and changed direction.

"Give me the gun," Fay said firmly.

"You can't kill him."

"I can. He trades in children," she growled.

"I have a job placement license," said the man squirming on the ground.

That he shouldn't have said it, he didn't realize until the Cyber sorceress kicked him in the jaw. Something clicked and he fell silent.

Fay cooled down a bit so I could finally get her out of the whirlpool of the tent town. Soon we got used to the stench of long unwashed bodies, fermented leftovers and decoctions from various protein cubes and pieces of bio-waste that need to be boiled long enough to stop being life-threatening and, most importantly, lose any flavor. These stocks were called the Prague stew. I think I'd rather starve than risk eating just one tablespoon. But the people of Pod Lipami never got to know anything else. They probably never saw a real linden tree either.

"Look," Fay said as we passed the City News holographic projection projected from one of the pillars of the overground subway. Mina was just appearing on the screen, explaining something to the audience. He seemed to be arguing with some guy. The sound did not work, probably someone had dismantled the apparatus from nearby installations, but the information bars showed that it was a pre-election debate. Usually, CN technicians quickly repaired damaged screens and projectors, but no one was brave enough to come here. There were not even broadcasting drones that "sealed the holes" in transmissions in places without screens and projections. The locals usually destroyed them, took them apart and sold them in nearby bazaars.

Soon we found the place we were looking for.

We were led by red flags with a yellow letter R.

* * *

"What do you want here?" The twenty-year-old guy, at first glance, said aggressively.

His head was shaved, and on it was a green beret with the letter R embroidered on it. Besides, a poorly torn shirt was hanging, as well as a jumpsuit that was apparently worn by a man fifty kilograms heavier in front of him. Or even several generations of such guys. In his hand he held a long iron bar. Judging by the sharp edges, he must have just grabbed it from somewhere.

"I'm going to see Caesar," I said.

He looked suspiciously at the bulge on my shirt that I had hidden my gun underneath.

"What for?"

"We're buddies," I said.

It wasn't true. I met Caesar less than six months ago, as a member of the security of this poor town, when cyber sorceresses were hiding here, and then I accidentally stumbled upon him by a cocoa booth. This meeting made me identify him with another character mentioned in the fucking Zodiac list.

The young man whistled a complicated signal and a group of young people emerged from the nearby tents. There could be twenty of them. Some had iron bars in their hands, others had plastic ladles, from which the precious remains of Prague stew dripped off, and two older men were equipped with long rifles. I don't know if they were shootable, but if they sold them to collectors, for the first time in their lives they could try meat other than rats or pigeons. They aimed them menacingly at us.

"I recognize the Security right away. Do you want to lock Caesar up? You are a bit too little. He'll fast run from..."

"I don't like having a gun pointed at me," I said.

And I already had the K100 X-TRIM in my hand. A little late they unsecured their shotguns.

"In the war I learned how to kill a man painlessly. And vice versa. Paradoxically, on the example of suicides. Put the barrel in your mouth and squeeze the trigger - yes, it looks very elegant and simple. The human thinks he will just shut down and that's it. And shit, shit, goldfish. You usually lie on the ground with half your brain leaked, suffering like an animal, and you'd give anything to get out of this idiot position. When the bullet hits you in one place you will die immediately, but if in the other you will be an even more moron than you are now and you will feel such pain that you will be begging me to kill you," I said, waving the pistol but holding them at gunpoint.

"What war did you fight in?"

I raised an eyebrow curiously. The question was asked by a girl of about thirteen in a patched sweatshirt and skirt that was probably once a tablecloth. The girl was holding a plastic bar, wrapped at the end with rusty barbed wire.

"With the Poles," I replied.

"Shit, there aren't any Poles. My brother said the Corporation Council made them up. Has anyone ever seen a Pole?" One of the young men with rifles pointed at me blurted out.

"Thousands of Poles, boy," I replied.

Armed youth began to arrive. Many of them were staring at Fay. Some recognized her.

Whistle - a relatively successful whistle caught our attention.

"Ave Caesar!" I said as hello.

"Hello, Mr. Vachten. Are you playing a toy soldier, or have you come to help us with the revolution?"

"Fuck, with what?"

* * *

The tent town had not only external parts, but also internal parts, invisible at first glance. As there was not enough space in the colony, one tent was adjacent to another, a hut for a shed. The makeshift roofs were structures made of torn foil and pieces of old coats. The cramped space helped to save on material, as the addition of two or three walls was enough to build the next apartments. In this way, families created their own apartments with a few small cubicles, and the only problem was that you had to move around in them. Caesar led us through such a labyrinth, accompanied by a thirteen-year-old girl, until we reached a kind of center of the estate. We passed groups cooking food, crowds of sleeping people, some schools where little toddlers learned to read and were preparing for the pickpocketing trade, until we reached a quite stable room enclosed in double sheet metal stuffed with old upholstery foam. It smelled musty, but there was a fan in the corner, its blades creaking bravely and scattering the foul air. A chewed cable ran from the fan to the ceiling, from which sparks sometimes spilled, but still - probably thanks to the solar panel - kept the ventilation and a scratched lamp illuminating the room. The dominant element was a red flag with the letter R embroidered in gold. Various materials were used for its production, because in many places various shades of faded yellow could be seen. Under the banner were piles of cushions, blankets, and pieces of plastic in the shape of armchairs. A blind girl sat on one of them. It was easy to recognize her disability because she had no eyes. Instead, only scars, as did the hands and one leg. The other leg was a prosthesis, which, like the armchairs, was made of insulation tapes, wires and cords. Feeling guilty, I tapped the floor with my bionic substitute, which, even after many years, remained one of the latest achievements of modern technology.

Caesar sank into an armchair made of bundles of yellowed newspapers. They must have lain here for decades. Then he motioned for us to sit down. Fay lounged on the old pillow next to the blind girl. I preferred to stand.

"It's nice to be here. And where are the staroste?" I asked.

Pod Lipami was a town as you look, it even had its own local government.

"He left two weeks ago and hasn't come back. It happens." He shrugged.

He was right. It happened often. In this crap it was enough for a man to wear a good coat and to operate the iron bar too slowly.

"You're in charge now?"

He shook his head.

"I don't rule anything. It's Aurora."

I looked at the blind girl.

252

"I heard you in CN how you treated this murderer. I wouldn't expect something like this from..."

"Security?"

"Yes." She nodded. "You know, we don't have the best experience with the Security here," she added.

I shrugged, even though I knew he couldn't see it.

"Toothless from the street who incites the crowd."

"What?" Caesar frowned.

"This is from the message that this prick left for us with one of the murdered. He was kind enough to give us a list of future victims. You are among them," I explained to Caesar.

I'd like a drink of something. My throat was dry, but the water was left in the parked hovercraft.

The young man just smiled.

"That's nice of him. He calls himself Zodiac, right?"

I nodded.

"Has anyone ever threatened you? Someone was following you? Or tried to kill you?" I asked directly.

"Yesterday. The GEZ security guards. They fired volleys of rubber bullets at us." He smiled and unbuttoned his shirt.

The skin beneath her was dotted with bluish-purple blotches.

"Reason?"

"Revolution," his mouth twitched.

"I can see that R. What is this revolution?" I got interested.

"There will be neither rich nor poor. Everything for everyone. The production capacity is enough to create enough artificial food, but the corporations don't want that. They maintain a degree of scarcity which does not cause famine, but also does not meet the needs of the population. This allows them to raise their prices. If production capacity is controlled by the people, we can change that.

I looked at the blind girl with surprise.

"I don't mean to offend you, but you figured it out yourself?"

Caesar chuckled.

"No, it's from Sejmen," he replied for her.

"The owner of the ARKAS corporation?" I wanted to make sure.

"Yes. He likes to tell stories. About trade, production, production capacity," said Aurora.

"He also likes to rip off little girls' legs and gouge out their eyes. Then he has a stronger erection," Caesar explained, and Aurora fell silent.

I tried to gasp for air. This girl couldn't be more than seventeen. There was a silence that could be used as an ingredient in Prague goulash.

"Lucka?" Aurora said, breaking the silence.

A thirteen-year-old girl in a tablecloth skirt stood by the entrance the whole time, clutching a barbed bar in her hand. Probably so she could go for help in case something went wrong.

"Will you show Mr. Vachten the Hole?" She asked after a moment.

The girl just shrugged.

"I'm afraid I don't understand." I frowned.

"Caesar will explain everything to you. It was he who discovered this stigma on her. The sign of Pisces, Mr. Vachten."

"What?"

"Yesterday in the CN they said that the killer who murdered this actress leaves signs of the zodiac on the victims. She also wears one on her forehead. I think it might help you," she said.

"Any more victim?"

"Yes, and it's quite old. Dry like shit on the sunny side of the street. Crazy Merklová. Nobody saw her for several months. I thought rats had eaten her, but the children found her body when they went downstairs to fetch the water. When I saw it, I knew immediately that some freak must have killed her. But what kind of type Aurora did not understand until yesterday," Caesar explained.

I looked at Fay.

She just shrugged.

"Okay. I better see her myself. How much do I owe?" I asked Aurora.

She got up and held out her hands. At the same time, she relied uncertainly on an artificial leg made by a home-made method. I was wondering what to do now, but Caesar nodded at me with his head for me to come closer to her. Aurora touched my face lightly and ran her fingers over it. I felt a slight tickle on my nose.

"You'll never understand us. Never. But please don't get in our way," she said in a voice so firm and determined that a shiver ran down my spine.

* * *

Lucka led us through the tent town, to its very edge, where there was an old U-metro ventilation shaft. Its top had long since been torn down, and the bricks and iron had vanished to appear in the foundations of some poor mud hut.

"The hatch is quite narrow, but enough for children, they can even pull a barrel of sludge through it," Lucka explained.

Only now have I noticed that, like Caesar, she has Roman numerals tattooed on her hands. MMXCV. Not on the fingers, but around the wrists.

LeCa DaMy, I thought of an old saying to help identify Roman numerals, and read the number, 2095. Probably her birth year. So she was twelve or thirteen. So I hit the mark. There was a long burn scar just beside the numbers.

"Why do the kids go for this slime? There are a lot of adults at Pod Lipami and most of them are unemployed," Fay asked.

"Adults are killed by sever men. And the kids don't. Nobody knows why that is, but a bastard like this under ten can wander there without a problem. If you look older, they'll eat you," Lucka explained.

"Yes, I know something about that," I sighed.

"It's clean around the Hole. That is why we managed to get there. Recently, the underground has been somewhat restless. We watched it, we were concerned that the sever men were preparing something for us, and so we discovered the place where they stopped showing up. And it led us to The Hole," Lucka said and descended the spiral iron stairs.

I took a deep breath. The more I hated the underground lately, the more I had to go there.

* * *

We walked about a kilometer in total darkness and silence. We hiked, passing curves and paths, and after a few hundred steps I realized that I don't know how to get back without navigation anymore. I was tempted to turn on the cell band so that it would remember our way, but I believed the girl would walk us back later. She must have walked this way from an early age, because although, like us, she could not see anything, she walked very steadily and without stumbling.

"We're there. They don't come here anymore," she whispered, and at that moment the light blinded our eyes.

It came from a few archaic light bulbs hanging from the ceiling. They were placed along the corridor, brightening the walls covered with a thick layer of mold. We took a few steps and saw a large circle carved into a green and black wall. The remnants of dried mold lay on the ground.

"Ascendant," the girl whispered.

"I've heard about him. This is some kind of sewer sect, isn't it?"

She shrugged.

"They have been talking about him for many years. Caesar thinks it's their god, but Aurora says it's not that simple. The sever men believe that one day he will return from his journey and carry them to the surface. Caesar told them the revolution would save them, but then he had to flee because they wanted to eat him and offer his bones to the Ascendant," she whispered.

I had to smile. Belief. It has always been able to find its way to people's hearts. Be it in the Palestinian desert or in the concrete jungle of Prague. After all, it was always there to make sense of life. At the same time, it obscured the minds. Whether it manifested itself in the form of fairies, messiahs, creatures from the sewers, or in the form of a revolution was of secondary importance.

"Why don't the sever men come here?" I said inquiringly after a while.

"They are afraid. They used to show up here all the time, but now the Hole is cursed by them. I think it's because of this corpse," answered the girl and continued down the corridor.

There was no light left in several places, so our expedition plunged back into the darkness to enjoy the next stretch of archaic fluorescent lamps illuminating hundreds of square meters of mold. Eventually we came across a metal door, covered with rust for a change.

"Prague's Capital City Communications Company," Fay unscrambled the inscription on the logo.

"It's probably been here since the Middle Ages," Lucka summed up wisely and opened the door.

"Fuck," the cyber sorceress announced, then whistled in surprise.

* * *

"This corpse must have been lying here for at least two months, or maybe longer," I said, looking at the woman's body in an advanced stage of decomposition.

It was difficult to estimate her biological age, but given her meager and misshapen bones, she might already be in her eighties. She was lying on a long table, and there were frozen puddles of burned out candles all over the place. Beside it were dozens of dead bodies of headless rats. Someone had drawn a familiar circle on the wall behind the table.

"Sever men do that to these rats. This is some kind of a ritual in honor of the important dead," Lucka explained and, regardless of the surroundings, sat down in the archaic armchair, from which a cloud of dust rose.

I finally decided to turn on the cellular band to illuminate the corpse. I also started scanning them with the police application that I installed on the armband. Caesar and Aurora were right about this sign. The two opposite, as if inverted brackets connected by a horizontal line were the old symbol of the Pisces zodiac sign. The shape was only preserved because the killer had engraved it deeply on the victim's forehead. Of course, with a military knife. The blade marks were also visible on the victim's body. They were covered in a crust of dried blood, but when I broke it, I could know their depth and number.

"At least seven, maybe eight, very deep wounds," I said.

"Was she already naked or did you take off her clothes?" I asked after a while.

Lucka just let out a "bleh" and grimaced her face.

"We're not that desperate. I wouldn't touch anything the mummy was wearing," she added.

261

"He raped her or something," Fay said.

She carefully shifted the corpse's right leg.

The mummified skin showed signs of injuries sustained shortly before or immediately after death.

"Yuck." The girl in the chair shuddered.

"Maybe he just wounded her there," I wondered. "Who was this Merklová actually?"

"Solve problems."

"What problems?"

"Too much mouth to feed."

"So she was selling children like Aurora to be toys for rich perverts?"

Lucka shook her head.

"She looked after them and looked for a new home for them. Simply, when someone could not support the child, or for some reason did not want him, he would put him at the entrance to the Hole, from the other side. Merklová picked up the children and looked after them. Some grew up here, others found a family or something. She did not eat them. She also looked after the children of sever men. I've seen her here several times. She was scary, but people said you'd better give her back than anyone else," she explained, casually folding one leg over one leg.

I shook my head. The more bodies we found, the more complicated the matter became. Why would Zodiac kill someone like that? Plus, it looked like it was his first victim. I tapped on my cell band to send the recorded scans to Karel and the Security technicians, when suddenly a message popped out from him: "At 11:00 pm in the old barracks in Škvorec. Come alone. Important".

"Something happened?" Fay asked.

I just shook my head.

"We should go now. I still have to call Hynek. He's on that moron letter too," I replied and confirmed to Adam that I would come.

Then I bent down and took the spare K100 out of the leg holster.

"You know how to handle it?" I asked the girls, waving a protected gun in front of my nose.

"Caesar taught me something." Resigned, she shrugged.

"Happy birthday. You have a full magazine here." I stuffed the gun in her hand.

Her eyes lit up.

"Don't think I'll suck you for this, dude," the watchful twelve-year-old said.

"That's what he got me for, honey," Fay said amused.

"Take it, while I give and use it in your defense when the worst comes. All that is happening tells me that a girl like you might be in trouble soon," I growled and took one last look at the mummy of a harmless old woman.

* * *

The conversation with Hynek was brief, as expected. He told me that he had known about the letter for a long time and that I should actually take care of myself. I wished him good, if he was having dinner, and flew back with Fay to Belch's. After a short break for one powdered sour rye soup on a laboratory-grown sausage and artificial coffee, I took the hovercraft, pulled a new spare weapon from the trunk and headed for the barracks.

I did three months of military training after volunteering for the military police and went to defend my homeland, as it was once said. Of course, I wasn't defending anything. I tracked down people who traded ammunition and weapons instead of fighting, and

264

investigated crimes against civilians. It's just that the cop will always be the cop.

Before Prague was completely closed to the outside world, tens of thousands of refugees poured into it, not only from Moravia and Silesia, but from all over the country. Therefore, after the dissolution of the army, the barracks turned into a refugee shelter. Since the border started just around the corner, people eventually had to get out of here. The first generation of PRAGUETECH automated murder drones had the nasty feature of firing at moving targets in all directions, but not always where they needed to be. Therefore, a series of grenades hit the shelter, killing several families. Security has cleaned it up. At that time, CN was broadcasting a live broadcast of the carnival in the city center. No unauthorized person found out about the incident. Except for Mina, that is, who had plugs and information about events everywhere - often before they even happened.

These outskirts of the city were mostly occupied by production plants and warehouses. I flew past the last skyscrapers and reached the factories. Most were originally owned by DEZATEG, but now anyone could own them. They were working at full speed, as evidenced not only by the noise and lights, but also by the huge container trucks on which the goods were loaded. On the way, I tried to call Karel, but he didn't answer. For the hundred and fifty-eight time it has occurred to me that I need to get myself a security application that will force each cellular band to pick up the phone when I call someone. I think the guys and girls from Security must have had a lot of fun with it.

I turned sharply around one of the factories on the edge of the safety zone. It swayed a bit. I didn't have any implants that I could control, so I handled it by hand, no matter what.

When I reached the dark building of the old barracks, I was hit by an EMP bomb - a charge that reliably destroys all electronic devices.

* * *

Fortunately, the hovercraft was just two meters above the roof and at quite a decent speed. For that reason alone, at the moment of impact, I did not collapse like a peeled pear from a tree, but came to the landing like a paper airplane - gliding down and making a powerful whistle.

Obviously, I wasn't strapped in, so the foam airbags opened and I bounced off them and flew through the windshield onto the hood, then rolled onto the nanopap roof.

I cursed and sprang to my feet quickly. My pants were tearing at my knees and they were bloody. Despite the dramatic situation, I remembered a few similar falls when, as a fast-growing child, I could not co-ordinate my limbs and landed on the ground every hour. Instinctively, I pulled the pistol from its shoulder holster. At that moment, the rear of the hovercraft lifted due to kinetic energy, then it hovered in the air for a few picoseconds in an infinite time bubble before finally returning to its place, and this time it was a hard landing. The hovercraft certainly didn't look as kitschy now as it did before.

I tried to activate the wristband, but it did not respond. It had built-in self-healing mechanisms, but it's hard to say what the force of the load was and when or if the wristband would start working again. Same with the hovercraft. He looked completely dead too. In the distance, I saw lights illuminating the loading bay of the nearest factory, which meant the EMP outburst must have been local.

I crumpled and moved as far away from the hovercraft as possible. I took my steps carefully so as not to fall into a trap in this darkness.

"This is Vachten, Petr Vachten. I'm a cop."

It was my voice. He was speaking from several loudspeakers at once, which were hidden somewhere on the roof.

"This is Vachten, Petr Vachten. I'm a cop."

I took a deep breath and paced the roof step by step.

"This is Vachten, Petr Vachten. I'm a cop."

I stopped. He was playing with me. He prepared a trap.

He sent an EMP bubble on me while leaving his devices shielded.

"This is Vachten, Petr Vachten. I'm a cop, I used to torment little animals as a child. I had a dominant psychopathic mother who never loved me."

My voice was from CN, but the sentences were slightly modified. It was easy. Even a child could do it.

I smiled. I got that bastard ass, and now he was trying to get mine.

"This is Vachten, Petr Vachten, I'm fucking with dead bodies, because I wouldn't be able to stand up with the living."

Until suddenly I saw him. And then seven times. They appeared around me. It was a digital projection, but almost perfect. They looked exactly like in live broadcast next to the crucified corpse of an actress, whose name no one remembered anymore.

"This is Vachten, Petr Vachten, I am worthless garbage."

I stopped and cramped even more. He could be standing in some place with a sniper rifle. It is possible that traps were placed everywhere, dozens of Zodiacs armed with vending machines could run here. Anything could be out there.

As Sun Tzu used to say, "If you know your enemy and you know yourself, even if you fight a hundred battles, you will never be defeated. If you don't know your enemy but know yourself, sometimes you can win. If you don't know yourself or your enemy, you will surely lose every battle." I don't know if Zodiac read The Art of War, but he followed its advice - he tried to get to know the enemy, and it was me. I think he did it consistently. That is why he caught his victims so easily, which would never have happened if it had not entered their heads. I tapped my watch. It still didn't work. The surrounding lights were still off, only the noise in the distant factory indicated that the world was still working. There were even drones guarding the border zone of the happiest city in the world. One was less than a hundred yards away from me. I noticed it because the self-charging solar stand caught my eye. In the five-kilometer zone that covered the city, there were hundreds of thousands of similar filth, automatic smart mines, ambushes, and shooting positions. In addition to the automatic fire function of moving objects (mainly people), they also had automatic defense mechanisms.

"This is Petr Vachten, I am..."

"Shut your mouth!" I shouted my own voice and fired fifteen rounds of magazines at the drone, and immediately after that, though probably around the same time, I fell to the ground.

"K hundred" shoots, if necessary, at a distance of more than one hundred meters. The drone shoots at a distance of several kilometers, since we are already talking about it.

Bang, bang, bang, bang, bang! - a volley fired at the walls of the former barracks swept through space.

"This is Petr Vacht..."

* * *

The corner of the barracks literally exploded with a series of missiles that burst through the walls and the darkness. Several of them flew right over my head, along with fragments of the retaining wall of the former barracks. The Electronic Zodiacs are gone somewhere, and with them my modified voice. I crawled to the other side of the roof, so furiously that the hovercraft, lonely in the darkness, was speechless for a few seconds.

The shooting stopped after about ten seconds. Even the automatic extermination system can save on ammunition, especially when it determines that it is no longer in danger. I changed the magazine and looked into the darkness below. The top window, like most of the others, had been smashed. I grabbed the edge of the roof and jumped through it into the room. Chunks and bits of plaster crunched under my feet, but I landed standing and in a few strides ran to the nearest wall. I took out my gun again.

Inside, I was greeted by darkness. Only a faint glow fell to the floor through the window. I slipped around the corner and pressed against the wall. Then I noticed tiny glowing arrows on the ground. If I normally went down through the hole in the ceiling, it would have led me to an adjoining room. Someone must have drawn them especially for me. Who - I didn't have to think too long. He was standing at the next corner. On his shoulder was the Twardowski 07 machinegun. Like the electronic Zodiak, he was wearing a hoodie over his head, and I could assume other props, including that idiot sign on his chest. But in the dark, I couldn't see any details.

It wasn't the real Zodiac - I was sure of it now. Whatever his plans were, he surely wouldn't be in the front line of fire. I reached in my pocket and felt the muffler. Fortunately, I cleaned and lubricated all the equipment from the VEP armory. I felt the oil run down my fingers and the weapon part clicked slightly into place.

The guy was upset. I could feel it. Maybe it's just an imagination, but I felt his body tremble slightly. Probably because he stamped his foot under stress. I have no idea what Zodiac found out about me, but my basic strategy was that I wasn't playing by anyone, or actually by any rules.

The guy with the vending machine wasn't alone here. Just a few meters away, in the opposite room, I saw a black silhouette of a man creating a slightly darker background in space. They set apart so that they could see each other. There could be even more of them here. I will attack the first one and the others will enter the game. It's like a primitive smoke warning system. Only well-armed people made it here.

Near Zodiac number three there was another arrow that led down to the corridor. I had a vague impression that there used to be an electronic warfare training room there. I quietly moved a few meters away to the room with the third guy, looking for the fourth. I have not found.

What would Sun Tzu say? All I remembered was: "If the advantage increases, take action; if there is no hope of success, stay where you are." I wasn't sure if I had any advantage, but I preferred not to stay where I was. I took two steps to see all three. It was a bit like a shooting range, but it's clear that no target with a mother holding a painted child in her arms will not appear.

Bang! Bang!

The first shot pierced the silhouette in the darkness, and the second hit it as it slid down the wall to the floor. I aimed at the next one. I saw him turn around quickly, pick up the gun, his finger resting on the trigger.

But I already had my finger on the trigger.

I cleaned it up with two shots. A Polish machinegun fell to the ground, followed by a limp body.

But the third guard had already fired.

* * *

I was lucky. We opened fire on each other almost at the same time. I fired five bullets at him, he thinks four. I hit it and he didn't. I saw it fall to the ground, so I ran to the first. I fired one more shot at him, just in case, and after a few steps another one was still wheezing, so I put another bullet into his lungs and jumped straight to the third. It was not a perfect hit. I hit his collarbone, but the force of kinetic energy made him fall, and the pain and shock knocked the weapon out of his hand. Now he felt in the dark to find it. He still had the strength. He was bleeding profusely, his body making strange noises, but he kept trying to fight back. I dug up Twardowski two meters away and leaned over him.

"Who are you?" I asked.

* * *

I whispered. I don't know why. The noise of the shots must have reached the workers on the loading ramp of a nearby factory. With my free hand, I tore off his hood and in the dim light I saw a man in his fifties. Tired face full of wrinkles, scarred on the left side.

"Zo..."

"Shit," I interrupted him. "You're not Zodiac. Just his bum. Cannon fodder. Do you know for what purpose?"

As a precaution, I pressed my back against the wall and out of the corner of my eye watched the space around me.

"Blue... Comp... any... always," he said, as if his soul was escaping.

He made a show especially for me. Suddenly he quickly pulled out a spare weapon with his left hand - a good old K22. He had it in his pants pocket. It was enough to reach for it.

I shot him in the heart.

* * *

He didn't make show one more time. He died.

* * *

274

I noticed something flashing metallic next to the hole in which I was storing a nine-millimeter bee. The bullet passed by and even licked it a little. I tore his sweatshirt open. I got blood on my hand, but I felt a small plaque near the heart.

"What the hell is that?" I growled.

At first it occurred to me that this was some sort of medical implant, but the object was too primitive.

I started searching the guy, but he had nothing essential with him. Not even a cellular wristband. Nothing to explain.

I wiped the blood on his sweatshirt.

A light went on in the room.

* * *

It blinded me for a moment. I blinked, opened my eyes a little and saw through a narrow gap that there were autonomous fluorescent lamps mounted on the ceiling, which were now operating at full power. Instinctively, I jumped up. There were still nine rounds in the magazine.

"I admit it was too easy. But now the real fun begins, Vachten."

I knew this electronic voice all too well. It sounded exactly the same as it did during the live broadcast of the actress's execution.

* * *

The lights went out and I went blind again. The only thing I saw, as soon as my eyes got a little used to the darkness, were the phosphorescent arrows on the ground pointing somewhere backwards.

I did not react. I leaned over the body and continued my search. I picked up my sleeve and saw the famous Blue Company tattoo. Another veteran. How many of these bastards could have survived and returned to Prague? Several dozen? The soldiers, most of them at least, stayed together often. Classic war syndrome. They did not understand the people around them, and they did not understand them.

I pulled the plate. It was stuck to the skin.

"What the fuck is that?"

I tore it out, along with a few of his hairs. The guy wasn't feeling anything anymore, so you couldn't care less about how he felt. The item looked very dated, but I figured it was for a veteran's heart rate monitor.

"You bastard." I spat in the direction of the arrow.

He's not here. He's just not here. He's got a fucking riddle room ready for me. If they got me, I'd get a bullet in the head and they'd throw me into the sewers somewhere. But if I got my way through security, another show was waiting for me.

"Fuck you," I growled.

"As you already understood, you have no choice. One of them will die. Who do you choose?" An electronic voice rang out.

I must have missed something.

* * *

I guess I had to play this game anyway. I followed the arrows that led me to the lower floor. There were several spotlights illuminating the entire room. In the center of the room was an old electronic clock that was counting down. It indicated eight minutes. Now only seven and fifty-nine seconds, fifty-eight..."

"Vachten!" A familiar voice came from my cell band.

Pirate Tom. He has clearly installed a self-receiving application on my camera.

"You were hit by an EMP bomb. What happened?"

"Old…"

"Everything's fine?"

"Eh?"

"You are drunk?"

I shook my head.

Tom had probably set up some kind of electronic guardian for me, so when my new cellular band was shocked and shut off, an alarm went off for him. We're kind of like good buddies, but this unwanted over-protectiveness should be the subject of a fundamental conversation.

"Sorry, I'm in a bad situation. Karel Adam and Lota Dejčerová are here."

"Swingers party?"

"Unfortunately not." I pressed a few buttons and activated the camera.

It wasn't easy as not all functions were restored, but Fat Tom at least shutted up.

They really were here, Karel and Lota. They were both seated in old chairs, and both had huge iron hoops around their necks and taped lips.

I ran to Karel and took the tape off him.

"How many did you kill?" He asked.

Surprisingly, he looked very calm. He was wearing his work jacket, now a bit dirty and torn. He certainly didn't get caught easily.

"Three," I replied.

"Cool. There are probably ten of them. You have to kill everyone."

"But?" I shook my head not understanding.

"The chief fucker isn't here. He controls everything remotely. Prick, a fucking prick," Karel growled angrily.

"Tom, get the Security. We have to get them out of this," I said, but I was sure help was on its way.

Tom saw it all, and he certainly wasn't waiting for me to ask for reinforcements myself.

"They won't be on time. I'm dead," Karel said, nodding his head clockwise.

"The rules of our game are as follows. When time is up, rimmed blades will slit their throats. This is one version of the ending. The second is that you can choose who you want to save. The rims can be easily removed. Just unlock the clasp. But if you open it with one person, the other person will die immediately. Good luck, I wonder who will you pick. See you soon."

The electronic voice went silent and the room lights went out. It was lit only by a countdown clock.

* * *

"Fucking asshole," I sighed heavily.

* * *

"Tom?"

"Yes, I know, I think about it. I'm looking for a way to remotely disable it, but can't pinpoint anything. It's some kind of antediluvian technique. Looks like military."

The old pirate was right. It looked military and antediluvian. Some old fucking torture device. It even had the old logo of the Czech Armed Forces. Could we really do this shit before the war?

"Promise me, promise me you'll kill that motherfucker and all his people. Promise you to shoot his balls, shoot his eye, and then riddle him like a sieve."

"Karel?"

"Promise me!" The Security chief screamed.

"Okay, I promise, but now we have to figure out how to get you out of this," I replied.

I started sweating. I could think of nothing, not even a quote from Master Sun Tzu.

"Listen to me, I'll tell you everything that happened and what I know, okay?"

"We can do it. We'll get you out of this," I said.

Karel screamed at me again

"Shut up, Vachten, and listen. I spent a fucking hour here so I thought it over and I won't let him kill me. You're gonna shoot me. You put a bullet in my head. You need to aim well, I don't want to die slowly with the half of brain like General Beck, do you get it?"

I nodded my head.

"Tom?"

"I'm working on it, man, working on it," the pirate said.

I looked at the clock. Five minutes left.

"They came over to my house," Karel continued, "a few bastards in their disguises. They broke the door open with a pile driver. I shot one, his blood is on the floor. They are soldiers. Damn veterans, well organized. They didn't say a word. Only here did this asshole tell me everything from some loudspeaker. He must have been planning this for a long time. Maybe he's related to some big player like Albert Viktor back then. Maybe he worked in the police before and knows how to cover his tracks. That DNA was dropped off, you were right."

I listened to Karel's every word, but no matter how hard he tried, the information was useless to me, because I had known it all for a long time.

"All information about the deceased is on file, which you can access through my personal Pranet access. Nick is KarelV10, password Sigma, with a capital S," he continued.

He was breathing hard. His heart was pounding loudly. Or maybe it was mine.

"What if I decide to save you?" I asked.

He smiled.

"You wouldn't do that. And if you did, you wouldn't forgive yourself, and neither would I. We're from the old school. She is a woman. Even if it were the most conceited knitted cunt, it would have to be me anyway," he said.

"What if it was a trap? Test? Trick? He knows that I will choose to save the woman. Instead," he will kill you both as punishment.

Karel shook his head.

"Shit. He's tormenting you. He wants to find out who you are and how to get at you. This is the way."

"Like Sun Tzu," I sighed.

Time was passing too fast.

"What's your gun?"

Karel started shaking. Adrenaline buzzed through him.

In me too. I took out my gun and showed it to him.

"K hundred. Okay. My grandmother came from Žilina. All right," he smiled and added. "You believe in God?"

Three minutes left. I prepared the gun. I took a few steps behind Major Karel Adam's back.

"Tom?" I tried again.

"I got nothing, damn it! By Saint Bartholomew, by all the pirates, I have nothing!" Tom replied.

I had to act fast. I didn't want him to wait for this. During the war, I liquidated a few convicts who were imposed the death penalty by a field court. It was part of my duties. I knew the seconds to wait for the bullet were the worst.

"What do you mean?"

"Come on, God. Jesus, the one from the Bible, and the angels, and..."

* * *

He did not answer.

* * *

I dropped the gun on the floor and ran to Lota's. I wasn't thinking about anything, only the two shots rang in my head. I loosened the clasp on her neck, and right behind me there was a click and the metallic creak of the blade of the other rim. She was crying. She stared at Karel's shattered head. In fury, I released her from bondage. I literally yanked her out of the chair and made her stand up. Her legs were numb, so she moved like a puppet, but finally she stood up by force of will. She wore canvas trousers smeared with blood and a light green tunic with a stain of blood that was certainly not hers. I figured there would still be time for an explanation, and I ran over to Karel.

"Get me a hovercraft. The unlock password is 78x916f2", I said, picking up the gun.

I took the body in my arms. I had to put in a lot of effort to lift Karel, but I wasn't going to leave him here. The countdown continued. It was approaching the last minute.

I kicked the window scraps. A hovercraft floated beneath it. It wasn't very steady, but at least it worked. I stood on the windowsill and jumped into the backseat. Karel's corpse slipped from my shoulders, but I finally grabbed him and put him in the backseat. Blood was flowing all over the place.

Lota jumped into my arms. As soon as I threw her on the passenger seat, I grabbed the steering wheel and started up the hill. The hovercraft didn't really listen to me, but it was quite manageable.

"It couldn't," Tom's voice said after a while, "nothing could be done. Nobody would have stopped it remotely," he added quietly.

"I know," I whispered, flying to the roof of a building that once belonged to some private high school.

There were still the rusty hoops of basketball baskets in the courtyard. Behind us, the barracks building exploded. Zodiac was cleaning up after himself.

A few minutes later the cavalry arrived.

They had wingers, hovercrafts, flamethrowers and won in the air:

Look, the drops are rolling

I have more of them in my hand than you do

You are the mistress of the waters

And I am asking if for your hands

My drops are OK

Mina's return

Lota was abducted on her way to a party. She flew secretly, only in a covered hovercraft. Along with two foretellers who were shot.

"Ivana warned me, but I thought it would be an adventure."

She was still crying. She realized she had made a mistake. It didn't matter. I knew he would get her anyway, or use another person. In my opinion - maybe Belch or someone else who could compete with his longtime colleague.

I wiped away a stream of tears and smeared the "n" and "p" marks on her neck - the markings for the sign of Virgo. I turned to Karel. The bastards made an arrow around his neck - the sign of Sagittarius. It faded slowly under the layer of drying blood.

After twenty minutes, the cavalry had grown considerably.

An armored hovercraft accompanied us almost to the N-metro station, where Ivana caught up with us. Her new vehicle, in addition to rockets, was also equipped with an anti-aircraft gun and three pairs of rotary machine guns. It resembled a military helicopter of the Polish army.

Dozens of combat drones were circling around.

Lota changed over without a word.

"Are Fay okay?" Ivana asked.

"She's at Belch's. He keeps saying that he won the war and the Czechs are a piece of cake for him," I smiled.

Ivana looked sadly at Karel's body.

"If necessary, we will have a place for you. Do you know about it?"

I nodded.

"Perhaps we will take advantage of this. We'll see."

* * *

I reached the seat of Security alone. On the way, I also called Fay. Everything was fine with her. She sat with Tom and the other sorceresses at Belch's. It's a bit weird, but I didn't know where Karel actually lived. From what he said, he was alone. Taking him to the Security base seemed the only logical solution. I felt exhausted and my thoughts were running in all possible directions, so I didn't notice that, in addition to a few Security hovercraft, there was also one with the City News logo at the airport.

When I landed, Mirka Divišová ran up to me. It might have been two in the morning, but like Prague, City News also refused to sleep in these new times.

"Lieutenant Vachten, right?"

I turned to see her in one of the more defiant outfits. Probably it adjusted them to the needs of the respondents. This one had two chest openings that protruded boldly from a purple suede blouse. There were two small glass ladybugs on her nipples as ornaments.

"Yes?" I turned to her and jumped out of the hovercraft.

"We informed about the disappearance of the Prague Security Commander Major Karel Adam. We found out at the base that he flew to meet you," she said and waved her hand to the guy who was controlling the two transmission drones that hovered over her head with two cellular bands.

Then the reporter noticed a body in the back seat.

"Fílo, we're on the air!" she dropped and jumped to me with her breasts.

"City News reporter here, Mirka Divišová. We bring the shocking news that... damn, this is Adam, right?"

"Yes, that's him," I said.

I just wanted to carry Karel's body to the building and disappear, but Divišová barred my way.

"The Security Commander is dead. Who shot him?"

"What?" I frowned.

"He's dead in your hovercraft. He was at a meeting with you. Do you know who shot him?"

I was standing still. I looked at the screen that was broadcasting CN news. I was on it. In all its glory, plus two constantly changing close-ups - one on my bloody hands and the other on Adam's corpse.

"Do you know who shot him?"

"Me. But it's all more complicated, this bastard..."

"You just heard the confession on the live stream. The Security Commander was shot dead by his subordinate. Why did you do this? Was it a power war?"

Divišová was standing, her breasts with ladybugs sticking out menacingly towards me. I realized that at least half of the city's ten million inhabitants are looking at me now. And I just said I killed Karel Adam. Fuck. Media. Hell's bells! Why don't they prefer to broadcast Dirty Lopez? Well, one of the main stars is dead. Hell, my head wasn't working properly. Did I really say I shot Karel? It's true, but it wasn't me, not me, it was Zodiac...

"It's not fucking like that. That son of a bitch kidnapped him and wanted to kill him, I had to..."

"Do you take drugs? Are you under the influence of any psychotropic substances?"

"Damn it, go to hell," I lost my temper.

I picked up Karel's dead body from the damaged hovercraft and headed for the entrance. An apathetic Security guy stood by him. CN drones flew overhead, and Divišová trotted past. The screens and projections that I saw in the distance showed me and a dead body.

"You don't understand? He kidnapped him and wanted to kill him. Him and Lota Dejčerova. He wanted me to shoot him, so he wouldn't die at the hands of that bastard. I'll get him, but you guys show crap. It is all complicated."

I was walking, and I already knew that I was at the bottom. I can't get out of this.

"How do you feel as a murderer?" The reporter asked.

"Get Král back up the ass, you stupid cow!" I jabbed her elbow.

I didn't care now. I slipped by the Security guy and yelled at him not to let her in. It wasn't until the first office where I put it on the table that I realized I had screwed it up completely.

* * *

Fat Tom and Belch were shouting something at me from the blindfold, but I didn't listen to them. I passed a few dumbfounded Security guys, washed my hands of the blood, and took the elevator downstairs. Right after that, I went out into the street. CN screens and projections attacked me from all sides. The same image was repeated over and over again - the relentless face of Divišová and me, who poke her elbow and say: "Get Král back in the ass, you stupid cow!" And worst of all, people have looked at it. They really watched it. They stopped in the street, looked away from blindfolds or pieces of paper with inscriptions, news and announcements stuck to the entire subway, and stared at the news. And in them on me. I looked down and at each station I changed to a different car. But they almost always recognized me anyway. They stared at me, showed me, whispered. They looked at the repeated messages with me in the lead - like I said I killed Karel Adam, how I carry his

292

corpse, how I elbow a reporter and say: "Get Král back in the ass, you stupid cow!"

I got off at the Dejvická station and ran outside. It was no accident. Tom shouted through the blindfold a few times for me to get out there. I made my way through the crowd and heard a whistle. Tom and Fairy Fay were sitting in an old hovercraft. I walked over to them. The Cybersorceress threw her Hello Kitty sweatshirt at me. I pulled it over my head and put the hood on.

"You'll be out of sight for a moment..." Fay whispered unhappy.

"Please go ahead," I gasped and climbed into the backseat.

* * *

I woke up and it was dark all around. I closed my eyes to fall asleep again but couldn't. There was a thousand thoughts in my head that did not allow me to do this. I saw what happened yesterday in all too bright colors. Tied Lota, Karel and finally that cow Divišová with transmission drones.

He knew me. I don't know if he really knew himself, but he knew me and thanks to that Zodiac is able to defeat me. He repaid me for the humiliation I gave him when he killed Pipa, or what was the name of this actress? He paid back with interest. Now he could only finish me off.

"My God," I whispered, opening my eyes.

293

I saw glowing Fay implants in the dark. They illuminated her beautiful figure. She was naked. She probably just got out of the shower. The light of the implants was reflected in water droplets that sparkled with all colors. She walked over to me and sat on the bed. I reached out and brushed one drop off her body with my finger. She smiled and moved closer. She shook her breasts slightly and a few drops fell on my face. I licked them on left breast. They tasted like strawberry chewing gum. She stroked my cheek, then slid her hand down onto my hips. I slept naked.

"But..."

The rest of the protest vanished into a haze of excitement. Fay didn't even have to use digital tricks. After a while I had a really solid erection and started sighing uncontrollably. The sorceress kissed me carefully, then sat on top of me. Thanks to her own excitement, I slipped into her easily and without making any efforts, with a few movements, she brought herself to orgasm. She leaned on my shoulders and continued. After a while, I went to meet her. With both hands I firmly grasped her buttocks, squeezed them and guided her movements to get more pleasure for myself.

"More," she gasped.

Her implants glowed even more intensely. They glowed with blinding light. It was a natural process that she couldn't control, it was triggering automatically.

"God," she groaned, and shivered again.

"Shit, there's a war in town and you're fucking that trans-whore of yours," said Fat Tom, standing in the doorway.

He was wearing his favorite Scottish skirt made of a material so thick and strong it would have lasted these thirty years or so long without any problems, and with it only a white T-shirt with a few spots on it. I hoped they did not come from Belch's kitchen and that they did not remember the times of the republic. He stared at Fay, fascinated, even though he had just called her the trans-whore. I wasn't surprised by him. She was really beautiful.

"I don't care now," I gasped as I rolled Fay onto her back.

I grabbed her ankles, lifted her legs in the air, and before Tom could close the door, I squirted at her after a few jerky movements. I hugged her ass and rested for a while. Only then did I slide onto her breasts. She was still glowing.

"You're not guilty. None of us are guilty," she whispered.

"I'm guilty," I sighed. "Prepare the bait to lure the enemy. Pretend confusion in your ranks and crush it. That was what Sun Tzu advised - and that is exactly what Zodiac did. And I let him lure me and crush me. When Karel died, I thought it was all over, but he somehow lured that bitch off the TV and destroyed me," I added.

I closed my eyes and snuggled against Fay's chest, it was best for me there. It didn't take long, however. The door opened. Tom was standing in them again.

"Look, Hynek needs me back on my post, and I know you won't be able to fuck for too long, even with that trans-whore, so get the fuck up."

* * *

The restaurant was closed. Only Wojciech and Tom were sitting in the kitchen. Given the condition of their glasses and bottles, they'd been sipping their brains from the morning and watching City News.

I was only wearing boxer shorts. I sat down next to them, picked up a bottle of a special Polish drink and poured it on two fingers.

"The sorceresses are now safe in the VEP-tower," Wojciech informed me.

I nodded with satisfaction and watched the news with fascination. The armed men wore bulletproof vests and weapons that revealed they were working for ARKAS, but armbands with the word Security Prague glittered on their sleeves. They headed for the old town hall building. After the death of the old mayor, who had been replaced by the Corporation Council with an avatar, the town hall was empty. Now, Mina and the security were going there with a determined step.

"Due to the unstable security situation in the city, the leading politician of the Republic, Maria Ingrová, took the position of mayor of Prague with the full support of the Corporate Council. Both the Council and Security immediately pledged obedience to her. Maria Ingrová took office this morning. Until proper elections are planned, the mayor will rule by decrees that will gain legal force," the voice of an invisible presenter informed the audience. This was some kind of news summary, as Mina's press conference had previously been broadcast live on CN, as evidenced by the material displayed. Now only the most important fragments were shown.

"We care about the safety of all residents of Prague. Therefore, we call on all political groups and activists to respect the transfer of power and to wait peacefully for the elections. However, given the current situation, the actual elections have to be postponed by six months to get everything back to normal. Our goal is nothing more than security and prosperity. That is why we ask all employees to return to work calmly, and we prohibit any gatherings of more than fifty people per fifty square meters," she said in a decisive voice.

I smiled. It is difficult to say what exactly is a gathering in the streets of Prague, because people lived side by side and every major street looked like a demonstration was taking place there.

"The Security is also looking for criminals in the city who caused so much pain and chaos. They will all be caught and properly judged," Mina said, and the studio was shown on TV.

There was an emaciated thirty-year-old man with curly black fringe, and next to him a ginger of forty, a good twenty centimeters taller. I've never seen them on the CN news before.

"While the interim mayor hasn't said the criminals they are talking about, the Security has already published a long list of names in Pranet. It is headed by a former policeman suspected of killing the security commander, Karel Adam, as well as an anonymous perpetrator known as Zodiac. Moreover, there has been speculation that it is about one and the same person..."

"What?" I said, and almost snorted the last sip of moonshine.

"They gave you a nice picture there again, man," Belch replied amused.

He was right.

They picked up an old photo of me in a military police uniform from somewhere and enlarged it, and behind it they displayed shots of me carrying Karel's body and screaming at Divišova the busty cow.

Tom's cellular band vibrated.

"Hynek. We have a conference. Mina is probably not the only one who makes political plans," Tom smiled.

He looked sad rather than amused. Pirates lived underground for a long time. The Corporation Council put them on the list of enemies of the new state, and they were there for so long that in the meantime, everyone forgot about them. But they did not forget the inner-city network, Pranet, and rummaged through it, stealing, sniffing and selling what they had acquired - to the mafia, traders, and who knows who else. They also worked for Mina. I was wondering what their attitude was to this problem now that Mina was connected to the rest of the Corporate Council.

"Listen, did you find something about this reporter, or a list of the members of the Blue Company?" I still managed to ask in a hurry.

Tom shook his head.

"There is not only no Blue Company on Pranet, but nothing at all about the 51st Airborne Battalion. All military records are gone. The entire archive of the last forty years of the former Ministry of Defense. You don't exist either. Mention of the war has disappeared from the digital news archive. There is nothing on the Pranet or even in its underworld. Someone used the base code it was constructed on and it's gone. No trace, no print. Not even the fucking stench is left of this shit."

"How the fuck is that possible?" I poured myself another glass of moonshine.

"Army software. The Pranet was built on the original cut-off Internet and on the programs of the then government. It was guarded by the military, a department called Hybrid Threats or something like that. They got the highest priority programs. They could erase whoever they wanted, and now they have erased themselves. Their remnants still existed in Pranet. Someone had access to them and did a big reset. This is called divine intervention."

"Army. Everywhere I turn, I encounter an army," I growled.

Tom just shrugged. He was nervous, he was going to be late.

"I have to get out. If needed, I'll be in the Kingdom of Swords. I picked out such a busty girl in armor there." He winked at me as if he didn't know that in unofficial porn games all busty women in armor are guys.

"I cleaned your cellular band so that no one would break into it. All you have is a VEP account and unlimited calls wherever you want to call,

" he tossed over his shoulder and left the sanctuary.

I sat down on the table next to Belch, who listened disinterestedly and watched the news at the same time.

"Look, your girl friend." He nudged me with his elbow, and with a snap of his fingers he turned the volume up on the television.

This friend meant reporter Divišova. She was standing on a hovercraft in her decent attire. No wonder, because it was near the wreckage pyramid, where Cyber Messiah was talking.

"More than a hundred thousand people have come for today's sermon, and others are flocking to the nearby streets. Most of the faithful refuse to leave this place. They occupy skyscrapers and other facilities in the area. They think it's a sacred zone. Cyber Messiah called on the interim mayor to lift the assembly ban and immediately ban the malicious enhancement of people with cyberimplants. He also calls for the removal of Pranet and the opening of the city limits. His appeals remain unanswered for the time being."

The reporter looked like she had just discovered a way to make gold from her own shit. Although that was basically how television worked. Fortunately, her face disappeared from the screen and was replaced by an image of a couple in the studio.

"Civil disobedience was also declared by a group called Revolutionary Troops. They, on the other hand, have begun to occupy houses and other points in neighborhoods where rents are low. Pod Lipami Street, not having a good reputation, became the center of the movement. According to Security, these are criminal gangs that also want to take advantage of the situation, but order in the area will soon be restored."

I stared at the footage of a drone flying over a skyscraper covered in red banners with the letter R. It seemed that Aurora had decided to fire the first shot.

Fay entered the closed room, completely naked. It's not a provocation - she used to walk like that a lot. She showed herself like that to the crowd of fans, so she saw no reason to hide from her buddies. She poured the last of moonshine from the bottle and sat cross-legged on the table.

"It's good that the others aren't here. You can imagine what they were doing here while you were playing Lieutenant Columbo," Belch sighed.

"Well, I was just having fun, unfortunately," I grumbled.

Fay turned off the TV with her eyes. Of course, not just by looking, but by means of her improvements. But it was as if she did it with a wink. I think that's why cybernetic sorceresses fascinated people and terrified them so much at the same time.

"Pranet lives in a beautiful world," she said, her implants conjuring a perfect three-dimensional projection of the main interface of the citywide network.

Her mind shifted about the messages generated there, the most popular social networks, discussion forums on porn servers, everything looked as before - only the intrusive CN news module was gone, and the news announced that the city was welcoming the new mayor and looking forward to the elections.

"Pirates?" Belch asked.

I shrugged my shoulders. Pirates were capable of many things, but that was not their style. I think that's what caused Tom to leave. The former rebels must have realized that their five minutes had passed and found a new place in this world.

"More like Mina. It is very possible that the CN has broken off the chain, but Pranet is still in the hands of the corporation. After the break-up of DEZATEG, they shared their influence and competences. The CN originally belonged to VEP, so I suppose

ARKAS or GEZ have the Pranet keys, so that's what it looks like," I thought as I stroked Fay's back.

"What's your plan?" He asked after a moment.

"The beginning and the end of the story lead to the army, or rather to the Blue Campaign. That is why Pajac was one of the first victims of Zodiac. He knew the army backwards and forwards. He was in the war, he must have known something. He disappeared so as not to reveal the secret, just as the military files disappeared. For the same reason, Zodiac had to kill the underground babysitter Merklova to shut her mouth. But I really have no idea what she might have to do with the military. He would kill others later just to keep things moving forward, to bring about what was happening now. But for me it's just smoke and mirrors. This circus is only part of a plan, but if I keep concentrating on it, I will never find Zodiac."

"You won't find him anyway, because you don't know any living man with access to veterans."

"I have to get out of here." I nodded as my agreement.

"From where?" the Pole did not understand.

"From Prague. We both know there is world beyond it. The fact that the city has closed within its borders does not mean that the outside world has ceased to exist. Only it ceased to interest us. After all, there was the Internet and all sorts of things in it."

Belch gave a loud whistle.

"And if it's not on the Internet?"

I shrugged.

"This information must be somewhere. If I've learned something, it's that nothing can really go away. You just must search. I've thought about it, and I think it's the only way. Who knows how many years he planned it, how long did he prepare for it. I run on his pitch, but he mowed the lawn, set up the players and also set the rules. I have to go to a different pitch and I don't care how long I look for him," I explained.

The Pole grimaced and stood up. Without a word, he walked over to the bar, opened a shabby old safe, fumbled in the contents, then threw a military ID at me.

"You didn't tell me you were a colonel." I raised my eyebrows.

"I didn't tell you many things."

"Actually, why did you leave Poland, after all..."

"Pst, there are questions that I have already refused to answer you several times, so don't ask them anymore." He waved his hand in the air and looked at Fay.

"He has a hole in his head, but you have a memory better than the average person. I will give you a set of passwords with which you will get into the Polish intelligence system. If there is internet or something like that, then our repository is there. It parasites on foreign servers and migrates all over the world. The passwords change, but the original ones still work and will lead you to the old passwords," he said, then dictated to Fay several sequences of numbers, letters, and symbols.

He was right. I forgot them before he even finished saying them.

"What's this ID for?" Asked the cybernetic sorceress.

"If you come across the Polish army, show it to them along with the slogan "Boruta". After that they will know that I gave it to you of my own free will," he explained.

"I owe you," I said.

"You are. And not only for those unwashed dishes. Someday you will repay. Or not. That's life." He smiled and shook my hand.

I squeezed it tightly.

* * *

We packed the few things we had and headed outside. I made an appointment with Ivana and discussed my plan with her.

A man can make plans, but the crowd will thwart his plans anyway.

* * *

We barely got dressed when Fay grabbed my arm. Her grip was really strong. I turned to see her scared face.

"The girls are in trouble."

"Sorceresses?"

She shook her head.

"Cyber prostitutes from the Drank Payoff. They sent everyone an SOS signal and a warning," she explained, then just ran outside.

I waved to Belch and followed her.

* * *

The hovercraft Fay had picked up from the garage of my company flat yesterday looked very ancient retro in the daylight. I think that something like this only flew in old series. I was surprised it still worked but yesterday brought me here from the metro and this skill was all we needed.

I tossed Fay's belongings bag behind me and jumped into the passenger seat. As we traveled together, she was driving. It was easier for her, and I didn't have that strange prehistoric urge from internal combustion engine men to prove masculinity by holding the steering wheel. I could sit in the passenger seat, wear a Hello Kitty sweatshirt, fuck Mickey Mouse's ass with a dildo, and that didn't detract from my masculinity at all. I was wearing this particular sweatshirt. I pulled my hood down over my eyes and put on mirrored glasses. While the drone's facial recognition programs could identify me quickly, I felt better being a little cloaked. Over the course of the day, I went from being a Security officer to a search target, made famous by the news, almost like Dirty Lopez. But I didn't really enjoy it.

We flew outside the air corridors. Navigation protested for a moment before Fay fried her with one of her implants, then we flew there by heart where she wanted. However, it had its own navigation, which flawlessly led forward at maximum speed. Along the way, we brushed against two overcrowded garbage truck hovercraft flying from some better neighborhood, and we even knocked down one Security drone. It honked furiously but was fortunately unarmed.

We came too late.

* * *

The place Under the Drank Payoff was besieged by a crowd. And not just any. Given that many of these people wore simple white jackets, it was clear at first glance that they were followers of Cyber Messiah. They looked as if they were fulfilling their sacred duty.

We practically had nowhere to land. There were two hundred people standing in front of the pub, one next to the other. There was a small circle in the middle of which there was clearly something going on.

"Where do we stop?" I asked Fay.

"Nowhere."

"I see, but we have to get there somehow."

She shook her head angrily.

"There's an EMP bubble. I can feel it. It will eliminate not only the hovercraft, but also me," she explained.

"Okay. Bring me down here. I can handle."

I took off my cell wristband and tossed it over the backseat where Fay's bag of things lay. Meanwhile, she circled over the heads of the people standing in a place where the crowd was thinning. I saw a bit of free space and jumped to the ground between a guy in a jacket who was probably passing by and wanted to see what was going on, and a young girl who was smoking a menthol cigarette was listening to the Rainbow Fairy through earrings studded in her ears, and I think she was waiting for someone. She probably didn't know that a few meters away, she would have pulled these screws out properly.

Upon contact with the ground, I focused on shifting the weight of the body to the bionic leg. The knee gave a faint crunch, but it was also reinforced with fake metal alloys, so I managed to land standing with only a slight stab at my hips.

The EMP bubble also had its advantages - I didn't have to hide from sniffing drones. I left the hood on my head but put my glasses in my pocket. I took the first few meters of the way, squeezing deftly between people, but then it got tighter. So I had to put on more confidence and work my way with my elbows. Most people follow a simple mechanism - when they come across someone who seems confident and pretends to know where they are going, and their goal is to get ahead, they just pull away to make room for them. This is the rule of thumb for any crowd. Just like the fact that in the end such someone always comes across a tough guy who won't like it. This one was wearing a DEZATEG coverall and reeked of spirit.

"...why are you pushing?"

"I thought the followers of Cyber Messiah were expressing themselves appropriately," I replied.

I made him a little off balance, but only a little.

He licked his black fringe and frowned. He probably thought.

"I mean, where are you in such a hurry?"

Somewhere in the middle of the crowd, there was a scream. Feminine.

"Sorry, I don't have time right now." I rolled my eyes and when he licked his fringe a second time I kicked him with my knee between his legs.

He howled and fell to the ground.

I left his moans and curses behind me and made my way to the brink of a hurricane unleashed by the crowd.

Fay was right. Cyber hookers were fucked up.

* * *

They weren't looking too good. The EMP bubble hit them well. And not only it. Nine cyber prostitutes were crowded in the center, along with the bartender from Uncle Neny's place. All naked, or they had leftovers of clothes that were torn off by the crowd. Some have seen bloody wounds or fresh bruises. One of the girls was torn from the breast implant, which was now lying bloody on the ground next to the dead gangster. They probably dragged him out of the pub with them. Someone smashed his head with an iron bar or something. The Security apparently cut and run.

"...so righteous our savior that those who defile their bodies with technology are an insult to God and his love."

The words were shouted out by a guy I also knew.

"Hey, what with getting yourself two extra penises is not an insult to God and his love?" I screamed.

His robe was originally completely white, but now from the waist down it was splashed with blood in many places. Several women who looked like security in Cyber Messaiah's sermons were standing around, along with other dudes in straitjackets, but there were also plainclothes men crowding at the side of the crowd. The bloody stains on their clothes proved that they, too, were involved in the lynching. I wonder how many dead bodies they left in the bar. They all had some kind of weapon in their hands - knives, machetes, kitchen cleavers, rods or broken alcohol bottles. Pretty expensive alcohol. Unfortunately, uncle Neny doesn't break their balls for this anymore. Apart from Three penises, women were definitely more sacrilegious than men. One had all her hands bloody and carried a long razor in them. That torn implant was definitely her job. Behind her stood an old sow in a straitjacket, holding in her hand a suitcase disruptor EMP with a former symbol of the Czech army on it. Probably pulled him out of some historic military warehouse, or who knows from where. In any case, the sight of bloodied women did not surprise me at all. Women have always been able to make life hell for other women, that is, those who behaved differently from them. "A woman to a woman is a pig," my grandmother used to say. I mentioned her words a long time ago, when in our course in social anthropology we dealt with the history of circumcision of women in Africa. A nasty practice that women were more demanding to follow than men, especially those who had gone through it themselves.

They turned to me.

I saw the bartender's eyesight.

"Kill me, please let it stop," she said.

I narrowed my eyes and shook my head. I finally pulled the hood off my forehead.

"It's him, the killer. I know him from CN." One of the women pointed at me.

She pointed her hand at me with such vigor that a few drops of blood fell to the ground.

"He's the protector of the devilish trans-pigs. He definitely has implants too. I saw him walking down the street with them. He's one of them," the guy with three penises shouted.

The thugs in the crowd took a step towards me.

* * *

"Stop!" I shouted firmly. It worked.

I mean usually. But not now. The crowd moved. I might be able to fight off a few, but not all. They tasted the blood already. There was only a small difference between mine and the one that ran through Neny's veins - in the content of e-snow and expensive alcohol.

So I shot.

* * *

I chose a target without hesitating even for a moment. Another blood stain appeared on the straitjacket of the guy with three penises. This time the blood was from him. There was a bullet hole in the center of the new stain. Nine millimeters of solid Slovak work went through his heart. If he didn't have two more, he had a few seconds left.

Everyone froze as if they were participating in a children's game of statues.

* * *

I bent down and pulled the gun from the spare leg holster. I looked like an amphetamine-dosed juvenile gangster who wants to impress a thirteen-year-old chick, fresh from breast augmentation surgery, and who knows he has the charisma of a burned-out stove without a gun.

"Cyber Messiah said that whoever fears for his life will lose it..."

The words were spoken by the woman with the razor. After a while she dropped her to the ground as I shot her right in the forehead.

The crowd froze again.

It is actually a very nice phrase. Cyber Messiah stole it from the millions of similar prophets, saviors, and cheap sages who worked before him. I've killed two people and still don't see myself as a murderer. They are the murderers. Moreover, I stood between their thirst for blood and those to whom that blood belonged.

I looked at cybernetic prostitutes. Suddenly they seemed strangely ordinary, miserable, and helpless. Like ordinary women. They took the strength they took from the implants, deprived them of their confidence, beauty and sex appeal. They made ordinary victims of them. I hated people who made other victims.

"Whoever takes a step forward first, I will kill him. And the one who will be standing next to him as well. Just like that, because I like it that way. I still have twenty-eight rounds in my magazines. It is not a small amount at all. Enough for the first twenty-eight people to try to upset me," I said.

I fought myself against screaming, but calm was necessary to keep the face of a cold assassin. I had to control the space and minds of dozens of people around me. In fact, I wanted to shoot another bastard with blood on his hands. Great willingness! I was still staring at what they had done to the girls and Neny. True, Neny was a gangster, but he also had his honor. And those slippery followers of the guy they knew nothing about a month ago had none.

"Is it clear? The first to take a step towards me will die. I do not care. I am a murderer. You've seen it on TV. So step back, and anything that is in your hands that is not your dick, throw it to the ground immediately!" I shouted and turned on my own axis, holding two guns in my hands.

As a child, I believed that when I stood in front of the mirror at midnight and said: "Božena Němcová", a demonic succubus would reveal to me, who wrote the most terrible thing in the history of Czech literature, a novel titled Granunia, and would devour my soul. And now it looked like if I said the word "television" aloud, reporter Divišová would appear.

* * *

Either the military EMP disruptor was timed or not working properly. Behind my back, I heard the buzzing of the information drone with the CN logo on which someone had sprayed on it: "We are the only ones telling you the truth." I turned carefully and a few dozen meters away saw the CN hovercraft. They must have been waiting in a safe place for the bubble to disappear. I looked through the crowd at the CN screen and saw my back and the view of the corpse.

"Messiah said, do not be afraid of..."

She was one of the women in the bloody straitjacket.

I shot her.

The crowd began to hum. Some withdrew, but of course the drone was noticed by the others. It wasn't good. Television is a powerful medium. I remember it from the time when, in addition to stupid series, it was broadcasting real news, just like it wanted to do now. The possibility of a human being in the spotlight of television prompted him to do nonsensical things.

And to the pointless courage.

Sun Tzu said, "All wars are based on deception. Same as yours. Don't die for bullshit."

I threatened with my gun the group of women who were talking in whispers. Sun Tzu also said that the encircled enemy should be given an escape route. Not that I believe that I am holding the crowd under siege, but whoever is up against the wall must be given the opportunity to come out alive and well. Me and this crowd needed this opportunity.

"I'm taking this little group of women and we'll get out of your way. You," I pointed to the guy in the straitjacket who was standing in the place where the crowd seemed rarest, "make a way for us. You have half a minute to do so or I'll shoot you," I added when he realized I was talking to him.

It is remarkable how effective a death threat is.

Boom!

* * *

This time I didn't kill anyone. Maybe I should, but this girl wasn't wearing bloody rags. She was picking on that fucking EMP disruptor. The bullet bounced off it and landed on the ground without hurting anyone.

"Drop it here, you cow." I threatened her with my gun.

For a moment she looked confused, as if she expected someone to stand up for her, but I think her faith was defeated by her self-preservation instinct. I was in such a state that I personally would prefer to work together as well. I opened the device and fired three missiles at it.

Meanwhile, the guy prepared the way for us, like Moses, for the Jews escaping from Egyptian captivity. The prostitutes started to get up, and the ones who had more strength helped the rest. Only now did I notice that some of their hands were broken, and one even had an open fracture.

But there was one thing in all that gave hope - their implants gradually began to reset. It was easy to recognize. Some of the rage began to glow dimly, others gained much more energy and strength. Even the one with a piece of bone sticking out of her leg rose to her feet.

* * *

They walked along a prepared corridor, and I protected them from the back. The crowd didn't close behind me like the sea, but people started arguing about something fiercely. I think that is the usual saying in such situations, "Someone stop him, let's remember what Cyber Messiah said" and then, "Keep him yourself when you are so wise." I liked the people who pronounced the second sentence best.

My hands were sweating. I wasn't a cold killer. I felt my whole body shaking - you could see my adrenaline dropping out. Fortunately, we moved away from the crowd. About fifty meters from the last barrier of the bodies of Cyber Messiah's followers, I felt a slight tingling sensation. This turned out to be incredibly calming.

"Thank you," came the bartender's voice from behind me.

I turned to her. She was flickering slightly, as I had seen from Fay before. I nodded and smiled at her. A few more steps and we reached Under the Drank Payoff bar. It had broken windows and broken doors. Next to them was the corpse of someone from security, and next to...

"Damn it," I gasped.

"She was defending herself. In one of those freaks she got an erection and..." the bartender explained.

I remember that girl from the bar. She was one of Uncle Neny's favorite prostitutes. Half Asian with long black hair. Now she was lying naked, legs unfolded, and you could see shards of glass from the broken windows they had hammered into her. It was as if the shards had nailed her to the ground. But it was just that. Ordinary glass would not pierce smart asphalt. But her body deprived of the protection and magic of technology - yes.

320

The CN drone almost flew in front of my face. I swung at it like a fly, but he calmly circled me and filmed us from behind. The crowd followed us cautiously. At the same time, they were watching on the ubiquitous screens.

"How many people have you killed, Mr. Vachten? Is that dead work of yours too?" Said the reporter Divišová's voice, amplified by the loudspeaker.

Her hovercraft dropped about ten meters from us. She was sitting there with two men. One seemed to be driving, and the other was constantly adjusting her makeup. Today she was wearing a blue coverall, which made her look a bit like an auto repair shop mechanic disassembling stolen cars. She was smiling at me through the bulletproof glass of the transmissive hovercraft.

I tried to ignore her. I took a deep breath. I needed to think about it, but she wouldn't let me.

"Mr. Vachten, an arrest warrant has been issued for you. Will you fight the Security? Do you want to make a statement?"

I think she was making fun of me. The escapade with the dead Karel Adam turned her into an ultra-star overnight. Not even Dirty Lopez had experienced anything like this, and even older women had tattooed him on their chests. It was for this reason that his face was somewhat elongated in those images. Divišova must have known I was not a killer, but I was her case and hot topic, and she was going to get the most out of it.

"Fuck you media bitch," I spat.

But when I finally chose to ignore her, someone else distracted her from me.

* * *

I heard impact, the crackle of bent sheets and the clink of broken glass. I turned just in time to see the CN vehicle drop to the ground, pushed by a Fairy Fay hovercraft.

* * *

Hovercraft had systems that prevented them from hitting themselves or hitting a human. But it was an old hovercraft that Dejčer rode in as a boy. In addition to its bizarre design, it also had the advantage of playing Olga Hepnarova[4] with it.

* * *

The broadcast vehicle crashed to the ground, laying to its side. And as he slowly turned, Divišová jumped out of him, along with her little asses. Then Fairy Fay lifted our ride a few meters higher and hit the TV car with all her power. It flattened on the road before a second hovercraft hit it.

Cyber prostitutes clung to the wall, while confused TV workers tried to pick themselves up from the ground. Of course, it was all filmed by the CN drone kept at a safe distance. Fay literally flew out of the hovercraft and in a few hard strides ran to the reporter, who had a slightly chafed face.

"As you can see, independent journalists were attacked..."

It is admirable that she continued to hold on to her role. But she fell out of it the moment the cybersorceress grabbed her by the suit by her throat and hit her using head.

Divišová started screaming. Her nose turned into a rubber ball, droplets of blood dripping from it on successive punches. One of the staff members wanted to come to her aid, but it was enough to show him the xtreme barrel for him to change his mind and devote himself to examining the road surface within a radius of one square meter.

"Please, please, it hurts," the reporter screamed as the sorceress frantically served her blow after blow.

"Fay," I said carefully.

She turned towards me and I showed her the CN drone stuffed with cameras. What was happening with Divišova was watched by the whole city. And what else.

Fay took a deep breath and snarled. With her left hand she was still holding her overalls and her right hand was gripping her hair to make it easier to drag her to the dead prostitute.

"It's not a fucking show, bitch. She's an innocent dead girl who was just trying to survive in this fucking city!" She screamed and tossed the reporter at the feet of the dead body.

"You fucking understand that? What you are looking at is not a show. They are dead people. Dead. Just because someone didn't like what they were doing. Can you stop being such dicks?!" She roared towards the drone while tears and blood dripped from Divišova's nose and from the scratches on her face.

"Stop broadcasting. Make that drone disappear or I'll kill her," I stated and pulled the trigger.

* * *

Divišová turned, terrified, towards the drone. She stared at him with wide eyes and her mouth whispered, "Please."

She wasn't talking to me, but to the one who was controlling the drone and managing the broadcast from the street to screens and projectors all over the city.

"Please," she whispered a little louder.

"It used to be said: the show must go on. They don't care about you. They want me to kill you. Understand? You don't mean anything. A week ago, you were broadcasting only lies. Now you re-broadcast it, just imagine it's true. But the truth is so complex that you can't show it with a camera, one shot, one word. The truth is a complicated girl," I said a little to Divišová and a little to everyone who looked at it.

Fay threw it to the ground and I carefully released the trigger and secured the gun.

"We have to go. Most of the girls need medical attention," I said, ignoring the TV reporter and the drone.

Rebels

Bearing in mind that our hovercraft, after a collision with a CN transmission vehicle, could only serve as a reinforcement of the pyramid for Cyber Messiah's sermons, we left it to its own fate. From the trunk, all I took was a bag with clothes, spare weapons and magazines. What's more, thanks to digital prostitutes, our trip has grown so much that even with the best intentions, not all of us would fit there.

I gave one gun to each one that could stand on its own and hold the gun. As expected, there was no need to explain how to use the gun. Most of the girls made their way to their destiny in a complicated way and were not able to experience growing up in an environment full of love and security.

We ran down an empty street. It was a strange feeling. Something I have never experienced before in Prague.

Fay threw my cell band at me and helped the most cruelly scarred girl.

I tried calling Tom but he didn't answer. I didn't even find it in the agreed place - in a virtual game. But it came from the Security. First, a spy drone flew over our heads, and then one of the girls alerted about a flying pair of hovercraft with the Security logo. Due to the fact that the traffic in the area shifted to the higher air corridors, it was easily recognizable from a distance.

"Over there!" I pointed to a Vietnamese restaurant on the ground floor.

It was closed, but with two kicks on the door, I changed the opening hours.

* * *

As soon as we burst in, the door and shop window were showered with bullets from a rotary machine gun.

* * *

Fortunately, we didn't find anyone inside. We ran through the kitchen to a warehouse full of canned and dry pasta from the DEZATEG labs and made our way to the next door. I kicked it and we ended up in a neighboring place. This time we were welcomed by an interior full of clothes, with a young girl with red hair and a shotgun in her hand.

"These shirts are really expensive," she snapped and pointed at my face.

* * *

I had a gun in my hand as well as five out of ten girls. We aimed at each other. You could say there was a stalemate if you thought about what a cartridge from that shotgun could do to his face.

* * *

I looked around the store. The t-shirts featured humorous illustrations with references to the retro pop culture that was now hot. Various variations on the Rainbow Fairy theme dominated, but also Hello Kitty. The sweatshirt I was wearing looked the same. Therefore, probably the girl came to the logical conclusion that I am a fan of her goods and I came to rob.

"It's beautiful here," I remarked to the point.

It was beautiful.

"It's closed now," she said.

Her hands were shaking a little. Who knows how many years this weapon has been handed over from seller to seller and whether anyone thought to lubricate it.

"We were just passing by," I explained.

"Passin... what?"

"We have the Security and religious fanatics on our backs who want to kill us. Could we go this way?" Fay asked.

The saleswoman finally stopped looking at me and looked at the wounded women.

"Oh fuck," she said understandingly, and lowered her gun.

* * *

We walked through the side entrance to the second street. I tried to call Ivana but she didn't answer either. We had to get lost, and in this city, the metro is the best. The nearest station was less than half a kilometer away. Old, good Legionářská. Old and good because it was equipped with three levels, and thus it was possible to change lines to different lines.

The saleswoman led us along the corridor to the barred balcony overlooking the street. He was two meters above the ground, it was enough to jump off it.

"We use it to unload the goods," she explained as she opened the bars for us.

I jumped onto the street and helped others safely descend, although such a jump would probably not hurt them anymore. We ran across the street without complications, and finally found ourselves under the protection of the pillars bearing the S-line on top of them. This area had a somewhat old-fashioned atmosphere for me. In addition to a few restaurants in the neighborhood, there were mainly skyscrapers with premises for rent. Ordinary people lived here. People who started families raised children who studied at a virtual school until noon, and in the afternoon, they walked in relatively safe streets where they could run freely, not just on an electric treadmill. In one side alley we even passed a football goal painted on the wall. But now, apart from the garbage cans that have not been taken out for two days, and whose displays have been calling in vain for regular emptying, we have not seen anyone here. This only changed at the entrance to the subway. There was a group standing there discussing something fiercely. Fortunately, they were so passionate that they didn't even notice us at first.

We ran the last section to the subway with all our strength. A Safety hovercraft appeared between the skyscrapers, rotating machine guns exposed at the sides.

Before TV was off the chain, they would just have massacred us. They would have done it without hesitation. While the blood, guts and dreams would be drained from us and the gathered people, the eighth episode of The Doctor from the 150th floor would be on the CN. But before the others managed to take the appropriate shooting position, out of breath, we reached the subway vestibule, and behind us was a tail in the form of two CN drones, which the boys in the combat hovercraft, fortunately, noticed in time. About twenty citizens stood there - normal inhabitants of Prague. Some in work clothes, others dressed up for a party. One girl, about a fifteen-year-old girl dressed as an Easter bunny, argued with two older bellies about the price of double anal. We blended in with the human crowd, and before we broke through, I understood what was going on.

They were afraid.

For the first time since proclaiming an independent, free city of Prague, isolated from the rest of the world, they were afraid to do something.

"After all, television is good for something," Fay said, trying to catch her breath.

My instincts said, "Get out before they shoot." There was something fascinating about this situation.

"Rita can't make it," the bartender from the Under the Drank Payoff interrupted my thoughts.

She meant the girl who had the implant removed. She was bleeding and looked very pale. Her eyes grew dim. It wasn't looking good.

"Hey dick. Get on the subway," said Tom.

Classic. When someone starts talking to me, ten more people join him.

* * *

"I need..."

"I know. I've seen everything. We're also screwed. I had to go. The base is in disarray. We stand with Bacon at the Hřibova station. He will help you."

And that's all. I mean, not everything, because people in the vestibule started staring at us, and then someone blew up the Security hovercraft.

* * *

A grenade hit ii and fired a ping-pong ball like a racket. Only the remains of the hovercraft flew towards the pillars of the S-meter and instead of bouncing off them, they immediately fell to the ground.

Another hovercraft, about half a kilometer away, was on the conscience of the attack. It was the Ovčáček 2 manual rocket launcher. It was used during the war. It was named after a monk from the times of the republic. I've never seen this stuff in town. I didn't have to think too long about who it might be.

"We need to get to the metro," I said.

"It's not working."

"What?" I turned to the bunny.

Her clients realized that really bad things were happening around them, and immediately felt like not having sex. They were now running in the opposite direction of where the hovercraft had exploded. And not only them. Most of the debaters stopped chattering and, driven by their self-preservation instinct, went to their homes.

"They closed that line. About three hours ago. Because of some bandits who are robbing the Pod Lipami skyscrapers," the girl explained, looking at us and the burning Security hovercraft.

"Thanks. And you run, maybe you will catch up with these guys yet." I let her go.

"How will we deal with them?" Fay asked desperately.

This question had to be answered quickly.

* * *

"Don't fight if your position is not favorable," I replied, grabbing the injured prostitute in my arms, and started down the stairs.

The Prague metro was never closed. As far as I can remember, it was still driving, bustling with life all the time. It didn't even have a door or gate to lock. The fact that they stopped traffic at those stations and turned off the lights meant nothing. It was enough to run down a few steps to see people with nowhere else to go, which is why they were sitting here. They sat everywhere. And they stank. More than usual. This was due to the limited air flow. Since the trains stopped running and the lights and air conditioning were turned off, the air had grown more dense than the atmosphere at a home party when the organizer's mother suddenly bumps into her.

In addition to the people at the station, there was also a train. It had the door open and dozens of people were lying and sitting inside. Some lived there on a daily basis, but it was clear that many did not voluntarily end up here. Religious riots raged outside, and they just didn't get home. In addition to the light coming to us from the outside world, the entire space was also illuminated by displays of cellular bands.

"We have to follow the rails. It's about five kilometers to Hřibovka," I explained to the cyber prostitutes.

"She won't survive this," the bartender said, looking at the girl who was moaning softly in my arms.

I stopped on the platform next to a group of seated workers, who did not spoil the good mood by the failure of the metro, reinforced by cheap schnapps.

"I don't think we are either," Fay pointed to the vestibule.

Six masked men appeared there with the rays of the sun on their backs. They were holding Polish machineguns, but even without them I knew what was squeaking in the grass.

I ran to the metro control cabin. Although it operated automatically, the control cabin had enough space for regular maintenance. It basically contained the good old control panel, although most of it was taken up by a large touchscreen.

"If there was electricity," I muttered.

"There's no need. It is equipped with batteries that allow the train to travel to the nearest station in the event of a power failure."

Fay surprised me with this knowledge.

"One of my mother's guys worked on the metro. As a girl, I secretly rode in these," she explained and put her hands to the door.

It sparkled but didn't even flinch.

She turned to the other cybernetic prostitutes and a strange shiver ran down my spine. I think they were just getting along telepathically through the implants.

Fay, the bartender, and another woman held hands, and as soon as the cyber sorceress touched the door, it opened.

A gunshot rocked the metro.

* * *

The bullet brushed against the door and hissed into the tunnel somewhere. But the impact shook the entire station. People started screaming, falling to the ground, some jumping straight onto the tracks. Others fell into the carriages of the abandoned train and went under the seats where some people were already sleeping.

Fay and the bartender jumped into the control booth and I carried the wounded woman to the first car. I put her on the ground and entrusted her to the care of others. I unlocked the gun and was about to go off-guard when the car flashed its lights and the door closed.

"Dear Travelers, the train to Longing Station is just leaving, tudududu," Fay's voice echoed through the speakers.

This last sound was probably meant to simulate an old train honking, but that's just my guess. Rather, it sounded as if the sorceress had accidentally sat down on a hedgehog.

The train started and stopped a second later. Those who did not sit or lay down fell together. I readied the gun again, but the roster regained power and plunged into the tunnel.

* * *

Running the train also enabled CN transmission in the side projections. At the bottom, an information strip scrolled with a list of people who had died in the streets. The destroyed Security hovercraft was displayed in the background. After a while, CN switched to Mina's press conference. She changed her appearance. Now she was wearing a bulletproof vest and was surrounded by a group of duffers in combat suits. Shots from the square in front of the government skyscraper appeared instead of the information frame. Fully armed boys and girls hopped into the armored hovercraft, wielding automatons. Someone sprayed the Safety logo on all hovercraft, but so many people never had Safety. Corporations have had to repaint their small private armies. ARKAS and GEZ stood behind Mina. I guessed that the heirs of Petlán, by dividing his billions, figured out whose side it was worth standing on, and the tough guys from PRAGUETECH had also stuck the Security logo on themselves. Nobody could oppose it. No one. Now all that mattered was how many people Mina wanted to massacre to regain power after decades of patient waiting.

"Our units are still working on the closure of the area around the central skyscraper of the VEP company, which was banned, on the basis of clear evidence, for Charlotte Dejčerova's involvement in a premeditated murder. I hope Miss Dejčerová will put herself in the hands of the Security, which will ease the tension. Soon, the situation with the so-called rebel zone in the Pod Lipami region will also be resolved. Order will be restored in the whole city soon," Mina thundered, and those around them were applauding enthusiastically. But she wasn't talking to them. She was talking to the cameras. She was talking to people.

"Is it true that security officials had to withdraw from this area after the so-called revolutionaries defeated them in fighting in the houses and on the streets?"

The voice belonged to a young CN reporter who wore a perfectly fitted beige jacket. He looked a bit moronic, but he didn't flinch under Mina's stern gaze.

"The Security is working to restore order, and reinforcements are on the way," she replied.

"Supposedly you are meeting today with a religious leader known as Cyber Messiah?" - the reporter asked another question, but at this point the line-up stopped and immediately turned off. Right after all the doors opened.

* * *

The passengers we practically abducted began to peek outside curiously. There were a huge number of people at the station. And many of them aimed their weapons at us.

* * *

I cursed and looked around. The citizens with the guns looked quite ordinary. No special equipment, just shotguns, pistols or older automatic guns. Only a few wore vests with the Security logo, but they were certainly not safe.

"Everyone to the floor!" A woman's voice came from the archaic megaphone.

He reminded me of someone.

"Hey, my wife is dying. Can this floor be put off until later?" I said, hands above my head.

"Shall I shoot him, Colonel?" The man in his fifties turned to Lucka.

The thirteen-year-old changed the tablecloth skirt for long pants and a luxurious pseudo-leather jacket. Considering she wore three gold watches, about ten rings, and four cellular bands, I guessed the revolution had begun to reward her children.

"Look, the TV star is back," she laughed and motioned to her men to leave us.

* * *

She wasn't the only person I knew here. The entire Hřibov station was located in the back of the rebel zone, so after the battles with the Security it became a kind of a field hospital. And his central figure was none other than Dr. Bacon.

He cut an ulcer out of my ass several times. Unfortunately, not only figuratively. Back in the time of the Czech Republic, he was briefly the minister of health, who became famous for his statement, in which he stated that when the money for heating hospitals runs out, the staff will manage somehow, for example by discovering the quilts of patients with the highest temperature. If I am not mistaken, he was serious. After the separation of Prague from the collapsing state, he disappeared into the socio-political underground and hid in a pirate base.

As always when he operated, he had a cigarette in his mouth. He once explained to me that cigarette ash is perfectly disinfected by heat, so even if it falls on an open wound, nothing will happen - and it calms him down, which is beneficial for patients. He was just sewing up a wound on the head of a boy about twelve who was clutching an automatic rifle that was only a few centimeters smaller than he was.

"Doctor, I have an emergency here."

* * *

"Are you fucking them all?" Bacon asked me greeting me, putting on the last seam.

"No, just this one and this, this and sometimes that one," I replied.

The girls frowned slightly, but I think they realized this is exactly the crap type of joke some guys like."

"She's dying." I showed the woman in my arms.

"Shooting?"

I shook my head.

"They cut out her implant. Cybernetic prostitute," I explained, placing her on the bloody plastic rectangle that served as the operating table.

Bacon spat the rest of his cigarette, pulled a second one out with a bloody hand of his pocket and snapped a lighter.

"I'm in, but I will need assistance." He winked rather lasciviously at the half-naked bartender.

She shrugged and rushed to help him.

The other girls sat around.

Finally, I was able to get a good look around the station. At one end the arms dealers organized, while most of those who found refuge here just sat and waited to see what happened next. So is Tom, who is perched on some plastic barrel. As I got closer, I noticed the logo of a famous brand that produces luxury lingerie for the rich. Immediately I thought I probably knew who might be wearing it now.

"They locked Hynek," he announced, absorbed in the virtual world of the computer game.

* * *

Mina wasn't stupid. She used a group of archaic hackers, and then simply shut them up for what they did decades ago during the Corporate Council overthrow. She knew pirates would not strike a deal with corporations. Bacon reportedly left their hideout a few days ago when he chose to avoid the upcoming political adventures, and Tom stayed because of me, so he only arrived after their old base was taken over by the ARKAS tough guys.

"Who's playing with fire..." I shrugged.

"And who says this. You worked for Mina too," said Tom.

And he was right. Only now Mina was following me like a rat after the remnant of a Christmas dog.

"Here." The last free pirate elbowed me and handed me a flask.

"Bison grass vodka?" I sniffed.

"I blew it on the Pole as he stared at the tits of the trans whores," he chuckled, and then said to Fay, "No offense."

Fay just rolled her eyes.

"What are you doing now?" I asked.

"Bacon is playing Hawkeye Pierce, so I'll wait until it's finished and then we'll hide somewhere," he replied.

I had no idea who he was talking about, but Tom was from the old school. Sometimes he used comparisons and phrases from the last century.

"Security! Quickly, get to your seats!" Someone shouted from the entrance.

I waved at Tom and we ran in that direction.

* * *

About twenty armed men rose. They were led by Lucka, who still had the gun I gave her. We broke through between the wounded and the resting people and went out into the street. The skyscraper was burning right in front of us. It wasn't just one window or a floor - black smoke was coming from the middle parts of the skyscraper. Shooting sounds were heard from the surrounding buildings. The streets were lined with barricades made of discarded furniture, hovercraft and whatever was at hand, reinforced with PVC cubes that were once used as curbs. One of them was flown with a red flag with the letter R.

I grabbed Lucka's arm. I mean, Colonel Lucka. I suspected everyone was a colonel or a general with them.

"Thousands of well-armed and trained soldiers, equipped with the latest killing equipment, are rushing straight at you. None of you will survive."

I practically yelled at her.

Everyone around were irritated.

At this point, for some strange reason, she was in command of not only teenage street children, but also some adult guys and two women reaching their sixties. One tied a handkerchief around her head and drew two black warlike lines under her eyes. Now they were torn by mixed feelings that it was probably not fair for an aging man to shout at a twelve-year-old girl.

"It's our city. We know every corner, every hole. We will resist as long as they do not accept our demands," she replied. Her eyes sparkled.

"Demands?"

"Yes, Aurora made ten demands of the revolutionaries to negotiate with the usurper."

"She means your ex-boss. "Fay winked at me playfully.

"What demands?" I did not understand.

"Free healthcare, better working conditions for all corporations, access to clean water, sharing..."

"They'll kill you all," I interrupted her.

Only now I noticed that Lucka has blue eyes. She opened them unnaturally wide.

"We could have ended up worse," she said.

"How worse?" I did not understand.

"Do nothing. Vegetate like sewermen and wait for the mythical Ascendant to bring us to light and give us food and clean water. We don't want this. Aurora believes..."

I didn't listen to her anymore.

Faith. That was it. Everyone believed in something and followed it, even if they were executed. Faith gave people the meaning of existence, although it also often took it away. I didn't believe in anything. Perhaps only that I will get my tormentor. But he got lost in the haze of whirling events. They didn't understand it. Everything was wrong from the beginning. They closed the city and built a beautiful utopia in it. It doesn't matter how much you tell everyone that they are doing well, that they are leading a wonderful life. Eventually, something in them will begin to crave what is out of reach. It was not the fault of the sorceresses or Cyber Messiah. The blame was to blame people's heads. Goddamn people. Only problems with them.

Boom!

A rocket from a Security armored hovercraft exploded nearby.

Fortunately, cavalry arrived shortly after. For the first time in my life on time. And from its speakers we heard:

I am a rainbow fairy

And who am I?

I have the sun in your gaze

* * *

The Security vehicle, which had attacked several rebels, was struck by a volley from a hovercraft's rotary machine gun... yes, painted in the colors of the rainbow. Immediately afterwards, two rockets fired at him and killed him. At this point, rebels from barricades and surrounding houses began firing at the rainbow battleship.

"Tell them to stop, this is help!" I shouted to Lucka.

She understood and issued a series of orders to one of her cyberbands. She was doing pretty well.

The rebels focused again on shelling Security's hovercraft. But they weren't the only problem. Behind them came units of modernly equipped and armed to the teeth soldiers, and combat and spy drones flew over their heads.

I experienced it during the war in Ostrava, which turned into one huge battlefield filled with death. Fighting in the city was the worst and most difficult thing that could happen. Maybe Lucka was right about those holes and corners where they would hide in order to survive. When the city turns to ruin, drones and good machine guns cease to matter, and a person only dreams of surviving for a week in a concrete hideout. Drink your piss, shit your pants and wait for the shit to harden so that it can be easily scraped off and used as kindling. Persist until the enemy weakens, loses their vigilance, changes position - and then shove a bullet in his back. But this was based on the assumption that Prague would be left as rubble. Or at least from this part of town.

"Prepare to transport the girl and anyone who doesn't want to stay here and die," I said to Fay and ran to the barricades.

* * *

This time I didn't call Ivana, she spoke up herself.

"The eagle is about to land."

"Who?"

"Eagle."

"Well, such a coded message that I'm here," she explained.

"The military doesn't say that," I replied.

"I saw it in the movie," she said.

"If it was a cartoon, that would explain a lot," I muttered, gasping for breath.

We were walking with a group of Lucka's towards the barricades, and bullets were whistling over our heads, which the attackers fired at people defending their positions. They didn't have to save on ammunition - unlike the rebels - and they just pounded as much as they could. In addition, they were supported by drones and hovercraft from above.

"What exactly is an eagle?" I asked after a while, moving to the barricade.

Bullets pounded on the top of it.

"This," she replied, and at that moment hundreds of bullets rained down from the sky.

Windows in the high-rise buildings that had survived the first phase of the fighting exploded, probably for a good two kilometers. The missiles hit not only hovercraft, but most of all Security drones. For a moment, a fire of hell broke loose over our heads. It came from five rainbow hovercraft. Then the rotary machine guns began to mow the street. I climbed the barricade and watched as boys and girls with armbands and the Security logo fell to the ground looking for shelter, others disappeared into skyscrapers. But they still responded with fire. One of the propeller vehicles was hit by drone fire and several projectiles. After a while, it fell and exploded. Since it was all in the middle of the main avenue, the fire and smoke created a barrier to potential reinforcements.

"Who is this?" Lucka asked.

While others tried to blend in with the street, she climbed upstairs with me.

"Eagle."

"What?"

"The eagle has landed."

"What?"

"Kind of allies," I finally explained, then grabbed her head from behind and focused her gaze on one of the hovercraft. Its owner will not fly away anymore, because the shells have made a colander from the roof to drain the pasta.

Behind him crouched one of the armed men who placed a missile launcher on his shoulder. The second was just arming the launcher with a new rocket.

"Hey, everyone to me!" She screamed, and I started firing both guns at the rocket launchers at once.

The others joined me.

They took a few bullets, but the bastards were wearing bulletproof suits.

Someone from across the street hit the second rainbow hovercraft. It exploded just above the ground.

"Eagles, get out of here!" I shouted to the cellular band.

Ivana didn't answer, but the last three fired a burst in the direction where those who had taken out their buddy were shooting.

I threw away two magazines and loaded spare ones. It's good that we cleaned this VEP squad.

"They're aiming at us!" Cried the twelve-year-old and her unit scrambled back over the barricade as she started firing where I was.

I fired both magazines at the same time again. One of the bullets passed to the safety guard through the gap between the vest and the helmet. The dude fell on his partner and at that moment he activated the launcher. The missile hissed almost vertically into the air, where it searched in vain for its target.

"I hit him quite well," Lucka smiled.

I looked at her, at her enthusiasm and at the delighted glances of her companions.

"Well done, Colonel," I commended her, then saw the missile spin and fly back after a few hundred yards of fruitless flight up.

"Oh, fuck." I ruthlessly grabbed the girl by the hair and threw her off the barricade. Then I rolled over behind her.

* * *

Poof!

The missile exploded about ten meters in front of the barricade. The shockwave threw the entire barrier a good two meters. Some PVC cubes flew out as if thrown by experienced pavers who had come through the tunnel of time to the future. Only smoke and dust everywhere. I was lying on top of the girl I instinctively protected with my body, and a few pieces of fortification hit me so hard it took my breath away. I tried to gasp, coughing from the smoke, which I inhaled greedily into my lungs. I felt dizzy and heard a whistle in my ears. Sure, it's always better than the Rainbow Fairy, but I still prefer the buzzing of the electronic bees that replaced the living ones in Prague twenty years ago.

"Hey, get up. She is twelve years old," someone was shaking me.

I rubbed my eyes and saw Fay.

"Twelve? This is ok." I spat the dust and rolled to the ground.

Lucka only had a scar on her forehead that was bleeding slightly. But it made her look more colonel-like now.

I got up and ran to the subway while she sent her unit back to the barricade.

* * *

Foretellers in combat suits flew out of the hovercraft. I knew two of them. They replaced flamethrowers with rotary machine guns. Together with the others, they formed a fairly decent unit to patrol the area. Fortunately, the nearby shooting was weakening.

"Thank you," I said to Ivana.

She stood among the hovercraft in tight-fitting black pants and chunky boots of the same color. A VEP CZ 06 pistol was hidden under an unbuttoned, dark green jacket in a holster under the armpit.

"They're sisters," she replied. "Trans whores. We're kind of a sister community of cyber whores," she explained as she became aware of my dull gaze, partly due to the sharp whistling in her ears.

"We can take twenty men," Fay said, and made sure, looking at the other three hovercraft.

The sorceress ran into the subway with three women in combat suits with the VEP logo. To my surprise, neither of them had wings.

"Mina said on TV you were besieged by her," I said.

"Mina can only talk." She waved her hand.

"Although the VEP-tower looks like a pimped out palace, Václav Dejčer once equipped it with an arsenal that could raze this whole city to the ground. It was he who read to me The Art of War, and as Master Sun Tzu said: 'The Art of War teaches us not to hope that the enemy will not come, but to rely on the fact that we are ready to welcome him; not to hope that it will not attack, but to rely on that we have made our positions impossible to conquer'. After the first drones downed, they simply withdrew and now want to negotiate. They have bigger problems here." She nodded towards the barricades. I would not agree with her here - the people behind the barricades had more problems.

Fay returned shortly after, carrying an injured prostitute. Bacon took good care of her. She was dozing, but that was probably because he had injected her with something. The bartender followed, leading the rest of her chiquitas along with some children and two young girls.

"Where are Tom and Bacon?" I asked.

"They stay here. They say it's the best thing they can do," Fay replied.

More women and children followed her.

"Only twenty. More people won't fit there," Ivana said firmly.

"Twenty-one," I said, and ran to the barricades.

* * *

"I can take you to a safe place. Now," I said to Lucka.

She tied a pair of black panties around her forehead, which she probably wore in her pockets. Beneath her feet were still packages from a luxury store that had been looted by the rebels.

"And why?" She asked, continuing to load the 9mm rounds into the Slovak xtreme's magazine.

"You're twelve."

"Do you hear those shots?" She pointed with a half-empty magazine at the opposite skyscraper, part of which was on fire. Its glass windows and heliports were fired into the streets, where Security was regrouping. "There are even ten-year-old boys. Born on the street, battered more than those little guys of yours, and they're fearless. Will you take them too?"

I shook my head negatively.

"Not enough space."

"That's the problem, man. There will never be enough space for everyone. I'm staying here," she said firmly, then looked at the cellular band. "Caesar is calling," she added, and I no longer existed for her.

Ivana

The foretellers, along with the cyber prostitutes and the children Fay had picked up from the subway, set off in the hovercraft towards the VEP-tower, and the only three of us were left - me, the sorceress, and Ivana. The shooting gained momentum again, so we went as far from Hřibovka as possible without hesitation. Here revolutionists, instead of fighting, merrily robbed.

We walked only three kilometers and, instead of shooting to the death, we encountered only hordes of people who did not attack the Security, but shops, especially those with food, and also tried to get to the highest possible floors in high-rise buildings. They didn't do that well, since most buildings had very strong security locks every ten floors. The top floors could not be reached on foot or by elevators. They were separate parts standing in other blocks, to which residents could only get through using hovercraft. From the thirtieth floor up, people led a normal life, while the revolution raged beneath them. Although it did not seem like a revolution.

We stumbled upon people who managed to break into a water store and now drank greedily - perhaps for the first time in their lives - pure mineral water. They looked drunk more than if they had plundered Nikka's 150-year-old whiskey store.

Fighting came from all sides. We didn't even go two kilometers when we came across groups of rebels and attackers. But we had something that was more important to this city than weapons - economic resources. At least now. One of the buildings belonging to the VEP was in the area occupied by the rebels. The first ten floors here had windows and doors protected by armored roller shutters and shutters. Fortunately, Ivana's miraculous armband led us inside and even sent a note to security in time so we wouldn't be shot at the entrance. So we rode to the 50th floor with the VIP elevator in the form of a capsule, there we appropriated one of the company's hovercraft and this way we got out of the clash area. We flew quite high, avoiding large communication junctions. Nevertheless, I had the feeling that someone was watching us all the time. But maybe it's the result of the stress I experienced in the last few hours?

A few kilometers away, everything seemed to be just a bad dream. The air corridors on all levels were crowded with properly moving hovercraft, thousands of people swarmed beneath us, and the S and N lines were hissing happily by subways. Only CN screens and projections showed that there was a shooting just a few kilometers away. In contrast to the rest of the city, it looked like it wasn't about the news, but some action series.

Suddenly the news changed.

"Stop!" I forced Ivana as we flew by the huge screen where Mina was greeting Cyber Messiah.

It was like some old country visit abroad - red carpet, smiles, a crowd of nervous people around, and among them a strange guy in a simple robe.

"The mayor today received a respected religious leader known as Cyber Messiah, who agreed with her that the situation in the city needed to be stabilized. He also promised to support her efforts to eliminate criminal elements in the streets and bring the CEO of VEP to justice. The entire company has already been banned by a decree, and its activities will be taken over by other companies that are part of the Corporation Council. After the meeting, the mayor announced that gatherings outside the zone where criminal elements are rampant are allowed. At the request of Cyber Messiah, any electronic enhancement of the human body was also prohibited. Anyone who fails to remove unmedicated implants within a month will be interned and their operations performed under the law."

The presenter who read the news spoke in a professional, calm voice, as if he was presenting the weather forecast for the next weekend.

"Old whore. She hosted me at her home not long ago," Fay snorted.

"She's prevaricating. She is afraid of him and concedes. There is nothing strange about this. She's a... politician," I said the word reluctantly.

I thought that someone had to lead people, but for the most part, it turned out that those who wanted to lead also had many hidden intentions that were not entirely compatible with leadership. Maybe she'll even throw an old friend and defender like Hynek into a crap so that he doesn't get in her way.

"Wait." Ivana grabbed my arm, pointing at the screen. "...Cyber Messiah has announced that he will run for mayor when the election date is scheduled."

The incumbent mayor welcomed his decision, saying he was looking forward to a duel over ideas about Prague's future.

"One worth another," Fay sighed.

* * *

We only stopped in one of the peripheral factory districts in the north-east of Prague. It was the VEP warehouse, apparently abandoned now. I mean by people. There were passive missile defense systems on its roof. Fortunately, Ivana had access to it.

We left the hovercraft at the entrance, and after scanning her eye's retina, the automatic door let us in.

And there a strange surprise awaited us.

* * *

"What is this?" I asked.

The warehouse itself was half empty, with only piles of old and mostly dirty clothes in a row of boxes. And on the opposite side were hangers with new robes in all sizes.

"Reloading point."

"Reloading point?" Fay didn't seem to understand.

"For people. For people like me," she added.

"Are you smuggling refugees into Prague?" I guessed finally.

She nodded.

"There will always be someone who wants to get in and doesn't want to get hit by drones and automatic fire systems," she replied.

I remembered what Lota had told me about her - that she herself had come to Prague as a refugee.

"Okay, how do we get out of here?"

"We'll go through the tunnel."

"We'll go?" I frowned.

"I know people from the outside who can help you. Without me, they wouldn't trust you," she explained, and suddenly froze.

"Something's going on. Right at us"

* * *

She made a gesture with her right hand - gently twisting her wrist, opening her fingers as if she was holding something delicate underneath - to show us what she saw in her head. The projection showed a point approaching, undoubtedly moving towards us at high speed. After a while, she switched to some sort of camera next to the warehouse and we saw a closed black hovercraft.

"Let me guess - are those bastards who tried to get us at that closed subway station? How did they track us down?" Fay turned to me.

"Maybe military satellites left overhead, or spy drones all over town," I shrugged.

"They're not really our friends, are they?" She asked Ivana.

I shook my head.

"Got it," she whispered, and at that moment we saw several bullets flying out of the magazine towards the hovercraft.

He opened fire in his defense almost immediately.

A hail of machine gun shells fell on the building. Missiles exploded nearby, and as soon as we ran on, one flew here as well. Fortunately, only a piece of the roof was torn off. But we were already headed underground. There was an iron door waiting for us there. Judging by the bolt on our side, the builders assumed the need to protect against what would come from there, not from here. I pushed it aside and opened the gate.

* * *

It was impossible to secure the door from the other side, but at least we closed it and rushed it to the front. We were greeted by a tunnel that resembled an old mine. It could have been three meters wide and two and a half high. The walls were reinforced with metalwork. Nevertheless, it was clear at first glance that this was some conspiratorial work. The tunnel had minimalist proportions mainly because there had to be a bloody problem in the city where the house stood next to the house, taking the soil out of sight and not involving more than ten people. Simple air conditioning was working, but no lighting was installed. This is what cybernetic prostitutes took care of. They could gently shine, which was enough for orientation while walking. The tunnel had a lot of turns, probably due to the unstable ground, but otherwise I couldn't see any junctions or side branches. Nobody could get lost in it. Unfortunately.

The darkness behind us lit up with a machine gun fire. Both cyber prostitutes darkened and clung to the wall. Another volley. The missiles hit the ground and bounced off the metalwork. One scratched my hip. Fortunately, he only tore his clothes apart.

Good thing the clothes were not for my money, I thought, recalling what had happened in the last few days with the things I was wearing.

We started running. First Fay, followed by me, and finally Ivan. The shooting grew more intense. At some point, however, Fay disappeared and I immediately understood why - a bend.

"Stop," I gasped, and pressed myself against the cool and damp earth that stood between the two metal-plastic hoops. I pulled out one of the two pistols and grabbed Ivana with my free hand.

She was breathing hard.

"We'll get them here," I said, and she slumped to the ground.

* * *

Bang, bang, bang, bang, bang!

Our pursuers did not intend to spare us and switched the machine guns to continuous fire. It was even dangerous to stick out a hand with a gun. Nevertheless, I fired a few balls into the dark. I fired like them, at random, only those motherfuckers on the other side had much more powerful weapons and more ammo.

"What's wrong?" I knelt down so that I could be closer to Ivana and at the same time so that I could protect us. In the dark, all I could see was its dim outline. Until it glowed slightly. She looked weirdly pale, so eerie, like comedians from fantasy parties in the VEP-tower.

"She got a few shots," Fay explained.

Her hands shone too. She turned Ivana on her side and groped her.

"Sorry," said Ivana.

"What the fuck?" I grunted.

"That I won't help you anymore, that…" she sighed.

In the glare of the light, I saw a dress streaked with several bullets on her back.

* * *

Bang, bang, bang, bang, bang! A volley of bullets flew overhead. One of those bastards ran up to us and, from five meters away, was shooting at the space he expected us to be in.

Boom! Boom! Boom!

I shot a full clip at him. I aimed for his underbelly, where he was not protected by a bulletproof vest. But in the glare of the gunshots, I couldn't see him very well. However, his next shots hit the ceiling. If not me, it was probably kinetic energy that knocked him to the ground. I jumped to him and took the other gun from him. I helped the first one fly away into the darkness.

I caught on his body. He hit me on the head with the gun and his free left hand stuck into my chest. So I was shooting a bulletproof vest after all.

But he wasn't wearing a vest. The first bullet from my backup weapon went through his jaw, the next one shot his eye, and the third bullet his head.

Bang, bang, bang, bang, bang! The shots of the rest of the company couldn't have come from a long distance - maybe twenty, maybe fifteen yards. I huddled next to the corpse and held it out in front of me. Thanks to the bulletproof vest and the pile of muscles, it served much better than the barricades around Pod Lipami Street. Several bullets hit him, but none hit me. I crawled back around the bend with that pile of meat, panting as my blood literally boiled inside me.

* * *

I dropped the body halfway down the hall and rolled to the ground. A few more bullets entered the corpse. My foot hit my lowered weapon, reached for it, and changed the magazines of both pistols.

I heard Fay cry.

* * *

I turned, panting, while the shooting in the corridor continued.

"Fay?"

"Sorry, Lieutenant," Ivana said.

"There is no need to apologize. We'll get out of here. Surely Sun Tzu would have some confusing, mystically obscure but true parable," I replied.

"Yes," she agreed.

"That's it." I nodded my head with satisfaction.

"Anger can turn into joy over time, bitterness into contentment. But once the kingdom has been destroyed you will not restore it, you will not return to the dead life."

* * *

I took a deep breath and gritted my teeth.

"Her heart... doesn't beat anymore. They shot it," said Fay.

"Only my implants keep me alive. But not forever," Ivana explained.

The sorceress helped her lean against the wall.

I fired another clip into the corridor, but it didn't relieve me a bit.

"Get out. I'll stop them," Ivana gasped and grabbed her gun.

As for her heart failing to obey her, she held her quite tightly.

"They will do something to you, something..."

"That they would kill me?" She interrupted me. "I'll take a little longer. I know what to do. Get out. Find Zodiac. Please do your job, Lieutenant," she said as I loaded the last spare clip into my pistol.

I leaned over and took her hand.

"I..."

"Words are redundant. Fay will explain everything to you. And please do not forget: 'The art of war teaches us not to rely on the defeat of the enemy, but on our own readiness to confront him. Not to rely on his inability to attack, but on our own steadfast and varied defense'. Now get the fuck off."

* * *

We were running through the tunnel in complete darkness, and we heard gunshots behind us. Gunshots and roars. A man's scream. It wasn't a scream of victory, but a roar of pain. Both sounds continued for a long time before we reached the end of the tunnel, out of breath. At this point, we were probably ten kilometers behind. At first the tunnel sank deeper and deeper until it reached its lowest point and began to climb again. In the end it narrowed so that it was impossible to run it anymore, but you had to walk on your knees and then crawl to the iron hatch, which also had a latch on the inside. We pushed it aside and entered the concrete chamber, full of dust and debris. We saw a light upstairs, so we climbed the ladder and found ourselves in a larger room, once protected by a door that was now balanced and rusted. Their function was performed quite well by dense shrubs of blooming lilacs. The smell seemed unearthly to me. We cut through it and found we had passed through some ancient water supply station, overgrown with moss and ferns. Behind the thickets there was a green meadow full of flowers and young birches.

"What is this?" Fay asked.

She looked dizzy.

"It's called nature, baby," I smiled.

Sadly, but I smiled as I thought of the woman who was dying downstairs now, in the dark and with no friends.

Blue Company

For the next hour we walked practically in silence and awake. I had no idea how many of these bastards had survived the fight with Ivana, and whether they would follow us beyond the water station. I grew up in a city and spent most of my life in built-up spaces, but somehow I knew subconsciously what to do to make it harder for my pursuers. So as soon as we discovered a rock in the forest - we just climbed it and then moved on through the densest forest. Only at the edge of a birch grove did we come across something that made us stop.

"Looks weird," Fay said.

We were standing on the edge of the pond. It probably had twice as much water originally, but the spring sun was burning, and I hadn't heard of rain since January. Still, the water in it was fairly clean and not overgrown with any filth except the reeds.

"I don't know. Or is it poisonous?" There was a sense of uncertainty in her voice.

Fay never left Prague. She knew only tap water and she saw it in a mafia spa, where she received clients. The pond water seemed unreal to her.

"You don't have to worry," I replied and undressed.

It was only then that I remembered that a bullet had grazed me in the tunnel and it seemed to have broken something under my clothes. My shirt dried to my wound, and when I pulled it on, my skin turned red again. But it is nothing serious. I took off my shoes and pants and went naked into the water. It was nice and cool and smelled strange. Not like the cleanest water from the top floors of Prague's skyscrapers, but somehow more authentic. Despite the burning in the wound, I made a few moves to warm up. After a moment of relaxation and utter blankness in my head, I saw Fay undress and slowly, cautiously following me.

"There's something soft down there!" She shouted at me.

I turned on my back and swam towards her.

"It's mud. Not the hideous, toxic underground from the Prague underground, but just mud. Some gravel, stones and sand, and… just mud," I said, and standing on the rock, I waited for it to come to me.

She spat out some of the water that trickled into her mouth, but it looked like she wasn't afraid anymore. She swam up and put her arms around me.

"I talked with her. In the head, you know?" She whispered.

"With Ivana?"

She nodded.

"We can do it. In a simple way. Pass on thoughts, feelings. It is very hard. You feel what the other one feels. That's why we're so good in bed. We know what excites whom, but we can also get to know his thoughts, feelings and fears. And the two of us can do even more."

I didn't know what to say to that, so I just stroked her hair.

"She was supposed to die there as a child. Not in the tunnel, because it wasn't there then, but on the way to Prague. You could say that Dejčer gave her a new life. I think she had the desire to die where her entire family died, shot by defense drones."

I closed my eyes and imagined Ivana. In all its artificial beauty, it was perfect in many respects. When we spent the night together, I saw more than her charm, sarcasm, roughness and intelligence. I also felt her sadness, so ubiquitous and indelible.

"Make love to me. Please. I need to feel alive," Fay whispered and started kissing me.

I couldn't immediately erect to the occasion, but the omnipresent water, the shining sun, trees, and the stress that was slowly leaving my body - all this allowed me to free myself from thoughts and focus on only one thing - the cybernetic sorceress. I kneaded her breasts, ran her butt. I gently dipped my finger into her crotch, and when I felt ready at the bottom, I grabbed her thighs with both hands, lifting it slightly, and slid my penis into it. She put her arms around me, and I moved carefully within her. Because we were immersed in water, things were different than on dry land. After a while I felt how excited she was, how inside she was embracing my penis with involuntary contractions, biting my neck and whispering: "More, please, more", and finally she sighs quickly, losing her mind.

I closed my eyes at her arousing body. The world outside of us ceased to exist until I gushed into her, pressing her body tightly against my own.

"Everything is fine, but you know that there are leeches?"

I opened my eyes and saw three guys in camo. One was aiming a shotgun at us, the others were looking at our weapons and clothes.

* * *

Fortunately, Fay had no idea what leeches were, so she just swam out of the water to the shore, and I carefully followed her. I still had a hidden weapon in my artificial leg, but I didn't want to get into a conflict without a real need. These three were not our persecutors. If only because they spoke first, and did not shoot. Moreover, the others had automatic guns, and the latter only had old-fashioned hunting rifles.

"You're not from a refugee camp, are you?" The guy asked while the other two eyed the naked sorceress.

I did it too, but for a different reason - I was looking for leeches. The man looked a bit older than me. He had gray hair, and in addition to the old camo, which probably remembered the times of the Czech army, black shoes from the same times. I wondered if he was too hot in these clothes. His blue eyes surprised me. The other two were much younger - they might have been thirty or twenty-five. Blade cutters with a razor that had more teeth than the average U-line passenger.

"We're headed there," I said as I stepped ashore.

It didn't bother me that I was naked. I lived in a three-shift hotel and spent some time in the subway cars. I lost my shame a long time ago.

"Pretty inadequate. We carried out executions for such an answer during the war," the oldest one grimaced.

"We have to get to the camp. There are people we need to talk to," Fay said.

She wasn't embarrassed either, but those hungry looks certainly didn't make her feel good. But what is surprising. Not only was she beautiful, but people outside of Prague probably didn't know the implants.

"And with whom, if I can ask, miss?"

"With Mayor Gajdoš," she replied.

I'd never heard that name in my life, but I understood that Ivana had passed on all her contacts to her.

"I'm already a little old for courtship," the oldest of them laughed.

"Ivana's sending us," Fay replied, and then I noticed a leech between her thighs.

The guy whistled and said:

"Finally. Everyone is waiting for the smugglers here."

I quickly took the leech from her and threw it back into the water. I was going to look for mine later.

* * *

Josef Gajdoš turned out to be a rather reserved man in the end, but when he heard Ivana's name, he let us get dressed and take his weapons. Immediately afterwards, they took us to a nearby clearing, where the Ibrahim 7 tracked vehicle waited. Military universal vehicle that was once delivered to the Czech army by Saudi Arabia as part of aid against Poland. Probably to get atheistic Czechs to defeat fanatical Catholics. But half of them were stolen before they were put into the army, and the rest disappeared in the first week of fighting for Ostrava. Typical for Czechs - which the sheikhs somehow did not take into account. We jumped on it, and five kilometers away we were greeted by a refugee camp.

Places such as this or the tent town at Pod Lipami Street had a lot in common. Both a peculiar disorder, and a kind of collective despair and social exclusion. But people had more space here. Instead of tents and makeshift shelters, there were wooden huts with children running between them, and a kilometer further there was an old town with a stone church. It was called Smildary or Smidary - as long as I had correctly figured out the rusty plate that lay overturned next to a road full of holes. Gajdoš led us to one of the stone houses, which was probably the town hall.

Before the war, as a young cop I traveled all over the country, but still, after years in a city full of skyscrapers, this open-air village, houses no more than two floor high, and all this trees and grass - it all felt like a virtual game.

Fay was even more fascinated. Confused, she stared at everything that surrounded us. The most stunning perspective was the space and horizon. You really felt as if you were in a different world.

We finally got to the town hall. People debating something there stared at us with curious eyes. They were dressed much like the mayor - simple coats, dark colors, and functional cuts - completely different from what we came in. But what fascinated them most was the cybersorceress. Her hairstyle, implants, it all looked to them as if Gajdoš had brought a sea mermaid from a long journey.

* * *

"In Prague you probably drink better, and here we only have apple booze. The potatoes dry up or rot, and most often both," he said, pouring us full glasses.

We sat in his office. There was a wooden table, a faded couch, a cracked leather armchair where he had settled into, and two wooden chairs that we had taken. The pendulum clock chimed behind him. He probably inherited the furniture from his grandfather. In Prague, a good antiquarian dealer would be able to sell it for a decent profit.

"We already have quite a crowd here. You are late. How many people will you take?" He asked bluntly.

Fay and I looked at each other.

"Nobody now," I answered truthfully.

"What?" He snorted apple moonshine.

"We can not. We just need to connect to the Internet. But then we'll come back and we can take some refugees to town," I added quickly.

"A few? I had a deal with Ivana. Three thousand people wait to get to their dream city, where food falls out of the vending machine and children go to school. And more come every day. I need to get rid of them. They are too lazy to dig latrines because they think that tomorrow they will find themselves in a coveted world of prosperity. If you came here to watch, go back where you came from." He pounded the table until the table top jumped, and our still intact glasses spilled a little vodka.

"Prague is not in the best position for refugees right now," Fay tried to appease him, but the mayor did not seem to accept it.

"Do you think it's here? The Federation of Czech Cities is hardly able to maintain security in the largest agglomerations, such as Pardubice or Hradec, just around the corner. Elsewhere it is ruled by whoever has the better weapons. This village is only holding on because these people give us money to wait here for their journey to a better life. And we have to pay for security, because Pardubice self-defense doesn't give a shit without it. Thieves' gangs come across Poland as far as the Caucasus. It is true that the Germans are sending humanitarian aid, but they are stealing those fags from Most, Ústí or Karlovy Vary. You locked yourself in your beauty, wealth and puffiness in front of the rest of the world and left us to our fate, and now you fucking tell me you've come to look at the Internet? These people have almost nothing to eat anymore, there is practically nothing to hunt in the forests, and you have come to the Internet? Are you kidding me?"

The mayor drained the rest of his glass and poured himself another.

"Sorry, bad things are happening in Prague right now," Fay continued.

But it didn't make sense.

I watched the reddish rays of the setting sun and didn't know what to do. We had nothing to pay here, there was no other option but to go further to Poland and believe that Belch's slogans would help us. But we would have to walk with no food and no water.

The mayor waved his hand and stood up.

"Take these people with you to Prague. That's what they're here for," he growled, then pointed to the door.

* * *

We went outside and my stomach rumbled. I haven't even had a moonshine, but the mayor will probably be able to deal with it. We sat down in the grass in a small park by the town hall, and I closed my eyes. I was tired. My body was telling me that he wasn't enjoying all this anymore, that he was exhausted, and that I should do something about it, preferably lie down and sleep. But we had nowhere. Fay cuddled up to me, and as she stroked my hair, I dozed off for a while.

* * *

I woke up after an hour or so.

"Do you see them?" Fay asked.

"What?"

"Well, the stars. You won't see it in Prague. Possibly over the tops of skyscrapers, but only in such a hazy glow. I never thought there could be so many," she explained.

I got up and looked around. There were fires between the wooden huts. It got quite chilly. There was no such thing in Prague either. Buildings absorbed heat and gave it back at night. Suddenly I felt cold.

We got up, I hugged Fay, and we walked towards the fires. The largest of them was used to roast a roe deer or a young deer. There were a lot of people around waiting for their portion. At one of the tables, I also saw the mayor and his companions.

"Real meat. And these people want to go to Prague," I smiled crookedly.

When they noticed us, Fay caught their attention again. Adults and children stared at her. One boy, about ten years old, finally found courage and ran up to us.

"I heard about you!" He said proudly, as if he knew something no one else knows.

"Yes?"

"You're a sorceress, aren't you? They made you in a factory, and you do magic, right?"

Fay smiled and stroked the boy's hair. Then she started to shimmer slightly and with her hand she "conjured" a glowing bird that flew towards the stars. With her other hand, she created a light butterfly, which sat on the boy, flapped its wings and melted.

"Fay," I nudged her.

Everyone was staring at us. Absolutely everyone.

"Can you conjure up food too? Apparently that's how it is done in Prague!" The boy said.

He probably didn't like venison and wanted something better, unaware we had nothing.

The sorceress unbuttoned her shirt and rolled up her sleeves so that more implants could be used.

"We know how to give people love and hope," she smiled at the boy and created an image of her companions and their performances.

A huge image that she projected in the sky. They were all there - Fay, Black, Long Liz, Kelly and Kuka, floating on the stage and surrounded by thousands of people, with dancing lights and strange images all around them.

I didn't even notice that the mayor got up, walked around us, and patted me on the shoulder.

"Come with me," he said, and started walking.

We followed him. What else was left for us?

* * *

We went up the hill above the village and saw Prague. It was fascinating. It glowed in the distance with millions of tiny lights that merged into one gigantic flickering diamond. Its lights soared up high in all directions, amplified by thousands of neon lights projecting images from the skyscrapers onto the sky. It was dark for several dozen kilometers all around, but Prague was beaming.

"I come here every night and look at her. Apparently, you can see it even from a distance of one hundred kilometers. It's because of all these skyscrapers and millions of lights. It is like a giant candle for human nightmares and nightmares. It looks like heaven, a gateway to a different, better world. I hate it, you know? That is why. People come here from far away, staring at the glow of the lights, believing that a better life awaits them there, just because of all those lights. I don't know if he's waiting for them or not - but because they believe it, they're not trying to make a better life for themselves here.

He paused and spat. I understood him too well. It is a pity that these people here had no idea what awaited them in Prague. That millions of people are much worse there than all of them here.

"I'll give you what you need, but fucking stop with your Prague spells. You're going out of here tomorrow and sending us real smugglers, okay?"

We nodded in agreement.

* * *

I woke up almost noon, on the couch in the mayor's office. I finally got a good night's sleep. Probably because until two in the morning we sat at Gajdoš's computer with a satellite connection to the good old Internet, looking for everything I needed. Not only did we get to the old documentation of Polish intelligence from the war, which Belch hid in the bowels of the Internet, but in the end, open sources helped us the most. We were able to recreate in the archival video library of one of the now defunct national TV stations all the wartime reports by Lukáš Pajac that had disappeared from the Prague Internet. Several of them concerned the 51st Airborne Battalion, as well as its third company. It was also called the Blue Company. But Pajac made films not only about the Blue Company. Before the war, he specialized in topics related to human fate, in such typical tear jerkers. He dedicated one of his videos to a woman named Marcel Merklová. The whole story suddenly made sense. If Zodiac didn't want to silence and erase these stories, I probably wouldn't be looking for them. But an old police rule was that the most suspect was a spot on the floor that someone had scrubbed thoroughly. It meant that blood had spilled there earlier.

* * *

We waited until it was getting dark and headed back towards the water station. I knew they would be waiting for us there. They are not stupid. Why chase us through the forests and hills when they can wait in the only place we have to go through to get back to Prague.

Sun Tzu said, "War is first and foremost a clever deception," so we took a group of armed refugees with us and agreed with them that in exchange for a promise that we would come back for them and take them to the city first - they are within a short distance of the waterworks do a little show. They had a pretty good gun that - about a mile from the entrance to the dungeon - launched a nice cannonade, and Fay joined her with a heartbreaking roar. The whole thing was to give the impression that some villagers caught the cyberworlder. To be clear, she glowed with all the implants. And then everyone just took a defensive position and waited for our pursuers to attack them.

And they moved on.

They were soldiers. Maybe they grew old - as I was - but still had all those instincts and ways to get around well in the field. I was lying far enough away from them, but I realized that even if I walked as carefully as possible, they would still get me. The one closest to me scrambled out of the bushes and ran to the next one who was waiting behind the tree. I slowly crawled forward. Fortunately, the fugitives along with Fay created a wonderful soundproofing that drowned out any breakage in the branches and the rustle of grass that I couldn't fully eliminate.

"Take it in the bow from the left, and you wait here."

Eventually I heard their conversation because they had been silent most of the time. The third one I picked up was still hiding behind the tree. I needed to target them all. I failed.

When the first veteran ran out into the dark, I had to act.

Boom! Boom!

I hit him in the head. In the light of the stars and the moon, I saw his skull shatter like a pomegranate.

I had one pistol in each hand and I fired. I just shot and walked. Speed and determination was paramount. I got the second just as easily. The moment the first one ran out, the other one was with his back to me. He took several bullets in the left shoulder. Crushed arm and collarbone were minor injuries. He fell to the ground and tried to catch his breath.

* * *

I fired incessantly. I counted the clips, hoping there weren't more, and headed for the tree. And from behind it a gun barrel peeked out and fired a series of shots.

I jumped to the side.

* * *

Maybe it was just my imagination, but I literally felt the bullets whistle around me. He fired blindly. He didn't know how many of us were here. He wanted to gain time.

I jumped over both bodies and saw him. He was getting off the ground.

But he didn't get up anymore.

* * *

I shot two bullets in his head. He could not have survived even with all the saints standing by him. The machine gun went silent and I scuttled behind the tree. I grabbed his gun and jumped to the guy who was curling in the grass. Blood was dripping from his hand.

"How many are you here? Quick, talk!" I growled.

He just sighed.

"I'll let you bleed out here. When you die, wild animals will kill you. Stray dogs roam everywhere. Do you know what awaits you?" I whispered when I calmed down a little.

I took his gun and clung to the plump oak - in case other members of the Blue Company tried to catch me.

"I want to live," he gasped.

"Speak."

"There is no one here anymore," he howled.

I counted quickly. There were six of us in the subway. If they hadn't received reinforcements on their way to the warehouse, there were five of them in the tunnel. Ivana could have killed two. It would make sense. But I didn't trust him.

"Fry in hell," I said and shot him in the head.

* * *

In the tunnel, next to Ivana's body, I made sure he wasn't actually lying. Plus, I figured the motherfuckers had drawn a Scorpio symbol on her forehead. I removed it and took her body into my arms. Even if it was the last good thing I could do, I knew I had to bury her outside of Prague, where her family had once parted ways.

Death of the cop

Sun Tzu forced the adepts of martial arts to realize that if they did not know themselves, their mistakes and strengths, and did not know the enemy, they would not have won any battle. And I finally met my enemy. And I knew he knew me. Therefore, I could not do anything that I would have done under normal circumstances. I had to find a safe haven.

We did not return to the happiest city in the world until two days later. We emerged from the demolished warehouse around seven in the morning. After a few days in nature - of the true nature - Prague seemed bigger than before. We walked through the ruins of the warehouse and after a few kilometers of wandering between the halls and factories, we reached the first U-metro station. We mingled with the crowd of workers returning from work and got onto the back of the train. The rear part of the train was usually occupied by those who did not travel from somewhere to somewhere, but over and over again.

You have a nice whore, man," a guy, about fifty, expressed his appreciation for Fay, with a long coat dotted with corporate logos and well-known product brands, mainly BublaFoli and SnicKofili. It even had a Happy Sausage stamp.

I suppressed the urge to throw up at the memory of not-so-distant events.

"Could she suck me? I have two energy bars," he added hopefully.

A mother with five children was dozing next to him. Each of them had an arm wrapped in a rope, the other end of which was wrapped around the parent's belt. A primitive but effective safeguard to prevent anyone from stealing her babies while they sleep.

"I could castrate you," Fay snapped.

"I think I've seen you before. I give my head that you've sucked me before," continued Mr. Logomaniac, undaunted.

"She blows for the crown, not the bars. Get the money, then we'll talk," I waved my hand and dragged the sorceress to the more distant part of the car, where a larger group of people slept under the cover of bags and boxes.

They stank terribly, but I was used to it. After the days spent in nature, it was like a return to familiar, home scents for me. This time, Fay was wearing a Hello Kitty hoodie so that no one could see her implants on her head. Fortunately, Ivana's hovercraft was still parked outside the warehouse, so we pulled out our weapons, ammo, and some clothes. But we were not going to use the hovercraft itself.

We sat down in an empty seat, I embraced the sorceress to protect her body from being groped or pissed by some roommate, and we fell asleep. While she was fast asleep, I would wake up every half hour, as my old habit dictated, constantly checking for new guests in the car, but surprisingly nothing dangerous happened for the rest of the day. Mr. Logomaniac finally fapped - in front of the family riding next to him.

* * *

"Is it morning already?" Fay yawned, suddenly awake.

"It's still morning here, darling," I replied and dragged her out of the car onto the platform.

Our seats were immediately taken by a barefoot homeless man who had been waiting for them for half an hour.

393

We got off at the Bořislavka station - the last stop of the U line before Dejvice. The affluent neighborhood did not have a U metro station. The reason was simple - people living in a better neighborhood did not want the poor to come here. Thus, it was the only part of the city to have the S-line overhead. As a result, people living in the lower parts of skyscrapers could receive more light.

The sun was just going down. You could tell from the vicinity of Bořislavka that we were approaching the district of the rich. There were much fewer homeless people, beggars, fencers, pimps and petty thieves, and many more people who did not stink. Instead of street stalls and kiosks, skyscrapers surrounded restaurants with gardens.

"They have soy duck, man I would eat it." There was a rumble in Fay's stomach.

I shook my head and dragged her to the public restroom. Another amenity that can only be found in better places. I tossed in a high five and we went through the revolving gate. We passed three brokers who were discussing DEZATEG's stocks so cheerfully that it was immediately obvious that the rest of the white powder on the sink must have been theirs. The sorceress pulled her hood over her face so they wouldn't know she was a woman, but I don't think they care. After all, who would pay attention to the people using the toilets there?

I knocked on the third booth from the left.

"Occupied," muttered a familiar voice.

"But I have to shit," I said.

The latch on the door clicked and I quickly pulled Fay in and closed the door behind us.

* * *

"I'll come up with a password next time," I snapped at Tom.

He sat cross-legged on a closed toilet seat. He had a large green backpack in his lap.

"There won't be a next time. They want to lock me up," he whispered and opened his backpack.

I took out two neo-leather jackets and scooter helmets.

"But for what?"

"Mina. She's afraid of me. The others have already been closed. Except for Bacon, that is. He stayed to make a revolution," he replied with a lopsided smile and handed me a cellular wristband. "I think she'll want to get you too. And not only her. I pimped yours a little, but I think it's better to replace it. In addition, this one is connected to scooters and you are set to navigate to this bitch there," he explained.

I handed him my armband. Tom tossed it in the toilet and drained it.

"Use Earthworms next time," he whispered, taking Fay's sweatshirt.

We already left the toilets wearing black helmets.

* * *

Using a new wristband, I called the scooters from the underground parking lot. The best that could have been in this situation - neither too new nor too old, but perfectly functional and inconspicuous. They were stolen, Tom bought them from fencing, but calibrated them so that they were untraceable. After all, it was one of the jobs pirates did for the mafia - outsmarting corporate software.

We politely joined the air corridor for scooters. We flew through Bořislavka and zigzag, along the marked path, around the European Avenue. It rained a little, but within a few minutes the rain had passed and a kilometer away there was no memory left of it, only an unpleasant stuffiness. We passed the screens and projections of CN that started airing the series again. At least for now. It probably meant that things had stabilized in the last few days, I thought. But as we flew over the N Dejvická Line, City News corrected me. A brief summary of the news showed several skyscrapers on fire in the area of battles with robbing criminals.

Two of these criminals have been shown. Caesar and Aurora. They lay side by side, their bodies full of bullets. The first thing I thought was that one day it would make a nice picture for t-shirts - but it was just my sarcastic Vachten trying to suppress the sadness. Aurora was cruel, but after what she experienced - no wonder, but Caesar? An idealistic kid who wanted to die for the things he believed in. Maybe I am seasoned, devoid of all ideals, rude and distrustful of all who hope that with one great act they will change the world for the better, but I really liked him. Sure, human fate was suck even without revolutions and wars, but from the bottom perspective, it probably looked completely different.

I instructed Fay to get off the scooter route a bit. The Security drone winked its lights menacingly at us, but we didn't cross the zone enough for it to intervene. The next report was about Cyber Messiah. He stood at the top of the pyramid with his arms outstretched and blessed.

"Cyber Messiah calls for immediate elections to end the mayor's rule. It also calls for the opening of the city limits. Meanwhile, his followers occupy other parts of the city and proclaim the so-called holy zones in them. For this reason, Security withdrew some units from fighting with rebel units. People with implants gather at designated protective points."

Divišová was, of course, the host of the report. It was enough for me.

I waved my hand to Fay and we headed back to the air corridor.

But not for long. The band alerted me to leave the route and go to one of the nearby skyscrapers. That was the problem. In such places, apart from the air corridors, only those who had a residence permit could move. In other parts of the city, such a thing was unnecessary, but rich people lived here, fearing that someone might be lurking on their property. Of course, this permission in practice was the proper calibration of the chip.

"Lobster delivery?" Fay smirked as we pulled into the 100th through 120th Residents Heliport.

With the help of implants, she could easily connect to my new band and find out under what cover we got here.

"It's Fat Tom's job. We might as well become sumo wrestlers on the way to a private lesson." I waved my hand as I parked the scooter between two luxurious hovercraft.

The delivery of the lobsters allowed us to enter through automatic doors into a wide corridor that further led to the individual apartments. We were spinning for a while until we finally found apartment number 1543.

Fay put her hands to the eye's retinal scanner, then she walked her way around the electronic system, and the door swung open. Internal security was not so perfect anymore. As the average safety guy would say: the rich lived here alone, and they don't commit crimes.

* * *

Due to the cameras, I only took the gun out of the door and took off my helmet and put it on a small plastic table. The Chinese lucky cat standing on it waved its paw at me.

Fay carefully closed the door and followed me deeper into the apartment. We walked down the long corridor, past the spacious bathroom and toilet, to the kitchen-dining room, where we heard muffled sighs.

"I think he has someone here?" Fay whispered.

I shrugged. This was not a problem that could not be easily resolved. I took a few steps and heard a faint growl. That already sounded suspicious. I unlocked my gun and stormed into the bedroom.

"Surprise," I shouted to the masturbating reporter.

It took a while for her to switch from the mental attitude I'm doing well to I'm in the ass. But in the end, she caught up pretty quickly. She dropped her realistic snarling penis and tried to grab the cellular wristband that was lying on the nightstand.

Fay was faster. She tried to fight it, but to no avail. Fay hit her, then grabbed her hand and twisted her behind her back. Then she pushed her down onto the bed and held her with her knee.

"Please don't scream. Because we'd have to cover your mouth with the thing that looks a little slimy now," I asked her.

She was shaking with fear. After all, the repertoire of our last meeting had guns and some violence.

"You came to kill me?" She whispered.

She probably imagined we could do something worse to her.

"I'd like some coffee."

"Coffee?"

"Yes. If you stay in bed and don't scream or make any sudden movements, Fay will make it to us three. But before that, she could also let go of her grip. What do you say?"

The reporter took a few deep breaths. She thought for a moment and realized that she had nothing to lose, or at least she would have a cup of coffee before she died.

"I have a capsule maker. It is in the kitchen. And I'll be... polite?" for a moment she was looking for the right word.

"I prefer naughty girls, but I'd be really grateful if you're being good now," I smiled encouragingly and motioned Fay to let her go.

"I also have a hot topic for you, but I need some answers first. I'll be glad if they are true. The Cyber sorceress is like a lie detector. If you don't tell the truth, she'll know it. And you imagine what you could do with that boiling coffee, right?"

I was bluffing. Cyber prostitutes didn't have that skill, but most people didn't know it. I was hoping for Divišová as well. But judging by her expression, she took the bait.

I put the gun on the edge of the bed and stretched my arms. It's gonna be a long night.

* * *

The next day I was left alone in the reporter's apartment. It was six in the evening, and I had practically never slept the night before. Using smart software in my apartment, I darkened the windows, made a whale mating sound, then sat back in my chair. Unfortunately, I did not have a cat, and - what is more - the chair was not rotatable. But I searched the nightstand of the reporter Divišova and found a collar in it. I put it at the entrance with an open bottle of red wine (made of real grapes - which made it impossible to drink it, because everyone knows that the best wine is Gotthard juice after three fermentation, based on energy bars with the taste of tutti-frutti, which passed the term of validity).

After a long wait, the door finally opened. For a moment there were murmurs from the corridor, and finally...

Good evening, Headmaster, I greeted Král.

* * *

He realized very quickly what was happening. He stood naked in front of me with the collar around his neck for only a few seconds, then just started running down the hall. Damn fast.

You will recognize the ex-soldier immediately. No matter how fat his body becomes, how comfortable he becomes and stops exercising, he still has two things - muscle memory and the awareness that he can do a lot. The first one cannot be completely deceived, weak muscles, overweight - all this eventually leads to the fact that after two hundred meters you get tired and start to gasp. But knowing that you used to be able to do a lot is worse. It can force the body to superhuman achievements. Once you remember that you could stand on your hands and even walk on them - even if you haven't trained for ten years, have lowered and put on weight, your head will persuade you to do it, just because it is encoded in the fact that you can do it. That's why I caught up with him only in the corridor. He trampled on his scattered clothes and

402

tried to open the door. His cellular band didn't work. Similarly, it did not work, as well as the apartment control system. It was down to the little EMP handy bubble that Tom gave me as a bundle with the scooter gear. But one thing was fully operational - my gun.

"You can scream and pound as much as you can. These luxury apartments are well-built. You know it perfectly well. And your security left in the corridor has other problems now."

"What?" The television director growled.

"Let's say that fate sent them demonic fairies." I winked at him and looked at his cock, which I think could crack nuts and kill elephants.

He took off to me. He looked like a rabid rhino with a horn bombing in all directions. He lunged at me with a few hard leaps, trying to crush me.

I jumped back, pointing at him, and shot him in the right thigh. He fell to the ground with a heavy thud. It felt like a safari.

I backed up two meters. He tried to crawl up to me and grab my leg. I kicked him in the head and jumped back.

"Come on, Corporal. All the perks are in my hands," I said, aiming between his buttocks.

"And now you will do as I say, which is to turn around and start speaking. You are not like them - a dull meat, ruthlessly loyal, bitter idiot who wants to fulfill the mission at all costs. You are smarter than those Zodiac has sacrificed. That is why you were the most precious to him and therefore, sooner or later, he would get rid of you."

I didn't made empty promises. I really thought so.

Král turned and grabbed the shot leg.

"I don't want to bleed out," he said.

I opened one of the drawers in the hallway and took out a bright blue dress.

"Wrap your leg with this." I tossed him his clothes and crouched down.

"So you already know about him," he said resignedly, trying to stop the bleeding.

He was still on the ground.

"Yes, I know about all the members of the 3rd Company of the 51st Airborne Battalion. And about your first degree "For Courage" award, which surprised me. You look more like a supplier." I smiled.

Král grunted under his breath.

"You changed. You were quite handsome. I wouldn't recognize you in old photos and recordings. I think it was a mistake you didn't change your name like he did," I explained and stood up.

Král tried to sit up. He hissed in pain, but with his leg tied he finally succeeded. He looked quite comical. I almost felt sorry for him. Almost - because I knew about everything he had done. For example, how he probably personally delivered Pipa to Zodiac so that he would perform a spectacular execution on her - while he himself acted out in front of everyone a devastated poor man whom they slaughtered like a pig's mistress during a live broadcast. And that he sent Divišova to the Security base because he knew that I would return there with a dead Karel, and then she would throw me into media hell, and then there would be riots in the city - that was a small matter.

"He claimed all Pranet information was gone. Everything. That he erased the past so that he could avenge it," said Král after a moment of silence.

"He deleted it. But out there is a whole world that has not forgotten the past. Birds are singing there, there is the Internet and there are a lot of things in it. For example, publicly available old TV reports. Like those of Lukáš Pajac. He killed him or is it your job?"

Král just grunted.

"The Blue Company always obeys orders," he said after a moment.

It could mean anything.

"One thing that interests me is why you? You come from a wealthy family. You went to war for adventure. After your return, you made a career. You fucked every actress and journalist you wanted..."

"The Blue Company always pays its debts," he interrupted me.

I smiled. I understood. Like the others, Král was also fanatically devoted to Zodiac.

But I didn't laugh for a long time. In one moment, he leaned on his good leg and threw himself at me with lightning speed, knocking over the table with the waving cat in the process.

* * *

The enraged rhino attacked again. He waved his hands at me. He wanted to knock me to the ground, gain the advantage of just crushing me and taking my weapons away.

But I was just waiting for him to do it.

Boom!

* * *

I shot him in the other leg. He fell again with a thud and began to scream in pain. I kicked him in the jaw, which calmed him down a bit, then I opened it and stuffed the barrel into his mouth.

"I wanted answers, but if you don't give them to me, Zodiac will give me them," I growled.

"You're not getting anything. Nothing. You are nobody. A cop that has neither the strength nor the courage. What do you do? You will kill me? People like you don't do that. You always leave the dirty work to others. You want to bring the perpetrator to justice, right? Then call the Security. And I'll call my lawyer," Král muttered and snorted into the barrel.

He thought he knew me.

"I'd do it. Until recently, this is exactly what I would have done. But you did three things to change that   you killed a lot of innocent people, you destroyed my beloved city, and then, dick, then that word you said. I hate attorneys," I explained and shot his brain out of his head.

The cop in me died a long ago.

* * *

Five minutes later the foretellers entered. From their looks, I concluded that Král's security has already been cleared and it is in the trunk of one of VEP's special hovercraft. All that's left to do is load Král there. Originally, I was going to hand him over alive, but...

"It looks like in a painting by Jindřich Göth. Now just put it in the gallery," whispered the foreteller.

He referred to the famous post-colonial postmodernist who shot his brain onto the canvas at the last exhibition. The resulting work was sold for the price of one older skyscraper.

While they were cleaning up after me, I went to the next room and dialed Mina's number on my cell band. I didn't have to wait for a call, I just spoke on her wristband. Tom finally uploaded the Security technology to me.

"What?" Mina snapped. She probably didn't have an easy life now.

"Give me five minutes," I said.

"Vachten?"

It wasn't hard to recognize me.

"You have a nice mess in town," I said, sitting down in one of the suede armchairs.

"I know that without you," she replied.

"I'll help you clean this up, but I need one thing."

"Everyone needs something. I need you out of my way now, so..."

"Once a kingdom is destroyed you will not restore it, you will not return to a dead life."

"Who said that?"

"Sun Tzu and one dead girl. A very good girl. This kingdom, your kingdom, is falling apart, Mina. It flows through your fingers. You play two jacks against a guy who has had aces up his sleeve for several years. I'll help you catch him."

"Zodiac?" She asked.

"Yes," I agreed.

"Except he's my the least fucking problem," she replied.

"I wouldn't be so sure. Give me one day. Get all your troops out of the rebel-captured areas and I'll get rid of that butt ulcer. Then do what you want. You can even issue a wanted poster for me..."

"I already did," she laughed bitterly.

"Mina, you're a cow, but you know I'll always get my killer."

She was silent for a moment.

"You have one day, Vachten, and then burn in hell."

"You too, mayor."

The Ascendant

Here, in a demolished disused warehouse building on the edge of town, we are witnessing an absolutely bizarre event. Someone placed an old corpse on a wooden cross and spilled an undefined flammable substance around it, which he set on fire. As you can see from a distance, the fire created a symbol associated with a serial killer known as the Zodiac. We were informed about this incident by workers from a nearby factory, who were alerted by the sounds of shooting. There is a man under the cross...

The report by Mirka Divišova was broadcast by City News in a special news issue. Content was flashing at the bottom of the screen. At this point, the drone zoomed in as Divišová commented on the broadcast hovercraft event. After a while my face appeared. I was standing in a bulletproof vest with an automatic machine in my hand and I was firing into the air.

"We're waiting for you, bro! Look, we got your girlfriend, you prick!" I shouted at the transmission drone.

Divišova's comment followed, in which she stated that it was about me, and she enumerated everything that I was accused of. It looked nice and dynamic. I turned off my cellular band and closed my eyes for a moment. Divišová had a drawer full of energy drinks. I snorted its contents like a junkie when my grandmother's late first aid kit was taken, and while it made my vision a little blurry, I didn't fall asleep - and that was the most important thing. I watched the recorded report that was broadcast live on CN two hours ago. I took a deep breath and looked at the oxygen mask. Two more hours left. Then I have to get a new mask out of the hidden bag and put it on as soon as possible. I did not risk running into sensors, cameras, drones, just nothing. It was clean and empty all around me. Just me and The Hole. I didn't hear them coming. But I knew it was them - the Blue Company.

* * *

Eight of them left. Pretty decent number. Considering that Poles reportedly killed the entire unit, quite a lot of them got to Prague.

Specialists for attacks on the rear of the enemy. Elite.

The elite he left out in the cold. Because he was gone. But they still felt wronged.

Like all veterans.

But this group was led by a freak.

* * *

They skillfully inspected the entire space. The place that sewermen and people from the Pod Lipami estate called Hole was not too big. They searched and checked it in less than a minute.

"It's clear."

"It's clear."

"It's clear."

The walkie-talkies crackled. The guys in the bulletproof vests commanded themselves "stand at ease". Then he appeared in the doorway. Messiah.

* * *

"Something's wrong," he said.

"Why?" One of the men asked him.

"He was here and left nothing behind. He provokes me as I provoked him. He's a good player. He would do something. Some kind of joke. Message. Even if only a diamond engraved on the wall. It's a trap," he said.

That son of a bitch got into my head more than I could have imagined. Exactly the same thought line followed Sun Tzu: "Who knows his enemy and knows himself, will not be defeated even in a hundred clashes. Whoever does not know his enemy but knows himself will sometimes be victorious and other times he will be defeated. Whoever knows neither his enemy nor himself will inevitably fail in any struggle".

He was sure I would have left him a message because he knew me. And that's exactly what I would have done if I had taken the body out of here, not Fay. If I was now sitting in the old VEP magazine, not my electronic version that Divišová together with Tom made, and then they aired a fake as a live broadcast on CN while I flew by the ceiling in anti-gravity boots, in combat gear and with a tank filled with napalm.

I pressed a button and the world began to burn around me.

* * *

I am a rainbow fairy

I have the sun in your gaze

I am already carrying the cloud

I am pink and white

I dance, look how!

I was singing. I could not hold back. I hummed silly words of a stupid song under the hood. The world was burning around me and I was singing:

My knight of the winds

I have to draw my sword

You have our destiny in your hand

I will throw myself into the trap

Your hot temples

I give the rainbow guard

Smelling like chamomile

Rises, the rainbow hall rises

The rainbow ball spins, the rainbow ball spins

As if I were playing in a fairy tale!

* * *

For five minutes, I flew over the heads of the Blue Company veterans, sending hellfires upon them. A few have fired a shot, but when you burn with the world around you, when the flames take away your oxygen, and the temperature reaches such a level that you have no chance of survival, even if you are not touched by the fire itself, you have no chance to hit. And they missed.

* * *

There were a couple of times the dry clank of my gun. If it weren't for my protective suit and oxygen mask, I would probably have suffocated and fried. Now I was looking down at the trigger. The bodies were on fire, as were the remains of The Hole's equipment. There was smoke and dust everywhere. Fortunately, due to the laws of thermodynamics, the heat was moving towards the exit and the temperature difference created a draft.

I flew around the room and counted the dead. I found eight of them. It wasn't looking good.

* * *

Several bullets hit me in the air. Some of them passed through the tank, five or maybe seven, I caught in protective clothing. Their strength threw me against the wall. I fell on her with my full weight. Someone grabbed my leg and pulled me down.

* * *

I was kicking, but it was to no avail. Several more bullets rattled against me. My shoe has come off. The lifting force stopped working properly and I crashed to the ground.

* * *

As I fell, I grabbed onto my attacker. I pulled him with me, and after a while we rolled in the dust on the hot earth. He took off my mask and tried to hit me. He swung, and then I turned and put the empty tank against him. I threw him off my back and hit him on the head with my elbow.

I could hardly see without the mask. Only darkness, smoke, swirling heat and the brutal stench of burning everywhere.

* * *

I felt the Twardowski machine gun. I grabbed the barrel with all my strength and the shot passed by.

Clash.

I have never enjoyed a dry fire so much.

* * *

The guy dropped the gun and sprang to his feet. He kicked me in the stomach. But my coverall protected me.

I hit him on the head with the empty tank and he fell to the ground.

* * *

I was breathing deeply, which wasn't the best idea. I was choking on this shit that was my making.

I grabbed his legs and pulled him outside.

Behind the Hole they were waiting for us...

* * *

Sewermen.

* * *

I sighed resigned. There were perhaps a hundred or more of them. Cyber Messiah gasped as I stopped. I saw them in the light of the burning remains of the Hole.

"Ascendant," whispered the woman at the head of the crowd.

She looked young and old at the same time. As if the young body had absorbed something ancient. She was wearing an old work coverall, painted white, peeling paint. Her hair was completely gray, but her face was unbelievably young. Judging by her, she could easily be twenty years old.

"No. It's a murderer. He killed her. A woman who lived in the Hole," I spoke.

The Messiah was beginning to regain consciousness. It didn't work to my advantage.

It boiled between the sewermen.

"It can't be," said the woman.

"He was one of her children. An abandoned, surface-born baby whose parents brought her to raise. And she did it. A woman who belonged to two worlds. She took care of him and then placed him in a charity school. And he killed her. He didn't want anyone up there to know where he was from."

And probably other things as well, I thought as I spoke the words.

"I am the Ascendant, he is the meat of the Ascendant!" Shouted Cyber Messiah, furious.

* * *

He jumped up and threw me to the ground. I tried to grab him but he dodged. I reached for the holster under the combat suit. There he hid both the military knives he used for the murders. One of them...

* * *

A few hands grasped my jumpsuit and knocked me to the ground. It was total chaos. I tried to defend myself but couldn't. It's like fighting an octopus. I squirmed, kicked, but was soon stripped of my protective suit and flying boots. Fortunately, Cyber Messiah stood to the side. He was explaining something to the sewermen, but there was such a buzz among them that I didn't understand.

"He the Ascendant. Such a prophecy," the gray-haired girl said.

Fucking prophecies. Fucking religions. It's just a load of rubbish.

I felt anger.

But if the surface people are stupid, why not fool those below. They had a million reasons for it, more than the ones at the top. If they had nothing to eat, at least they had to believe in something.

"He is the false Ascendant. He killed the woman from the Hole. I created the fire. After all, the prophecy says: "From the sewers, the Ascendant will emerge, kill the false prophet, and bring the people to the surface."

I said it in a raised voice so that at least thirty people standing closest could hear me.

The gray-haired girl looked at me in disbelief.

"Is that a prophecy?" She asked thoughtfully.

"Yes," I lied.

But that's the way it is with prophecy, right? It was enough to say with full conviction that what you are saying is an ancient prophecy, and most people believed it. At least I hoped so.

"What's this crap? I grew up here. Me! I am your Messiah!" Yelled the guy, whose real name wasn't Blažek, but Merkl. Ondřej

Merkl. He was given the name of the woman from the Hole and erased all traces of it. At least here in Prague.

I have no idea what he went through, why he loved and hated this woman, but I think he was a bit crazy. Maybe he really believed he was the savior of the sewermen and would lead them outside. But it was likely that the samaritan woman in the sewers had the idea of overthrowing the city, which had renounced it twice - once as a baby and once as a war veteran.

The former gave him access to the sewers, all their facilities, hiding places and plenty of worshipers, and the latter brought him a small but his own army of assassins, protectors, influential people like Král, and the technology by which he prepared for revenge. That's why he fought against cybernetic sorceresses. Their cult, which for some time had become poor, stood in the way of building his own cult.

"Yes, he is the messiah, but not yours. He's the messiah of those above," I shouted, pointing my finger at him.

The gray-haired girl was looking at both of us, weighing the knives the sewermen had taken from me. Finally she took one in each hand and stretched her arms out towards us.

"Who will survive, this Ascendant!"

* * *

I didn't wait a moment. I took the knife and attacked. The sewermen backed up a few meters, creating a kind of ring for us. Merkl jumped back, and I took a few steps back towards the closest standing, among whom there was a murmur. The opponent gripped the knife tightly and took a step forward. This time I backed up a bit. Under my bare feet - because I had lost my socks along with my shoes - I could feel the cool and damp ground. My gait was unexpectedly light and firm. I looked at him and watched his eyes. He was furious. Probably not even because I thwarted his plans, but because I took away from him what defined him - the position of the chosen one, the position of the preacher, the position of the leader.

"Putting it together turned out to be not that difficult. Who you killed to cover your tracks, like Merklova or Pajac, and who you killed just because you had fun or to destroy the top of the city," I said without taking my eyes off him.

"Two things I don't understand. Once you became messiah and mayor, what would you do with all of these here?" I nodded at the sewermen.

He attacked. He stabbed from below, throwing himself forward with his whole body.

I backed away cautiously. I still felt light. It's probably thanks to the reporter's medication.

422

"And the second thing that bothers me - did you fuck her while she was still alive or after her death?"

He attacked. Strong and fast.

And thoughtlessly.

* * *

He lost his concentration. I took a step to the side and his impact just brushed against me. I jumped towards him and stabbed him in the left shoulder. As he curled up in pain, I punched him in the stomach. He started to bleed.

He shouted something incomprehensible and tried to deliver a punch to my chest. With my free hand, I blocked the attacking arm and stabbed him in the hand that held the blade, slicing through his tendons. He dropped the knife and started screaming.

I looked at the white-haired girl. She stood still.

"I have very specific instructions. From Karel Adam," I said and pierced his eye.

Cyber Messiah wailed in pain. He fell to the ground and twisted like an earthworm.

"I was supposed to follow the order. The eye was supposed to be in second place, and I was supposed to take it out with a gun, but we'll talk about the details with Karel one day in hell," I said, and stuck the knife between his legs, and then a few more times.

"Now all that's left to do is puncture you like a sieve," I whispered, hammering the blade into his stomach as many times as he did to his victims.

* * *

They were waiting for me. A group of people next to one of their barricades. Fay and Divišová stood there with the rebels. There aren't many left. They were led by twelve-year-old Lucka. In the days we haven't seen each other, she seems ten years old. She was holding a dusty machine gun in her hand. She was sitting on some chest, staring into space. I think this one-sided truce came just in time. I got out of the subway, and dozens of unfortunates trailed behind me. Fortunately, it was dark outside, so the sewermen were not afraid to go out into the street. They looked around as if they had never been in the open air. This was probably the case with many of them.

"Is he dead?" Fay asked.

I nodded and hugged her.

"And they?" She pointed at the sewermen.

"They came to the surface, although it is not known what awaits them here. First of all, they will say loudly that they are also

424

human. Everyone, especially you, miss." I pointed a finger at Divišova.

"Are they really human?" Asked the cyber sorceress.

I remembered all the dead bodies in the sewers, eating children...

"Yes, they really are human. Only some of them have forgotten about it. And not only them." I shrugged.

I walked over to Lucka and held out my hand.

"Your gun."

She shook her head.

"It's over. Cyber Messiah is dead. You have one day to disappear and pretend you were never here. Tomorrow morning this city will swarm with bewildered believers who have lost their savior. They will quickly replace him with someone, and here law and order will return - whatever that means. And then cleaning will begin. And tidying up tends to die more than doing a mess," I said, thinking about Mina and how insecure her position is, and everything that awaits her now. And about the man who created the Aurora, and what awaits him when I finally find him.

"But I have nowhere to go," Lucka said.

She did not defend herself as much as during Caesar's lifetime.

"You'll come with us," I said.

"And where are we going?" Fay asked.

"There will always be someplace. It's Easter, my love."